JEN
INST

By the same author:

**THE DOMINO TATTOO
THE DOMINO ENIGMA
THE DOMINO QUEEN**

JENNIFER'S INSTRUCTION

Cyrian Amberlake

First published in 1994 by
Nexus
332 Ladbroke Grove
London W10 5AH

Copyright © Cyrian Amberlake 1994

Reprinted 1994

Typeset by T.W. Typesetting, Plymouth, Devon
Printed and bound in Great Britain by
Cox & Wyman Ltd, Reading, Berkshire.

ISBN 0 352 32915 7

Contents

1	An Auspicious Occasion	1
2	A Chance Encounter	11
3	A Remarkable Letter	24
4	Discussions and Devices	39
5	Tea, and After	50
6	An Interesting Departure	65
7	A Conducted Tour	82
8	Behind the Door	99
9	The Importance of the Alphabet	115
10	The *Ne Plus Ultra*	130
11	A Curious Fancy	146
12	Support and Stability	159
13	Pictures at an Exhibition	174
14	A Novel Tartan	189
15	First, Last and Always	203
16	An Ideal Position	218

To Susan, with affection
and Doreen, with feathers
and always and especially Ellen.

1

An Auspicious Occasion

The Professor's wife opened the door. 'Hello, Jenny,' she said. 'Do come in.'

'Hello,' I said. I hesitated on the step.

She gave me a smile of sympathy and welcome, and opened the door wider. She obviously knew why I was coming to see her husband. I went in. I thought it was a good thing their front door was shielded from the street by a deep porch, for apart from a choker of black velvet and a pair of black button-strap sandals, the Professor's wife was completely nude.

She shut the door behind me and took my coat. I had not put a jacket on that morning, preferring a soft white angora jumper, which I thought would be more practical.

'Cold for the time of year,' the Professor's wife said conversationally, rubbing her hands together briskly.

I'm afraid that rather made me stare, and I began to blush.

'Never mind,' she went on confidently, 'I expect you'll be feeling warmer in a little while, won't you?' And without further ceremony she ushered me in to her husband's study.

'Ah, Jennifer,' he said, pushing his chair back and rising to his feet. 'I'm glad to see you here so punctually.'

He too rubbed his hands together, though the

room was very warm, as it had been the first time I set foot in it. There once again was the cheerful coal fire burning in the hearth, and the ancient grand-father clock ticking in the corner. I was amazed once more how crammed the walls were with books, so many of them old books, in leather bindings. The study was lit only by lamps and the fire, and the shadows were many and deep.

The professor was, unlike me or his wife, dressed more formally this time, in a smart tweed jacket and dark grey flannels. His shirt was a white starched one, and he had put on a deep-red tie with a small em-broidered black and gold crest.

'Nervous, Jennifer?' he asked me. 'There's no need. This is all perfectly straightforward.'

Without seeming to, the Professor's wife had steered me to stand in a spot in the middle of the carpet, facing the broad desk. Now she was pulling forward another desk, a sloping schoolroom one with a built-in seat; simple and quite small. Its metal runners made a hush-ing noise as they slid across the carpet.

'Is there pen and paper, my dear?' the Professor asked his wife, and she took out both and put them on the desk; the paper square in the middle, and the pen in the groove above. I saw her bottom dimple as she bent and straightened.

Ignoring the clock, her husband pushed back the sleeve of his gown to look at a large gold wristwatch. 'Tea in forty minutes, I think, dear,' he ordered. Nod-ding obediently to him, then smiling and wishing me good luck, the Professor's wife left us alone together. I heard the study door click quietly shut behind her.

'Is that a skirt or a dress, Jennifer?' the Professor asked, nodding at my clothes. My instructions had said either would be acceptable.

'A skirt, sir,' I said. It was my good grey flannel

2

skirt with pleats. I was surprised how meek my voice sounded now that I was here, now that the time had finally arrived.

The Professor gestured. 'Up, please,' he said.

So it was to be as simple as that.

Taking a deep breath, I lifted my skirt. I hoped the Professor would approve of my knickers, which were white cotton and brand-new, and my suspender belt, which was white too, though that I had had for years. The instructions had said stockings were compulsory: black for preference, unpatterned, with seams. I had bought some specially, and made sure the seams were straight before ringing the doorbell.

'Good,' said the Professor. He reflected, lacing his fingers and bending them back as though to flex them for some forthcoming feat of manipulation.

'We'll have the skirt off straight away, I think,' he said.

I commanded my fingers not to fumble as I unhooked the belt and opened my zip. It was my first time, and in any case, I thought, it is only once in your life that you're likely to receive the honour of a personal initiation from an expert as distinguished as the Professor. Naturally I was determined to behave as correctly and obediently as I possibly could. All the same, it's hard not to feel butterflies in your tummy when you're taking off your skirt in front of a handsome man, especially for the first time.

The Professor, I believe, is in his late forties. His sandy hair is sprinkled here and there with silvery grey and there are nests of fine wrinkles at the corners of his eyes. His wife seems rather younger; her figure is trim, her hair glossy black. I wondered if she had been a student of his when they first met.

'Sit down, Jennifer,' the Professor said, and he gestured for me to come to the desk.

3

He and I both sat then, in our respective places. The plain wooden seat felt strange to sit on in only my knickers; and I would have been obliged to say, if he had asked, that I didn't see why I needed to take my skirt off to sit down. But of course the Professor knew what he was doing, and he certainly wouldn't be interested in what I thought.

'Now, Jennifer,' said the Professor, 'you're going to compose the prospectus – ' and he emphasised the word, as if it pleased him greatly, 'for everything we'll be running through today.'

I straightened my hair and picked up the pen, ready for dictation.

'At the top of the paper, put: Inspection,' he ordered; and I did. 'Well, you've passed that already,' he informed me. All I had done in that respect was follow his written instructions. Still, I couldn't help looking up at him with a smile of pleasure. He did not seem to share my pleasure particularly. Of course, passing the first test was nothing to be proud of; the Professor had surely expected nothing less of me, or else he would not have agreed to take me. If I had failed in my initial presentation, no doubt I would have been sent straight home. I had escaped that humiliation at least! 'Put a tick, and go on to the next line,' the Professor said. 'Examination.'

I wondered what that would mean and whether I would pass it too, but before I could discover, my instructor was saying: 'Now divide the page into three columns. At the top of the first column, put Device; at the top of the second, Position; and at the top of the third, put Area. So, Jennifer: Devices,' he went on, and he put the same emphasis on that word as he had on the word Prospectus. 'What do you think those might be?'

I remembered the entry on the history of punishment in the encyclopedia. I looked warily around the room, thinking madly of iron maidens, torture racks, stocks and pillories. I saw a globe of the world; a wicker wastepaper basket; a lectern with an enormous dictionary on. 'I don't know, sir,' I confessed.

The Professor tutted. 'Come on, Jennifer,' he chided me. But my mind was a blank. 'Well, well – oh, go on to the third column,' he said impatiently. 'There put, in your best handwriting, the word Bottom; and under it, Thighs; and after Thighs put a colon. On the next line, indented, put Back; and under that, Front.'

My pen was scratching busily. 'Have you got all that, Jennifer?' the Professor asked.

'Yes, sir,' I said, and cleared my throat, because my voice had come out rather as a squeak, and I did not think that was a polite and proper way to address a man like the Professor.

'Now then, Jennifer,' he said pleasantly, coming around the desk and leaning against it with his arms folded, 'let's go back to the first column, shall we?'

'Devices,' I said.

'Yes, Devices,' he said. 'What Devices do you think we might need to treat those three Areas?'

Blushing warmly, I stared at the paper. I wanted to speak, but my voice didn't seem to want to work. Eventually I took a deep breath, and managed to quaver: 'I thought you might use your hand, sir.'

'Good, Jennifer, good,' he said, much to my relief. 'The Hand. First, last, and always,' he said, smiling and leaning towards me. 'But you need write it down only once.'

I wrote down: 'Hand'. I looked up inquiringly. The Professor was smiling gravely at me. His head was on one side, his eyebrows raised. He was waiting.

'I suppose – the hairbrush, sir?' I said, apprehensively.

'Certainly, Jennifer, certainly, the Hairbrush: a traditional method by no means confined in usefulness to the nursery whence it originates. The Hairbrush you will encounter, I promise you, later; but before that, I think, the Ruler. You may put Rulers, in fact, with a colon after it, and underneath – '

'Indented?' I said.

'Yes, yes, indented – write Plastic; and then Wood. For though the Ruler can be quite sharp in either form, and most appropriate, hm, for measuring out punishment to a young lady . . .'

I smiled, acknowledging the little pun; though I did not feel much like smiling, at that moment.

'Yet it is lighter than the Hairbrush, and must precede it.'

I pushed my hair back behind my ears and adjusted the cuffs of my blouse. I wanted to be attentive, and quick to learn what he had to teach me. 'So does Hairbrush go next, sir?'

The Professor smiled judiciously, lifting an admonishing finger. 'Not quite, Jennifer,' he said. 'Still before that in the ranks of severity, let us consider another Device, equally traditional. This is another we may borrow, so to speak, from the nursery, where for generations little boys and girls have been made familiar with it by conscientious nannies.' He paused. 'Can you guess?' he asked.

I could not. I had never had a nanny, or a nursery either. I wondered if intelligence was part of the test. I was afraid there might be penalties for not guessing.

Deep, thoughtful, the Professor's voice went on, prompting me. 'Perhaps it will come to you if you imagine a scene where punishment might be required at the end of the day, when a little girl, or indeed a big one, is ready for bed.'

I gazed at the Professor's face in the golden light.

I could not think, or speak. I was hypnotized by the sound of his voice.

'She bends over the bed for nanny, tucking up the skirt of her nightdress, and as she does so she lifts one foot – '

It was a revelation. 'The slipper!' I said.

'Exactly,' said the Professor with satisfaction. 'The Slipper: flexible but firm, and so conveniently at hand in evening or early morning.'

I wrote down Slipper. Neither of us was wearing them now. The Professor's shoes were sensible brown Oxfords; mine were court shoes in peacock blue. I supposed the Professor and his wife might keep their slippers upstairs, in the bedroom. Perhaps they might be too far away to be conveniently fetched.

'And now, Jennifer,' said the Professor, 'we do indeed come to the Device whose acquaintance you are so eager to make – to wit, the Hairbrush. Hard and strong and true. No leniency there, dear me, no. Write it down, write it down, if you please,' he said. 'And under that: Strap.' His voice sank very deep on the word. 'Another flexible Device,' he explained, 'but one that is thorough in its flexibility; all-encompassing, you might say. It embraces the very curves of the miscreant bottom, or indeed thigh. And there I think we will leave it for today,' he said, and I was profoundly grateful for that.

Swirling the ribbons of his gown, he went and sat back behind his desk. I could feel the heat of the fire up my left thigh, through the nylon mesh of the stocking and up the bare flesh. The Strap! I had heard of it. More severe than the Hairbrush! Despite the fire, a cold shiver ran down my spine.

'Now, the second column,' continued the Professor. 'Which is?'

'Position,' I read.

'Position,' he repeated, with satisfaction, like some-one contemplating a favourite subject. 'Take these down,' he told me. 'Knee. Chairback. Desk. Couch. You'll have noticed, Jennifer, this room has no couch at the moment.' I had noticed nothing. My head was spinning too much to notice anything. 'For that, we shall need to ask my wife if we may borrow her sitting room. Put a colon after Couch, Jennifer, and beneath, indented as before, write Cushion, and then beneath that Knees Up. And finally in that column, put Toes. Have you done all that?' he asked, after a moment.

I had, though it seemed rather cryptic. I supposed I would understand in time. Perhaps then it would not be so frightening.

The Professor came and stood over me, checking my Prospectus. I was glad I knew I had done exactly as he said, and spelled everything correctly, so there could be nothing to make him cross with me so early in my career. I was determined to be the perfect pupil. All the same, the lesson did look as if it might be quite difficult.

There was something else, still, that was making me uneasy.

I had read, once, when I was a little girl, a story about big girls who attended an old-fashioned boarding school and what happened to them. Though I had not quite understood everything that was involved, one detail had stuck in my mind. My research had failed to clarify the general principle, and now I felt the time had come to find out.

'Please sir,' I said. 'Forgive me asking – '

The Professor waved a hand. 'Ask away, Jennifer,' he said. 'The Socratic method of question and answer is the very essence of education.'

I grew more confident. 'Isn't there something else we need to put down?'

'The cane, you mean? Seniors only, I'm afraid, my dear: you must work your way up through the ranks to that. We must learn to walk before we can run.'

I remembered a conversation I had had once with his wife, and wriggled in my hard, uncomfortable seat. 'No, sir,' I said. 'I mean, yes, sir. But don't you have to decide whether the bottom in question – ' I said, starting to blush again. 'Should be – ' How was I to put it? 'Clothed or unclothed,' I said, lowering my eyes in shame and confusion.

The Professor leaned over me, very close. I had to look up and meet his eyes. They were dark brown, very warm and steady. 'The question does not arise,' he said.

'No, sir,' I said.

'Not in this house,' said the Professor.

'No, sir,' I said.

Then the Professor showed me where our prospectus was to be hung, on a noticeboard behind the door, and I got up and put it there with a drawing pin. 'What's next?' he asked.

'Examination,' I read.

'Well, there we are, Jennifer,' he said, expansively. 'Now we come at once to the unclothing of the bottom in question.'

Uncertain as I had been, I cannot say that I was totally unprepared for this moment. Why had I put on brand-new knickers for my visit, and washed myself once again so thoroughly beforehand, if not in the hope of presenting a fresh, clean bottom, with no offensive stains or odours, if this moment should occur? The specification of particular kinds and colours of underwear had made it clear that that much at least was to be disclosed, like the girls in the story who had been told to raise their gymslips.

But underwear was one thing; nudity another.

9

Underwear or its equivalent, and what that revealed, could be seen any day in summer on a public beach. Though stocking-tops and suspenders were conventionally kept concealed, I knew perfectly well, as any woman does who ever wears skirts above the knee, that my underwear was at risk of casual and accidental display on any staircase, in any low seat, from any sudden, playful gust of wind.

A woman's bare bottom is not displayed, except to her husband and her doctor, unless she is a striptease artiste or a vulgar photographic model, obliged to put it on show for pay.

None of these conditions seemed to apply to this situation. The arrangement between the Professor and myself was strictly educational; to introduce me to a salutary system of practices and procedures that would be beneficial for me, and not before time.

A professor, I thought, is much like a doctor, and concerned only with the welfare of the individuals who have cause to visit him. I must put myself in his hands: literally, and absolutely.

I turned my back. Then, though my heart was beating like a hammer, I put my hands in the elastic of my knickers, and pulled them down to my knees.

'That's far enough,' said the Professor. He patted the desk where I had been sitting. 'Come here, Jennifer,' he ordered. 'Come here and bend over.'

2

A Chance Encounter

I had been fortunate enough to meet the Professor's wife at a party after a wedding. I was sitting talking to my boyfriend's sister when she came over. I knew who she must be as soon as I heard her name, and could not speak when Elaine introduced us, not even to say hello. I felt as abashed and tongue-tied as a schoolgirl meeting a film star.

While she and Elaine were talking I kept looking around secretly to see if her husband was with her anywhere. I had seen his picture in the press, and sometimes on TV too. I was sure I would recognise him if I saw him, but I could not see him there.

The party was crowded and noisy. They were friends of Kevin's who were getting married, and Elaine was the only person I knew, apart from him. I had drifted away from Kevin, as I always did when we were at parties, without really intending to. The conversation always seemed to move away from me, and I felt foolish and self-conscious standing beside him smiling and sipping wine while everyone ignored me. I could see him now, one of a circle of men over near the bar, smoking and talking loudly, and laughing. I knew nothing would move him from that spot until the party started to break up, but I kept looking across, as if I needed to make sure.

A gentle hand fell on my arm. It was Elaine: she

was on her feet, going to talk to someone else. She said she'd see me later.

There were so many people that I couldn't get up myself without looking as if I was trying to follow Elaine, and as she hadn't invited me to come with her, that would look silly. Also, I didn't want the Professor's wife to think I was trying to run away from her. I was sure that would be very rude, now that we had been introduced. I smiled shyly at her, wishing desperately that I could think of something to say. I couldn't. I looked down into my glass. I knew when I looked up again she would have found someone more important to talk to, and I began to hope it would be soon.

To my surprise, the Professor's wife asked me how I knew Elaine. She said it in the most natural and unassuming manner imaginable, and when I had told her, hesitantly, she moved closer, into the seat where Elaine had just been sitting. She began saying what a sweet and lovely person Elaine was, making me feel as if simply knowing her did me credit; and when I said something commonplace about Elaine and her virtues, she nodded as if I'd said something original and wise. She uncrossed her legs, with a shimmer of fine black nylon and leaned slightly towards me, giving me her full attention.

How gracious she was, I remember marvelling – just like royalty! She led me gently into conversation about dresses, about the bride and groom. She asked me whether I thought people still believed in marriage in the modern day; and she asked me what I myself felt about it. I hardly knew what my feelings were, but the Professor's wife made me feel I should have some, and that she cared what they were.

I told her I thought marriage was still very important to most people. Parents hoped their children would marry. Every woman I knew was either married or longing to be.

'I wonder why,' said the Professor's wife – not sarcastically or bitterly, but as if it was a genuine point of curiosity with her. Obviously she found people interesting, and liked to know why they did things.

I felt confident enough now to say that the women I knew seemed to think marriage would save them in some way from the anxieties and insecurities of a single existence. They would willingly trade the freedom for an end to the loneliness.

'But some of the loneliest people you meet are married women,' the Professor's wife said, sympathetically. She managed to say it in a way that suggested my experience must be just the same. The Professor's wife was doing me the honour of assuming I had a varied and interesting social life.

I leaned forward a little, my hands clasped, so as to show her without drawing attention to it that I was not wearing anyone's ring. 'Because their husbands are out at work?' I suggested.

'And they don't see anyone else any more,' said the Professor's wife, chiming in, as if finishing my thought for me.

Married or not, I realised, I never saw anyone but Kevin's friends these days. I never saw any of the people we used to see when I was with Michael, or any of George's friends, who'd been my boyfriend before Michael. I suppose it was the wine that made me feel sad about it, as if I had been falling through life all along, constantly losing touch.

'If anyone doesn't believe in marriage,' I said, daring to offer a thought I sometimes had, 'it's men.'

'Your young man seems very nice,' said the Professor's wife.

I hesitated again. I had been thinking if the Pro-

13

fessor's wife knew Elaine, she must know Kevin; but she obviously didn't. On the other hand, she must know who he was, which must mean she had noticed me with him, earlier. She must have watched us for a second or two at least, unless she was just being polite. I could not think she was so shallow.

What was even more surprising than the thought that the Professor's wife had noticed me, was that ever since she had started speaking to me, I had forgotten all about Kevin. I hadn't looked at him once!

'Thank you,' I said, a bit automatically, looking over in his direction. The crowd had closed up even more now, and I couldn't see if he was still there. Perhaps it was the sudden anxiety of losing him that made me miss what the Professor's wife had said to me next.

'What does he use on you?' she asked.

Puzzled, I turned back to face her. 'Pardon?' I said.

'What does he use?' she repeated. She made it sound as if she was asking what did he have on his bread: butter or margarine. 'The strap, would it be? Or do you have the cane already?'

I was shocked, completely bewildered. 'Oh, no!' I protested.

The Professor's wife sipped her wine. 'I suppose he must spank you quite regularly then,' she said.

'No!' I gasped. 'You're quite mistaken! There's nothing like that, nothing at all.'

I felt myself colouring. Why did I sound as though I was regretting it? I supposed I was sorry to have to say she was wrong – we'd been getting on so well. But what had I said to make the Professor's wife think I would let my boyfriend punish me? And why, when I told her he didn't, did the Professor's wife look at me like that? I swear I saw a moment of pity in her light blue eyes, as all the lonely wives she met must have seen.

She reached across the table with her white-gloved hand and patted my hand very lightly. 'Do forgive me, my dear,' she said, 'I didn't mean to pry. Oh look, there's Marjorie.'

I turned and looked towards the door. There was a constant stream of people coming in and out. I didn't know anyone called Marjorie.

'I simply must go and have a word,' said the Professor's wife lightly. 'Excuse me, Jennifer, won't you,' and off she went, into the throng. I sat alone for a moment, mechanically drinking my wine, feeling strangely small and overwhelmed, like a child lost in a department store. Though she was far too well-bred to show it, I knew, that somehow, I'd disappointed her.

When my glass was empty I went and found Kevin and hung around until he noticed me. We left early.

Kevin and I parted later that year. Nothing went wrong, there were no rows or unpleasantness of any kind. We drifted apart, that was all. Somehow he kept being out when I called. When I did manage to get hold of him and we tried to arrange a date he always had something else on. When we finally did get together, he brought me a box of chocolates and a bunch of flowers. After that I didn't hear from him until he phoned up to say we should stop pretending, and say goodbye.

I went on alone, untroubled. There was plenty to keep me busy. I discovered it was nice to be able to go out where and when I chose, to buy a coat or book a holiday without worrying whether it would please someone else. I refused the routine invitations I got from single men; in fact I suspect I was quite cold to them because none of them ever found a reason to ask again.

It was in another crowd – on a boat, on the river

– that I saw the Professor's wife again. It happened quite by chance. Leaning out to look over the water, my eye was caught by a head of jet black hair several rows further forward, and a fluttering neckscarf in bright lime green. She was quite a way off, but it was her, surely. And that head of wavy sandy hair beside her, that I just glimpsed for an instant as the boat rocked us all in our seats – I knew that must be her husband.

I was seized with an urgent, ludicrous impulse to push my way forward and speak to her, to presume on her kindness and remind her who I was – but I held back. I was gripping the rail of the boat with one hand, my other hand at my throat, as if I was wishing I had worn a neckscarf of my own. It was such a crush. There were children charging about, girls as well as boys, ragging each other, making a nuisance of themselves. The Professor's wife wouldn't remember me, I told myself. In any case, what was I supposed to say to her?

When I grew too agitated to sit still, I deliberately got up from my seat, stumbled and excused myself along the row to the aisle, then sidled and squeezed my way in the other direction. I went as far as I could, and leant on the stern rail watching the gulls wheeling and brawling in our wake, their voices bright and harsh as the sun that flashed on the water.

In a while I heard someone say, 'Jennifer?'

I turned, and saw her smiling face.

'Jennifer,' she said, warmly. 'I was sure it was you.'

I was filled with delight. We shook hands. Once again, her husband was not beside her. We spoke, or she spoke and I agreed enthusiastically, about trivial things: the changeable weather that summer; the flowers in the botanical gardens; a recent play we had both seen.

'Your young man isn't with you?' asked the Professor's wife casually, fixing me with her bright eyes.

For an instant I couldn't remember who she meant.

'Kevin,' I said suddenly, and she smiled, nodding her head as I imagined her husband must do when a slow pupil suddenly stumbles on the right answer to an easy question.

'I'm not seeing him any more,' I said, feeling a light blush creep over my face, not of embarrassment so much as shame – yet I was not ashamed to be unattached, so I did not know why I should be ashamed to tell her, a complete stranger, that I was. In fact, had she not said many encouraging things when we were first introduced, about the dangers of becoming a couple?

The Professor's wife looked at me now with genuine sympathy, as she had before when about to say goodbye to me. 'What a shame,' she said lightly. 'I had imagined you two – '

Rudely, I interrupted her. I did it without thinking. I simply couldn't bear to hear what she had imagined about me and Kevin. I did not want to remember Kevin at all, or any other man.

'I think I saw your husband,' I said. It came out more boldly than I had meant, as if I was challenging her to something.

Yet if I had been rude and abrupt, the Professor's wife did not notice, or at least she was polite and gracious enough to overlook it. 'Really?' she said. 'Where was that?'

I felt foolish again. 'Just now,' I said. 'Earlier on.' I hadn't wanted to admit I had spotted them and avoided them on purpose. 'I mean, I thought I did. Isn't he with you?'

What if he wasn't? I thought with dismay. What if it was a completely different man? To cover my confusion I put my hand up as if shielding my eyes from the sun. I gazed along the length of the boat, over the many laughing, chattering heads, trying to pick out his among them. The children got in the way, jumping and squealing at one another. I couldn't see that august profile anywhere.

I was startled and glad when the Professor's wife slipped her arm through mine. She was good enough to remember that I had never met her husband, without reproaching me with it. She simply said: 'He'd love to meet you,' and then before I knew it, she was guiding me forward and walking me through the crowd, which naturally parted for her as though the people were all made of smoke and sunlight.

Then he himself was before us, rising from the white slatted bench and turning to face us with a smile that looked more than polite; that looked, I thought to myself, peculiarly like triumph – as if he had just received a nice present, I thought, or won a bet.

'Darling,' his wife said, 'this is Jennifer.'

Although the Professor was wearing a pair of sunglasses that hid his eyes from me, I knew he was scrutinizing me as he shook my hand.

Of course I was expecting his wife to say something more, to help us over the first moment of meeting, which is always the most awkward; but all she did was let go of my arm, take hold of his, and hug it briefly, as though asserting her right of possession.

'I know who you are, of course, Professor,' I blurted out. 'I've heard you on the radio, many times. Your lectures are very popular. I came to hear you speak once, too.'

'What was that about?' he asked, naturally enough.

What had it been about? At once my head was empty. I could recall nothing but the distinguished

18

figure standing up in the hot packed hall. The bright lights of the stage had made his hair shine like gold. He had kept the fingers of his left hand inserted in his jacket pocket, I remembered, while his right sketched out for us in a series of neat and economical gestures –

'China!' I said excitedly, startling a woman nearby who looked at me as if I had said or done something very bizarre.

The Professor's wife laughed gently. 'How extraordinary, dear,' she said. I thought at first she was speaking to me. Then I realised she was addressing him; and he was chuckling now too.

'It was about the history of China and opium farming,' I said, pressing on determinedly.

The Professor lowered his head, tipped his sunglasses with a finger and looked at me with amused deference. 'Bamboo, possibly?' he said.

Abruptly, I remembered I had no idea what the Professor's speciality was, or even his field, even though I knew his voice so well. It was warm and dry and subtle as spice in a rich pudding. It was as familiar to me as if I had been hearing it since I was quite a little girl.

The Professor spoke to his wife, but I heard no words pass between them because of the chugging of the engine and the shrieking of the excited children. Now they were bumping into people and climbing on the seats in their chase. I thought they were far too old to be behaving so badly.

'Jennifer,' said the Professor's wife, 'if you'll excuse me.' There was not even a Marjorie this time, but she was gone again, as quickly as she had left me that day at the wedding reception. Again I felt absurdly abandoned, and somehow betrayed.

Helplessly I looked at the Professor, whose eyes

19

behind his sunglasses were quite unreadable. He had an encouraging smile, but he did not seem to be about to speak to help me out of my difficulty.

I opened my mouth. 'Well,' I said lamely, 'this is a lovely trip.'

At that moment one of the children, a girl of thirteen or fourteen years, barged into me from the side like a rugby player tackling an opponent, almost knocking me over. There was no apology. I caught a glimpse of freckles, a laughing mouth, flying pigtails, and then she had dodged away and was gone again. Staggering off balance, I hit two or three other people next to me with my elbow and shoulder, and reached out automatically to save myself.

I found I was clutching the Professor's sleeve, as if desperately trying to pull him towards me.

'I'm sorry,' I gasped, 'do forgive me . . .' And then I became very angry suddenly. 'These children,' I said. 'Where are their parents? I don't know what they can be thinking of.'

The Professor didn't seem a bit put out by the upset, or by my grabbing his sleeve like that. 'Have you any children, my dear?' he asked, in such a way that I was instantly made to sound like no more than a child myself, and he like somebody else's grandfather.

The suggestion seemed ridiculous. 'No,' I said, 'I'm not married . . .' And I felt myself start to blush again, feeling the same unreasonable shame as when the Professor's wife had questioned me about Kevin.

'But when you are,' said the Professor, helping me out, 'I can see you'd bring your offspring up more carefully than is generally the case these days.'

'Well, I hope so!' I said with surprising warmth. 'There seems to be no discipline at all any more, not in the schools, not in the home – nowhere!'

Suddenly, realising what I had said, I remembered

20

that strange question the Professor's wife had asked me when we first met. She had got the idea from somewhere that Kevin was in the habit of inflicting corporal punishment on me. Now, standing on that boat, having this awkward and uncomfortable conversation with her husband, I wondered where on earth she had got that idea from, and why. I knew there had been some husbands in Victorian times who had required their wives to loosen their stays and corsets and present themselves in their shifts for six with the dog-whip, but surely men these days didn't expect unquestioning obedience from their girlfriends, or discipline them when they misbehaved. I had never met any woman who let her boyfriend take down her panties and give her a good spanking. But what if they did, some of them, all of them, even, and didn't admit it?

Flustered, I tried to return to a proper sociable subject. 'Do you and your wife have children, Professor?' I asked weakly.

But he ignored my question as if I had never spoken. I heard the note of the engine change, and looking round, I realised we were pulling in to the dock and the journey was almost done.

The Professor was not. 'Do you believe, Jennifer,' he asked me then, as if he was an examiner and I was some promising postgraduate, 'that the young woman today, so independent, so ready to take the world by the horns, so to speak – '

I understood that like his wife he was complimenting me in his own fashion, and I tried to pay closer attention.

'Do you believe she would be better equipped for the hurly-burly if she had, let us say, a stricter upbringing?'

I tried to look into his eyes. All I could see was my

own face, distorted like some gargoyle in the eaves of an ancient church; all nose and no chin. People were beginning to push past us as the boat was made fast and the gangplank brought out. I knew I should make a brief, polite reply and then let him go.

'It's hard to know what to believe these days!' I said, trying to sound cheerful; but hearing myself, I felt only that I had let us both down: the Professor, who had been kind enough to pretend to be interested in my opinions; and myself, by not having any.

I saw an arm wave, and saw it was the Professor's wife's again, beckoning him ashore. What a kind, intelligent couple they were. I said goodbye to the Professor, and we shook hands.

He patted me on the arm, approvingly. 'Your ideas have merit, Jennifer,' he said unexpectedly. 'At least, they interest me, which is all you can ask of an aging fogey like me.'

For some reason, his words had the opposite effect, making him seem on the contrary quite young and virile. I supposed he was perking up now the boredom of talking to a lonely and empty-headed young woman was over and he could return to the company of his lovely wife.

'Perhaps you'd like to write them down and send them to me,' he said.

I was astonished. 'Oh, I couldn't possibly bother you.'

'I really think you should, my dear,' he said, rather sternly. 'Write them down and let me see them. Would you do that for me?'

Stunned, flattered, I had no option but to nod and say I would.

'I look forward to reading what you say,' the Professor told me. 'Goodbye now.'

As I stood back, watching him weave his way

22

through the departing throng, I was filled with an unaccustomed sense of purpose and determination. I would do it. Of course he was only being nice to me, in the only way a middle-aged man of learning knows how to be nice to a silly young woman; but I would take him at his word, and read up on the subject. I would write him a summary of my thoughts on the question of Discipline and the Modern Woman.

3

A Remarkable Letter

This is the letter I wrote to the Professor, at his suggestion.

Dear Professor,

You may not remember, but you were kind enough to give me a few moments of your time when we met this summer, on a trip we both happened to be making down the river. You said then that you would like to know my thoughts on the decline of discipline in our society, and the effect on the modern woman.

It seems to me that in history, our society was a good deal more disciplined than it is today. Everyone went to church several times a week, instead of only some people sometimes, the way it is now. Priests told them that if they sinned, they would be punished and go to Hell, and if they repented and tried to lead virtuous lives, they would be saved and go to Heaven. Right and wrong were very clear and indisputable. Everyone consulted the Bible to tell them what to do and what not.

The law was stronger then too, in the past, and more severe. People were executed for numerous crimes, or sent to prison for life, with no 'time off for good behaviour'. Criminals could expect to be flogged, or set in the stocks. Policemen were respected, and even hardened criminals would not put up a fight when they were taken, because they knew they had done wrong and the penalty was justly deserved. If you did something wrong, you would not expect to get away with it. People nowadays seem to think they have a right to go where they like and take what they want, whether it belongs to them or not.

The lives of women used to be very narrow, much narrower than men's. They were brought up with only one thought in their minds: to win a good husband, and after they were married to look after him and bear his children. Married women were ruled by their husbands completely, with no legal rights of their own and no easy and convenient divorce. Many husbands in all strata of society were like tyrants, ruling their wives and children with a rod of iron. I do not think this was a good thing, but then I am not married, as you know, and have no children.

In school, too, children used to be disciplined without question or appeal. The cane and, in Scotland, a leather strap known as the tawse were used frequently on the youngest children and the oldest too. In earlier times, there might be a birch in the corner of the classroom, consisting of a bunch of twigs of willow tied together around a handle and stuck in a large pot of pickle or brine. Fierce as they were, such methods gave children clear knowledge of how to behave correctly, and what would happen if they did not. Our children today are better protected. The cane is banished from the classroom, and thank goodness, many of them might say. But are the children better behaved or better educated as a result? No one seems ready to swear clearly and unambiguously that they are.

Today's young women have no such terrifying experiences behind or ahead of them. In fact many of them have never even known what it is to have their bottoms smacked, by a parent or anybody else. You can literally say that we are out of control! But do we know how to achieve what must replace that iron rod, that is to say self-control? I welcome wholeheartedly the challenge and opportunity the new freedoms give to my sex, but I can only speak for myself when I say that sometimes I am sure, life is harder as a consequence. If I am honest, I must admit I have sometimes wished I had been given some discipline that would see me through, like a soldier in the field.

Today we look in vain for an authority we can trust to point us along the difficult path between right and wrong. The church is divided against itself, and the law is a tangle of complications and contradictions. My own parents are very dear to me, but very gentle people, quite out of their depth in the confusion of the modern world. Sometimes I feel as if life is a busy main road, full of hurtling traffic, and I am stuck on the pavement, longing for a firm but kindly hand to guide me safely across!

Well, those are my thoughts on the subject, and I can only apologise for the muddle they are in and wish my mind was clearer. You might say the undisciplined shape of my thoughts is the proof of the very problem I have been trying to express.

I spent a while writing this, as you may imagine, drafting it in pencil with lots of rubbing and crossing out, then writing a fair copy in ballpoint pen. I had made sure to put in plenty of references to historical times, because I was certain the Professor would approve of that. But now I had finished it and read it through, I wished I had not said so much about different methods of punishment. I had never experienced any of them myself, so I looked things up at the county library. Now I thought perhaps I had got rather carried away. That aspect of the subject would never have entered my head, I decided, if the Professor's wife had not put it there. In fact I was becoming rather bothered and cross thinking about it now, so I folded the letter up and hastily pushed it into the envelope. Then I licked the flap, stuck it down and rushed out and put it in the postbox before my courage failed me.

For some reason, the next few days were full of anxiety. I kept making stupid mistakes, putting things down and not knowing where I'd put them, and forgetting what I was talking about in the middle of sentences. I kept finding myself thinking about my letter to the Professor; wondering if he'd got it yet, and if he'd read it. I remembered some of the things I'd said and grew quite hot with thinking of them; I was sure they were very stupid things. I was sure the Professor must think me a terrible bore and a waste of time. He must be cursing himself and wishing he had never asked me to write it; and then I wished I'd never written it; and then I poured the tea into the milk jug instead of the teacup, and swore, and thought what a perfect exhibition I was making of the modern woman's lack of discipline in her thought and life, if anyone had been there to see, that is.

After a while, things began to return to normal. I had just decided that the Professor was being kind to me in not mentioning my dreadful stupid letter, when a small white envelope arrived addressed in an elegant, educated hand. I had no idea what it could be or who it was from, but my heart was beating fast as I tore it open with my fingers, in too much of a hurry to pick up the paper-knife.

It was a card, printed with the Professor's address in copperplate writing, and underneath, in the same handwriting as the envelope, the date and a brief message. He thanked me for my letter and said he would be obliged if I would visit him to discuss it, and gave a date and time for that weekend!

I was filled with excitement and joy. I pressed the card to my breast and whirled into the kitchen. He had read my poor muddled thoughts and found something in them to interest him. Perhaps I was not so stupid after all! I wrote a note straight away to thank him for the invitation and to tell him I had pleasure in accepting it. Though it was a very short note, I was pleased with it. It seemed to have exactly the right tone of formality and dignity. Though the Professor had been kind enough to forgive it, I knew my letter had had neither, and I would not let myself down a second time.

I woke up early on the morning of our meeting, which was for coffee at eleven o'clock. It was hardly five, but I couldn't lie in bed a moment longer. I scrambled out of bed and pulled off my nightdress, and went hurrying into the bathroom.

In the long mirror beside the bath I looked at myself. My light brown hair was a bird's nest, my face flushed from sleep. I yawned and rubbed my eyes, which are either grey or blue, depending on the light and how I am and what I'm doing. They seemed quite blue this morning, though the whites were pink now from my rubbing them.

I ran my hands over my breasts. They are nice breasts, I think, quite high and pointed and not at all flat or floppy like some young women's. My nipples are a rather dark pink, almost brown, and small and round like squashed berries. I like the feel of rubbing my hands over them; I can do it for a long time and never get tired of it. When I get excited my nipples get thicker and stand out like push-buttons, and if I

28

rub them then, I get wonderful warm feelings deep inside me, as if I was a pan of something sweet and golden and melted that someone was stirring with a wooden spoon.

My nipples were like that now.

I took my hands away, feeling suddenly doubtful. I felt cross with myself. I was going to the Professor's house for coffee, that was all, I told myself sternly. I would sit on a sofa with the Professor and his wife and sip real coffee made from coffee beans, and we would talk politely about the deplorable state of society today, and the Professor would add some interesting and significant facts from history. It would be a grown-up, civilised meeting, and it would do me good.

So why was I standing naked in the bathroom, stroking my breasts and running my hands over my body, daringly slipping them behind me to feel my own bare bottom, touching myself between the legs? Why did I feel so warm there? Why were my fingers wet?

I stared at myself in the mirror in dismay. I lifted my hand to my nose and sniffed cautiously at my fingers. Good heavens! I smelt rich and salty, like fish and mushrooms and fresh-turned earth. The smell seemed to sink into my throat and make my heart beat faster. I caught my breath with a little snuffling noise like an eager puppy. I thought the smell was delicious.

Whatever was I thinking of? This was no time for playing with my body like a silly schoolgirl! The Professor and his wife were waiting for me!

At once I ran a basin full to the brim with scalding hot water, and scrubbed myself all over with the flannel and lashings of Camay. I wiped furiously between my legs, backwards and forwards, backwards and

29

forwards, until my poor vagina started to tingle in protest. I washed my breasts in a rush, forcing myself not to feel my hands as they hurried over them and round and round. I washed under my arms and behind my ears. I would be clean and nice and freshly scented for our meeting, and properly dressed too.

I hurried back into the bedroom and pulled on my newest white underwear: bra and panties, then a pair of plain tights in a light tan and a half-slip. I had decided to wear my suit, which is a dull dark blue that goes well with my eyes, and a white blouse, which I made haste to iron again, though I am sure there was not a wrinkle in it. I pulled back my hair both sides and fastened it with hairgrips. Then I realised that it was still barely six o'clock, and that there were five hours to go before the time of my invitation.

I made myself have breakfast, though my appetite was flown for some mysterious reason. What I ate would not have satisfied a fly. I hoped I was not going down with something. I went back to the bathroom and took my temperature. I thought it was rather high; but they said if you drank hot tea before taking your temperature it might come out rather high, which only stood to reason. I must calm down, I told myself.

I washed the thermometer, dried it and put it away in the bathroom cabinet, then went back downstairs and washed up the breakfast things. While I washed I twice caught myself leaning up against the sink, pressing my pelvis into it, and made myself stand an inch away.

Drying my hands, I looked at the time. Nearly half past seven. Plenty of time, though it was ticking away.

I made my bed, put some clothes away and others in the laundry basket. I wished I had not got dressed up already because my suit was rather stiff and confining; not at all suitable for housework. I actually had time to do a whole load of laundry, if I wanted. I took off my jacket and at once put it back on again. This was not a day for housework! This was a day for the intellect, for improving the mind with stimulating conversation on important topics and issues.

I went into the sitting room and sat down in an armchair to read the newspaper. There was fighting in Turkey, and at home developments in the economy that were creating grave concern among the members of the opposition. I tried to inform myself about them. It was hard to take it all in, even after reading it two or three times. I turned over the page and saw an advertisement for hairbrushes. At once, unaccountably, I started to wriggle in my chair. I scolded myself aloud, and sat still, forcing myself to concentrate. An article about traditional chair-makers bemoaned the dying art of caning. I flung down the newspaper in a temper, then picked it up in a fright when I saw what a mess I had made of it. I straightened the pages, folded the paper properly along the crease, and laid it neatly on the table. I went and switched the kettle on for a cup of coffee. Then I switched it off again. I didn't need coffee; I would be having coffee at the Professor's house, with the Professor and his wife, in only, only – two and three-quarter hours' time.

I sat and breathed deeply, and laughed at myself. I thought I would tell the Professor what a very undisciplined start I had made to the day, and he would laugh too, in his deep, masculine way, and the Professor's wife would laugh merrily and offer me another biscuit. Then I imagined myself telling them how I had stood in the bathroom stroking my naked body, and I grew hot and bothered again.

31

At last the time had passed. I had managed to catch a bus and ride out to the leafy edge of the city, where the houses are large and stand back from the road behind low walls and tidy hedges. I found the house easily, having happened to walk past it several times in the last few weeks. I went up to the porch, and knocked on the outer door, to be on the safe side; then, when nothing happened, I let myself in and knocked on the inner door which had pebbled glass in it. I knocked on the glass with my knuckles; then I noticed a brass bell-push at the side. Feeling foolish for not noticing it in the first place, I made haste to ring it. Then, of course, I realised how stupid I was being. They must have thought something dreadful had happened in the street, for someone to be knocking and ringing so urgently at their door.

A shape grew behind the pebble glass. The door opened, and the Professor's wife stood there, smiling to see me.

'Jennifer, isn't it?' she said, so warmly that I replied at once: 'Jenny, if you like,' though no one called me Jenny nowadays except my parents and Kevin, and I wasn't going to see Kevin any more.

The Professor's wife was wearing a pretty dress with large pink and green flowers on, which made me feel that my suit was perhaps a bit too formal. She told me it was nice to see me again, and I murmured that it was nice of her to ask me, even though it had been her husband who had asked me, of course. My hands were damp and I tried to wipe them surreptitiously on my skirt as I took off my coat.

'You wrote my husband an essay, I hear,' she said pleasantly.

'Oh, it wasn't nearly grand enough for an essay,' I began.

At that moment, as if activated by the sound of my

32

voice, the Professor came out of a room and along the hallway. He was wearing a cardigan, not even buttoned up, a blue shirt without a tie, corduroy trousers and carpet slippers. Now I knew I was over-dressed.

'Ah, Jennifer, delightful to see you, delightful,' he said, and put out his hand for me to shake. It was a large hand, and it gripped mine very firmly and con-fidently. It was warmer than mine, and strong. Hur-riedly I put my own hands in my pockets, as if I was ashamed of them.

The Professor's wife squeezed his arm again, in that proud way I had seen her do on the boat. 'Coffee in the study, darling?' she asked.

'Coffee, Jennifer?' he asked.

'Coffee sounds wonderful,' I said, as if the card he had written with his own hand hadn't said 'coffee'; as if coffee wasn't what you always drank at eleven o'clock in the morning; and as if I hadn't already drunk two cups before I left home. I think I would have said vinegar sounded wonderful, if he had of-fered me that. I must calm down, I told myself, and catching him looking at me, I gave him my most dazzling, and altogether brainless, smile.

His wife disappeared to the kitchen, and the Pro-fessor led me into his study. Then for the first time I saw the ancient grandfather clock, the globe, and the hundreds and hundreds of shadowy books hanging over me like dark cliffs.

There was a chair put out for me in front of his desk. It was an upright chair with a wooden seat. It did not look very comfortable. When the Professor indicated I should take it I sat down in some disap-pointment. Then I looked on the desk itself and saw, right in the middle of it, pages laid square on the pale green blotting pad: my letter.

My heart started to race again. We really were going to discuss my letter, as if it were a document that was supposed to make sense and have some importance. Why had I not prepared some more intelligent, better considered things to say? Why had I spent the whole bus ride in silly daydreams about the Professor and his wife, instead of reading the newspaper and forming some mature, considered opinions about the Prime Minister's speech to the dairy farmers?

Dizzily, while the Professor went round and took his seat behind the desk, I said: 'I see you got my letter.'

'Yes,' he said, with a non-committal nod. I remembered that last time we had met he had been wearing sunglasses, and I had been unable to see his eyes. I could see them now. They were brown. The light was too dim and the desk too wide for me to be sure what shade of brown. They were looking at me, and I thought how shrewd and commanding they looked.

I was still trying to find a polite way to apologise for my silly letter and the great muddle I had got into, when the door opened and the Professor's wife came in with a tray. She had brought two low, broad cups of beautiful fine pink china, and a battered silver coffee-pot which looked as if it had already seen years of devoted service and would see a good few more. There was a little bowl of demerara sugar, and one of white, and two tiny silver spoons. The Professor's wife put the tray down on the desk at her husband's elbow. She had not provided for herself.

'And now,' said the Professor's wife to me, 'I shall leave you both to get on with it.' She smiled at me, and at her husband, clasping her hands below the bosom of her dress, bestowing her blessing on us both. 'I know you have a great deal to talk about,' she said, and went out and shut the door.

I fidgeted with my hands in my lap. 'I hope my letter didn't bore you, sir,' I said.

'On the contrary, Jennifer,' he said. Then he frowned ever so slightly. 'It is Jennifer, isn't it?' And then he glanced swiftly at the end of the letter, at my signature, so childish compared to the assertive elegance of his own. 'Excuse me,' he said graciously. 'Too many – tutorials,' he said, with the tiniest and most fleeting of smiles.

I felt my cheeks go pink. 'I'm sure you're very busy,' I said.

'Yes,' said the Professor reflectively, as if I had made some new, unfamiliar proposition that needed judicious consideration before he could agree with it. 'Coffee?'

'Yes, please,' I said.

We sat and sipped coffee. I was too awe-struck to speak again. Let him tell me what he thought of my letter, and let me apologise for it and finish my coffee and get out, I thought.

'Some very interesting observations,' the Professor said slowly, fingering my cheap notepaper as though he could divine further information from the texture of it.

'Thank you, sir,' I said. 'You're very kind.'

'Oh, not at all,' he said, and he sounded almost surprised, as though the notion of his being the slightest bit kind was a complete and rather startling error.

We drank our coffee. The Professor put on a pair of tortoiseshell glasses and read a little of my letter to himself. I wondered which bit he was reading, and buried my nose in my cup. I could not bear the sight of my own writing across the desk, in his hands.

'From this I gather,' the Professor said, taking his glasses off again, 'that the Modern Woman finds herself in a most parlous state indeed. Most parlous.'

'Parlous, sir?' I said.

'Perilous, Jennifer,' he translated, making a little moue.

'I don't know sir,' I said. 'I just know that sometimes I feel very confused and don't know what to do. I don't even know what to think.'

'You shouldn't have to think,' said the Professor, in a most contradictory way. He sounded like the Caterpillar telling off Alice in Wonderland. I gulped my coffee, and apologised again.

'No, no,' he said, putting down his cup and giving a little wave of his hand. 'It wasn't a reproach. I meant to say, you feel you should *know* what to do, and what to think, for that matter, without, as it were, thinking.'

'Yes, sir,' I said doubtfully.

He picked up a page of my letter again. ' "The difficult path between right and wrong," ' he read.

'That's how it seems to me, sir,' I said, on the defensive.

' "Discipline that would see me through," ' he read. He put on his glasses and took them off again. He leaned back in his chair and folded his hands across his stomach.

'How old are you, Jennifer, if you don't mind my asking?'

I told him.

He scratched his ear.

My earlier sense of disappointment returned. This was not the stimulating intellectual conversation I had been promising myself. He obviously didn't know what to say to me at all, and his wife had left us because she couldn't bear to have to try to hold a sensible conversation with me.

'How did you know about the birch in pickle?' he asked.

36

I jumped, and began to blush again. 'I read it in a book,' I said stupidly.

He nodded slowly. 'And I suppose you know that in Suffolk and parts of Cambridgeshire, it was the custom right up until the Second World War to send erring servant girls and dairymaids out in their shifts to gather willow switches for their own thrashings?'

He spoke very precisely, but in a very matter-of-fact way; and he rubbed his jaw.

My eyes had grown very round during that little speech, and I had become unaware that my fingers were holding a coffee cup halfway to my lips. 'No, sir!' I stammered, spilling coffee in little drops on my skirt.

Hastily I put the cup down, clattering it in its saucer, and dived for my handkerchief to mop up the spill. When I looked up, the Professor was on his feet, coming round the desk to me, his hand held out. I gasped. What was he planning?

'Thank you for coming, Jennifer,' he said, quite heartily. 'It's been most stimulating.'

In a daze of dismay I held out my hand and let him shake it. His coffee cup was empty. I stood up, trying to drain mine as I rose.

'Sorry you couldn't stay longer,' he was saying, 'but we'll meet again soon.'

Would we? At that moment I must say I was far from sure.

With cordial farewells, the Professor sent me out of the room, into the care of his wife, who had come bustling along the hall wiping her hands on a tea-towel.

'Goodbye, Jenny dear,' she said, as though she had been a friend of my mother's and known me since birth. She gave me a fond smile. 'Have you made an appointment?' she asked.

37

I said I had not. 'He didn't say,' I said.

She waved her hand in the air. 'Oh, the absent-minded Professor!' she said. But she didn't offer me an appointment either.

As I went out of the gate and turned to close it securely behind me, I looked back at the house and had a strange hallucination. In the bay window of the front room, I thought I saw the Professor's wife standing watching me. I thought her dress had come off, and that she was standing there in her underwear.

I rode back home on the bus in a mood of black misery, and even started to cry at one point because I had made such a fool of myself. I was hopeless, worthless, completely unfit for adult society.

Three days later I received, neatly typewritten, his Instructions for young ladies about to receive Initiation.

4

Discussions and Devices

My knickers were down around my thighs.

I had not bargained for that. Clearly there were yet further degrees of distinction between nudity and underclothes. Between knickers on and knickers off, lay not a gradation of black and white, but a whole spectrum of greys.

It seemed not only less convenient but somehow more embarrassing, more lewd, to be required to leave my knickers where they were, at half-mast, so to speak, than to have to take them off altogether.

Nevertheless, my bottom was now bare. And of course, not only my bottom.

I must go to the Professor and submit to Examination. Yet I could hardly shuffle over to him backwards, preserving the last vestige of my modesty. It would be ridiculous; and not at all the conduct of a model pupil.

Head up, shoulders back, I turned to face him. Then I walked with as much poise as I could muster to the small school desk, and bent myself over it.

Then the Professor placed his hands upon me. Over-stimulated as I already was, I could not help it: I gave a little gasp. 'Quiet, please, Jennifer,' he said mildly. 'There'll be plenty of time for that later.'

Dizzy, I felt him squeeze my buttocks, gently, then more firmly, lifting them in his hands and separating them, running his fingertips down the cleft, then lifting each cheek in one hand as if testing its weight and spring.

Just like a doctor, I told myself again.

He pushed the tip of his bare finger into my anus. I squealed, and at once he took his hands quite away.

There was a pause. Then he asked, 'How much space is there on the bottom of that piece of paper, Jennifer?'

'Quite a lot, sir,' I admitted, reluctantly.

'Go and draw a line across,' he said, 'and under it put six ones. Don't make them too big,' he said, as I went over, crestfallen, ashamed of myself once again, and carried out his instruction. 'Leave room for more.'

Then I returned to my position over the desk, and mute and meek, allowed him to complete his examination of my bottom and thighs, and everywhere thereabouts. I bit my lip and screwed my eyes tight shut. Shivery waves of gooseflesh swept over me like the sea.

'Very suitable,' said the Professor, patting my bare bottom contemplatively. 'Perfect, in fact.'

I tried to feel encouraged by his praise, while his hand roved and roved. He pushed up my jumper and blouse at the back, as if to Examine the Area more generally.

'Can it really be true, Jennifer, as you were telling me,' the Professor asked languidly, 'that this perfect posterior has never yet felt so much as a single smack?'

'Yes, sir,' I said.

'Not even in childhood?'

'No, sir. I'm sorry, sir.'

'Oh, please don't apologise, Jennifer,' he said, his voice sensitive and low. 'It is a great pleasure to Initiate a complete – ' and his hand stroked lightly beneath my bottom, his fingers supple and sure ' – innocent,' he concluded.

'Thank you, sir,' I said, with another shudder.

'I'm simply amazed,' the Professor resumed, 'astonished, that any parent, any pedagogue, could forbear – could withhold their hand . . .'

I felt obliged to offer something. 'The midwife might have smacked me, sir,' I said, 'when I was born. They do it to start the baby breathing, sir,' I explained.

'A different case, Jennifer,' the Professor said.

'Yes, sir,' I said.

'The one is medical, the other moral.'

'Yes, sir,' I said again. Moral, not medical: I told myself to make a mental note of the distinction. It was becoming hard to concentrate.

'Well, well,' the Professor said. He took his hands from me, reluctantly, I felt. 'You may tick Examination,' he said.

'Sir?'

'On the Prospectus,' he said, impatiently.

'Yes, sir. I'm sorry, sir.'

'Well, pay attention,' he said, as I rose from the hard desk and hurried to the notice-board as fast as I could with my knickers still down. I was holding my breath, waiting for him to tell me to add to that ominous line of ones, in recognition of my lack of attention; but all he said was: 'Now read the first position.'

'Knee, sir.'

'Yes, Jennifer, Knee. By which we understand?'

I hesitated. I had a very good idea, but I was on completely unfamiliar ground, and unwilling to make any mistakes. 'I'm not sure, sir.'

'Then allow me to show you.' The Professor came

41

and took hold of me from behind, holding me lightly by the elbows. In that position I suddenly felt an extraordinary helplessness. I was a prisoner taken by the law, instantly and entirely subject to the penalty prepared for her. I allowed him to steer me round the broad, beautifully polished, dark oak desk to his chair, which stood pushed back a few feet, its seat of dark red leather gleaming in the gentle light. It was a rather large chair, with plenty of room for him to sit forward in it, upright, his feet flat on the floor, and indicate to me with a grace and economy born of years of experience the position he intended.

'Here is my knee, Jennifer,' said the Professor. 'In the course of the well-disciplined life that you seek, you will no doubt, on occasion, be required to submit to correction with the left hand; but I am right-handed, so you place yourself here, on my right, and bend over accordingly.'

Accordingly, I did bend over – rather clumsily I'm sorry to say; but the Professor soon had me balanced across his lap, bare bottom up, the yellow carpet inches from my face. 'Lift your feet, Jennifer, please,' I heard him say. Then I felt his capable hand strip my brand-new panties off my legs and whisk them away I knew not where.

It was almost a relief to be without them, free of the restriction between my knees, free of the fear that they might at any instant fall down.

'This is the most basic position known to man,' the Professor told me, his hand warm on my bare thigh above the stocking-top; 'and the most simple, one might even say most primitive, of all available punishments. To some pedantic minds, this is the only method that can accurately be honoured with the name of spanking: *videlicet*, spanking with the bare hand. All other corporal punishments, they argue, are forms of beating, and must be considered under an entirely separate heading.'

He stroked my bottom with a reassuring hand.

'Now I, Jennifer,' he said quietly and rather seriously, as though it was vital that he deliver this important lesson to me on the occasion of my first spanking: the message that lay at the heart of the mystery, 'I am not of that school. It is my contention, as I'm sure you know well, that "spanking" is the name that we give to a transaction between individuals; and that all the various methods, positions, preferences and paraphernalia are merely aspects of a single activity.'

Upside down, I supposed that this must be a speech the Professor always delivered to new pupils. I was not altogether sure that I saw the point he was making. It seemed to me, in my ignorance, that whoever looked at it, in whatever way, I was about to have my bottom spanked.

And I was.

It was not a hard spanking. I realised later that a disciplinarian as expert and considerate as the Professor would certainly temper the wind to the shorn lamb, so to speak, dealing gently with any young woman he escorted for the first time through the gates of personal correction; but I realised it, as I say, later. At the time, I was shocked, startled, and stung by the hard palm of his hand as he raised it and brought it down on me again and again.

'It hurts, sir!' I cried idiotically.

'It does indeed, Jennifer,' agreed the Professor. He continued. He smacked my left cheek, high and rather to the side, and then immediately the right, in exactly the same place; and while those two smacks were still stinging, he smacked the middle of my bottom, across the cleft – high at first; then just below;

43

then just below that, fetching me a sharp crack, the hardest yet, precisely across the sensitive pucker of my anus. My legs jerked wildly and I cried out, then reached up to stuff my hand in my mouth, recalling his prohibition against noise.

But he said: 'Feel free to cry out now, Jennifer. All authorities agree that the major part of the Initiate's suffering is in fact not pain but shock. When later she becomes familiar with the process, an additional requirement of silence may be imposed, either by means of a device, or as a learned discipline. Until then, the maiden may be allowed to shout the house down, so to speak; or at least vent her lungs in a healthy, natural way.'

Throughout this little lecture the Professor continued to spank me, but less severely now I thought, with the kinder, more sparing smacks of before. Not that I could have said for sure. By now the stinging in my bottom was continuous, the flash of each new smack hardly distinguishable from the strange (and, I must confess, not horribly unpleasant) tingle left by the one before.

I continued to cry out, though in less of a panic now that the expert had explained a fraction of my suffering to me; or perhaps I was simply beginning to be soothed by his calm and magisterial tone of voice. As he punctuated his speech with smacks, I clenched my teeth and tried to confine my cries to the pauses between word and word or phrase and phrase, so as not to drown out what he was saying. I did not want to lose the benefit of his education. As before, I wished to be the perfect Initiate, or at least a commendable one; and if, as he implied, there were those who shouted the house down when they were spanked, I made up my mind that I was not going to be among them.

44

Still I jerked and bucked as each smack fell, until the Professor was obliged to say: 'It would be helpful if you could try not to kick quite so much, Jennifer.'

'I'm sorry, sir!' I gasped.

'I understand that too is a healthy, natural reaction – '

'My legs – seem to fly about – on their own, sir,' I panted.

'Indeed,' said the Professor, smacking my right cheek as he spoke. 'Most understandable,' he said, smacking my left cheek. 'And of course, very familiar. Restraints are available,' he said, pausing. 'But I should prefer not to burden us with additional considerations at this stage.' He began to spank me again.

I tried to keep quiet, and I tried to keep still; but I regret to say that by now I was tiring and dazed. My self-control was failing and I was relieved when at last he sat back and said, 'You may stand, Jennifer.'

He helped me up, holding me by the elbows as before. I was very grateful, for though the spanking was over temporarily, and I had permission to stand up, I did not yet have the power to do so. My legs swayed, my knees refusing to lock. My bottom was stinging dreadfully and I clutched it without shame. I rubbed and scrubbed it with the palms of my hands as though I thought I could rub away the pain.

In a minute the Professor let go of me. When he saw that I remained securely upright, he laid his hand gently on my shoulder. He really was a very handsome man, I thought, irrelevantly.

'Very good, Jennifer,' he said quietly; and if my bottom glowed from the effect of my punishment, I glowed just as brightly inside at those simple words of praise.

The Professor put his hand under my chin and

tilted my head up to catch the lamplight. 'No tears?' he asked, unnecessarily, for my eyes were perfectly dry. 'Excellent. Yes?'

My voice seemed to wither in my windpipe.

'Well?' he said, smiling indulgently. 'Speak, child, speak.'

I swallowed, then sucked in air and cleared my throat, struggling for mastery over my own larynx, and a semblance of intelligent adult conversation.

'What are the devices of silence you mentioned, sir?' I asked.

The Professor gave me a more curious smile, as though my question had impressed him in some way; which I could hardly believe. Turning in his chair, he reached for a bookshelf and ran his fingers along it, searching for a particular volume. After a moment, he tutted. Clearly the book was not there.

He rose, ignoring me standing there still rubbing my poor bottom, and went to look along the shelves at the back of the room. In a moment he found it.

'Marion has been putting things back out of place,' he remarked, chillingly; and I felt for Marion, and wondered who she was: his wife; or a servant, perhaps. I did not envy her her next interview with her lord and master.

The Professor returned to his chair, and laid on the desk in front of him an old black leather-bound book, which he opened with care, out of consideration for its disintegrating binding. Pages of paper as thin and fine as a bible's slipped rustling through his fingers as he found the place.

He looked up at me. 'You've heard of the scold's bridle?'

'Yes, sir,' I said.

He showed me a picture in the book, an engraving of an old woman wearing a frightful contraption of

46

iron locked around her head. 'Similar devices have been produced through the centuries, of metal or leather, or plastic. Modern fetishists,' he said, as if these were a breed apart that one should indulge, or even study, but generally deplore, 'seem to favour a ball like a common table-tennis ball.' He held up his finger and thumb a little way apart to show me the scale of the device. 'Only painted black, of course,' he said, with a tone of the gentlest irony. 'Thongs, or a length of elastic, keep the ball in place in the miscreant's mouth.'

He turned some pages idly. 'Others recommend something that may be gripped between the teeth – a bar of soap is a particularly nasty one,' he said, with a grimace and a shake of the head. 'Or a block of soft wood covered in cloth or leather – rubber, in the tropics . . . some, you see here, even have metal studs on the underside, like the nails in a horseshoe, to depress the tongue completely.' He shook his head again, seeming to find this quite extravagant and almost depressing; and he shut the book with a soft clop.

The Professor steepled his fingers and rested his chin upon them, regarding me standing beside him. The clock ticked. The pain of my first spanking was subsiding in my bottom with surprising speed, I thought, giving way to a dull, throbbing ache.

'In my experience,' said the Professor, modestly, as if that did not amount to very much, 'a young lady's own panties, wadded up and popped into her mouth, are perfectly effective, and extremely convenient, logical, and charming.'

I blanched. Somehow, this proposition was more appalling than all the hideous apparatus described in his tattered book.

'Thank you, Professor,' I said, huskily.

As much, I think, to give me something to do as because it was the necessary next step in our protocol, he motioned me over to the notice-board. 'You may tick Knee,' he instructed, and I did so.

'And Hand, sir?'

'Not until we've worked a little on Thighs,' he said.

I looked down at myself. What were those little glinting patches at my crotch? Good heavens, was I becoming aroused again? Quickly I pressed my legs together. I was, I could feel it. The heat of my spanking had concealed from me an inner, more subtle heat of my own. How irrelevant! Could I not contain myself for a moment, just because a man had taken off my panties? I must, I thought.

'Should I take my stockings off, then, sir?' I asked.

'Let me look,' he said.

I stood facing him, legs pressed together, hoping I had managed to smear my unwary secretions into invisibility.

'No need,' he decided. 'Your lovely legs are quite long enough to leave ample room for punishment above the stocking. At least, at this stage.'

I coloured slightly at his unexpected compliment and fingered my hair self-consciously. I did not speak.

'Fetch that chair, would you, Jennifer, please?' said the Professor, pointing to a plain upright chair I had occupied at my first interview in this room. What an age ago that seemed now! I went and removed a pile of papers and learned journals from it, putting them neatly on top of another similar pile nearby, and carried the chair to the centre of the carpet, in front of the fire. It was terribly heavy.

'Chair-back,' I quoted, from the prospectus; and I was unable to keep a tremor of new apprehension out of my voice.

'Quite so,' he said, with a strange levity.

48

Boldly I placed myself behind the chair. It came up just above the bottom of my ribcage. I could see how you would do this. I leaned forward over the back, grasping the sides of the seat, and lowered my weight until my pubis was resting on the top of the chair-back, my head hanging over the seat. In this position clearly there was no danger of the tail of my blouse getting in the way, as I had feared when I removed my knickers. My legs, I supposed, should be pointed straight out behind me; but it was difficult to move now I was in the position.

The Professor's voice came towards me as he approached me from behind.

'You really should wait for the word, you know, or ask permission to go over. No, no – don't get up. You'll do very nicely as you are.'

There came a knock at the study door.

Resting his hand on my bottom, the Professor called loudly: 'Come.'

I heard the door open.

'Tea, anyone?' asked the Professor's wife.

49

5

Tea, and After

'Tea-time already?' said the Professor.

'Doesn't time fly,' she replied. Upside down through the legs of the chair I saw her, still nude, cross the floor and put a tray on the Professor's desk. 'I can see you're getting on famously, you two,' she said.

'I was just about to show Jennifer punishment above the stocking,' he told her.

'Don't let me interrupt you,' she said. 'I'll leave you the pot, shall I?'

'No, no, let's stop now we've stopped.'

'Oh dear,' said the Professor's wife gaily, 'I hope I haven't made him cross now, Jenny.'

'It's my fault,' I said. 'I bent over without being told.'

'Did you indeed?' said the Professor's wife. 'You are obviously well on your way.'

'Another way of saying that,' said the Professor almost boisterously, 'is *forward*, which is to say impertinent, which is to say undisciplined. Jennifer, get up, go and put another six at the end of the prospectus, then come and join us for a cup of tea.'

His wife was surprised. 'Would you like me to stay, darling?' she said, as I crossed the room and drew the fateful ones.

'She could hardly join *us* if one of us was in another room,' said the Professor, sounding like the Caterpillar once again.

His wife ran her hand over her perfect black hair; then down across her bare right breast, as though that might need smoothing too. She was as nearly flustered as I had ever seen her. 'No, my dear, of course not, how silly of me. But what I meant to say was, perhaps your pupil might object.'

'Well, there she is,' he said. 'You may ask her.'

Clasping her hands together, the Professor's wife swivelled to face me. Her pubic hair was thick and dark, and neatly trimmed. 'Will you excuse me if I bring my tea in here, Jennifer?' she said, lightly.

'I'd be delighted,' I said, and meant it.

The nude woman lifted her chin and raised her eyebrows the tiniest fraction. 'Perhaps you'd like to put your things back on then, dear,' she said, kindly.

I was mortified. However long would it take for me to learn the rules? 'I'm sorry,' I told her, ducking my head, 'I wasn't thinking.' And I hurried to get my skirt from the hook. Stepping into it and doing it up, I made an attempt to tidy my hair with my fingers, glancing all the while around the shadowy room. 'Professor, where did you put my knickers?'

I found them behind the desk, draped over a bust of Milton.

'I'd be a bit careful putting those on, if I were you,' said the Professor's wife, pouring the tea.

'Oh, yes, I see. Ouch!' I bit my lip, ruefully rubbing my bottom through my skirt. 'Sorry, sir,' I said to the Professor.

'You can relax now, Jennifer,' he said. 'Would you like to sit down?'

'Oh, yes,' I said easily, as if there could not possibly be a problem.

'That's the spirit,' said the Professor's wife,

51

bending down to pull a pouffe out from under a cabinet. I sat there, rather the lowest of the company, while the Professor's wife sat in the chair I had been occupying when she came in. She sat very close to me, but not so close that I did not suspect she was sometimes looking up my skirt. The Professor sat behind his desk, and we all took tea together.

'How are you finding it so far, Jenny?' the Professor's wife asked me politely.

I pressed my hand to my breast. 'It's still all a bit of a shock, I have to confess.'

'Oh?'

'Jennifer's just had her first spanking,' the Professor told her.

'Your first ever? My dear, I didn't realise! Congratulations!'

'Thank you,' I said feebly.

'We should be drinking something stronger than this,' declared the Professor's wife, but she toasted me anyway with tea.

I glanced nervously at the Professor behind his desk, to see how I should react. He was smiling abstractedly at us, and sipping his tea in perfect contentment.

The Professor's wife put her hand delicately on my leg. 'I really thought Kevin – '

'I shan't be seeing Kevin again,' I reminded her.

'No, but I quite thought – '

Her husband broke in: 'Nevertheless,' he said, and she became silent.

I wondered why she was naked. I wondered if there was any possible way I could find out without seeming to ask.

'This is lovely tea,' I said.

'Beautiful,' said the Professor's wife idly. She might have been talking about anything: me, or the occasion, or anything at all.

She put her hand on my knee again.

'I can't remember when I had my first spanking,' she said. 'I was terribly young, I expect. I was a naughty little girl, and my parents were very strict.' Her eyes seemed to sparkle in the firelight. 'They spent ages searching for a school where they would punish a girl properly, and not mess around with lines and detentions. The head caned, the teachers spanked, and the head girl and all the prefects used the gymshoe, though they weren't really supposed to. They had to keep it secret from the governors, or at least the governors pretended not to know. Where did you go to school, Jenny?'

'Park Street Comprehensive,' I said.

The Professor's wife looked across at her husband. 'I don't think we know it, do we, dear?'

'Know of it,' the Professor claimed. He was eating a macaroon.

The Professor's wife looked speculatively at me over the rim of her teacup. 'I don't suppose they . . .' she said.

I shook my head.

'No, of course not, silly of me – more tea, Jenny?' she asked brightly.

I looked at the Professor.

'Half a cup,' he said.

'Thank you, sir,' I said.

'And then we really must get on,' he said.

The Professor's wife poured my tea. 'I couldn't help noticing,' she said to me, 'I assume it's Thighs now, is it?'

I said it was, and drank my tea.

'And how's the Bottom?' she asked.

'Fine,' I said. 'Really,' and I drained my cup. 'Would you like to see?'

'Jennifer!' she cried.

'Oh, I'm sorry,' I said frantically, glancing at her husband, who was busy finishing his macaroon.

'No, no,' said the Professor's wife, 'I mean, I should be honoured! May I, darling?'

Chewing, he waved his hand. 'I don't see why not,' he said grumpily. 'She's about to take her clothes off again anyway.'

Slightly shy at the effect of my daring, I shed my skirt again and peeled off my panties. I did not think Milton needed them, so I hung them on the peg with my skirt. Then I went back to bend over the chair.

The Professor's wife was still sitting on it. She looked at me expectantly.

I turned round instead.

She did not touch me, but looked closely at my bottom. 'You are a bit red, dear,' she said pleasantly. 'Also your left stocking is slipping. May I?'

I stood still and felt her cool fingers adjust my stocking, refolding the top and refastening the suspender.

'Thighs are actually something rather different,' she said casually.

'Thighs have been known and used as a punishment area since well before records were kept,' the Professor observed. 'The slapping of the leg, and particularly the back of the leg, is behaviour often seen amongst mothers exasperated by their offspring in public places, especially if the little darlings are wearing skirts or shorts at the time. The punishment of a smacked thigh may be given to women of any age. It is a convenient punishment on the run, so to speak; in public, if necessary – which does not necessitate any derangement of the underwear.'

'Though a woman of an age to wear stockings,' said the Professor's wife crisply, her hand still lingering on mine, 'has to put up with the extra humiliation of lifting her skirt right up to her waist, to bare enough flesh for the process. Or having it lifted for her. On one side at least, in public.'

She stood up now, and put our tea things on the tray. 'It's much easier in summer,' she said.

I wanted to be helpful, not to let her wait on me completely, so I went and collected the Professor's cup and plate from the desk for her.

'Now, sir?' I asked him.

The lines at the corners of his eyes crinkled. 'Yes, Jennifer, now you may bend over the chair.'

'Thank you, sir,' I said, more bravely than I felt. I got myself into position once more. I could hear the tea things still being clattered about on the tray.

'My sweet?' said the Professor then. 'Would you like to witness this?'

'My dear! May I? I shall take the pouffe and sit in the corner, out of the way,' she said, doing so. 'I must say I do envy your posture, Jenny. Are you sure you haven't done this before?'

'Jennifer was learning all about the scold's bridle,' said the Professor, 'just before you came in.'

'Sorry, dear,' I heard her say, contritely.

The Professor laid his hand on my left thigh, above the stocking.

'For this,' he said, 'you will always bend over with your legs apart.'

'Sorry, sir,' I said.

'You weren't to know,' he said. 'But again, anticipation is not perfect obedience.'

His words had the air of a saying Victorian misses might have embroidered upon cambric and had framed and hung on the bedroom wall. Perhaps the work might have gone with them when they got married, to be presented, with a curtsey and a shy proud glance, to their new husbands.

The Professor helped me open my legs.

'You remember, Jennifer,' he said, smacking my bottom, 'the area we were concerned with just now was around here.'

'Yes, sir! Ow! Ouch!'

'The area we move to now is more in the region of here – '

'Ah!'

' – and here – '

'Oo-ch!'

' – and here.'

'Yes, sir!'

His hand flew lightly around the tops of my legs, smacking now in, now out; this side of the suspender, then the other. Both my legs were quickly stinging. The Professor seemed to be smacking both thighs at once. Upside down, it was impossible to tell.

'You appreciate, I suppose, how much this extends the range of even the simplest spanking?' he asked.

I did. Those few careless preliminary slaps he had given my bottom had not been incidental at all, but very cunning. They had revived the throb planted there by the spanking, and now my entire lower quarters felt as if he was kindling a fire in them. The sharpest sting undoubtedly came with the punishment that fell upon my inner thighs; though the fleshy back of the thigh, beneath the swell of the buttock, stung fiercely enough when a smack came rapidly.

But I held my tongue.

I think the Professor noticed. I am sure he did. There was nothing that he did not know, or recognise, or understand perfectly, about the behaviour of young ladies under corporal punishment.

I became aware that the spanking had ceased. My eyes were closed: I did not know when I had closed them. My face was hot from the fire, from hanging upside down, and from the extraordinary humiliation of my position.

Dimly hearing a drawer slide open, I reflected that alone with him I might not have been so sensitive to the lewdness and absurdity of my pose, not even when he parted my thighs. In my urgency to do my best and derive the most benefit from his tuition, I might have missed some of the moral force of this exposure. But in front of a witness! The Professor could not have found a more effective way to make me conscious of myself and stop me getting cocky.

I had received only one simple hand-spanking so far, albeit in two doses. It was nothing to be proud of. Some girls did the same every day of their lives. The Professor's wife had virtually said so. I was now under no doubt that she was appearing nude today as a punishment for some transgression of her own: a humiliation far beyond any I might fancy myself capable of bearing. For if she was my witness, was I not hers? Had I not been an unwished-for spectator of her punishment since the first moment she opened the front door to me? I wondered again if she was Marion, and if so, what would be required from her for disorganising the Professor's reference shelves.

'Bravo, Jenny!' called the Professor's wife. I was in need of encouragement, and grateful to her.

The Professor returned to me, beginning to speak again as he came. 'The Ruler,' he said, and I knew at once he had been to his desk to fetch one. I supposed it was plastic.

'The Ruler,' he said, 'is a deceptive instrument. In Plastic – ', and he caught me a stinging swipe on the left thigh, 'it has a most distinctive bite.'

Indeed, it made my eyes water.

'Yet it leaves virtually no mark, and may be used for a long time without any fear of injury – at least,' he amended, 'by a skilled practitioner. Yet in Wood – '

I was wrong. He had fetched both kinds of ruler.

'*Ow!*'

'It seems as sharp to the Novice as the dreadful Cane,' he said, in a voice like the villain of a Hammer horror film.

For a while he whipped my thighs with both rulers. Had he asked, I would have had to admit that after the first strokes, I could not have told which was which if my life had depended on it. I supposed it was like wine. How much there was to learn!

'What is the deceit in that?' he asked, suddenly and quite loudly, smacking me with what I supposed must be the wooden rule. I did not know what to answer, and said nothing; and then with relief realised the question had been addressed to his wife.

'Well, it's not properly a deceit, dear,' said the Professor's wife.

'It's a metaphor,' growled her husband. 'A pathetic fallacy. A quality of the subject is transferred to the object for dramatic or pedagogic effect.'

This analysis was underlined, you may imagine, by sharp whacks of the rulers to the rear of the subject. They had left the region of my thighs, and were creeping up my bottom.

'The Novice has made a mistake, that's all,' concluded the Professor's wife calmly, as if he had not spoken.

'And what is the Novice's mistake?' he asked, jovially, swiping freely at my bottom now. Quick and fleeting as the strokes were, I could feel how some were hard and rigid and hateful, while some merely stung and flared as if a solid object had not made them at all, but rather some lash of electrical force. Could I confidently identify the former with Wood, and the latter with Plastic? Or was it only the technical skill of the master that produced such a vivid range of contrast, such a dazzling chiaroscuro of effect?

'Jennifer? What was the Novice's mistake?'

So this question, like the rulers, was aimed at me. While the question buzzed and rang in my poor bewildered brain, the rulers were still playing energetically on all the bare skin above the tops of my stockings.

I could not answer; I did not know the answer. Not only did I not know, I could not speak. My teeth were clenched too tightly together for speech. Not only could I not speak, I am ashamed to confess that at that moment I did not even care what the Novice's mistake was, unless the answer might, in some mystical way, produce the immediate replacement of both the Professor's rulers in the drawer of his desk.

'The Novice's mistake?' said the Professor eventually. 'The Novice's mistake is what, darling?'

'The Novice's mistake,' replied his wife at once in a low voice, 'is that the Cane is very much worse than anything she can imagine.'

A terrible quavering whimper broke from my mouth.

At once, as if my tormentor had been waiting only for that signal, the spanking stopped.

I thought of it as a spanking, even then, hanging head first over a chair with my hands gripping the seat like talons and my eyes starting from my head. Though there was all the difference in the world between the effect of the human hand and the indifferent slice of the ruler, organic or inorganic, I knew exactly what the Professor had meant about the transaction being the same. The transaction was that I took off my knickers and he spanked my bottom; and I would defy any pedant who denied it.

Clutching my bottom I rose stiffly, painfully, very very slowly from over the chair.

'Dear, dear,' said the Professor's wife, bustling over to pat and cosset me. 'You are doing awfully well, Jenny, you know.'

In her hand I saw, dazedly, that she held a paper tissue; and while I writhed, bending my knees and flexing them, shaking my legs and turning restlessly this way and that, she surreptitiously wiped the back of the chair.

I was oozing again! I was absolutely mortified. Not only was I oozing, flowing hot and wet as never so freely before, but my nipples were shamefully erect. I was grateful they were still hidden beneath my clothes, for I could not have borne the Professor seeing them. He would have known then that all his labours so far had been in vain. I was obviously as little able to control myself and my unreasonable urges as the innocent young woman who had ridden there on the bus, little more than an hour ago.

'Tremendously well,' said the Professor's wife mechanically, though I did not suppose insincerely. Her skin was white and smooth where she brushed purposely against me. I smelt her scent: a light, spring-like fragrance. She looked me in the eye and smiled.

'Here,' she said, and openly handed me the wet tissue.

I thought she meant me to go and throw it in the wastepaper bin. Certainly there was no concealing it now, or what it signified. In my embarrassment, I wished it would vanish into thin air.

Then I saw that the Professor's wife was signalling discreetly to me. The tissue was to wipe the sticky juices smeared up across my belly and trickling down my thigh. Sighing unhappily, I mopped myself, then went and threw the horrid thing away.

The Professor was sitting behind his desk. I could not meet his eyes. My nipples, I realised, had deflated. Perhaps this embarrassing little episode was over.

'Tick Thighs: Back,' he called.

Gratefully, I shuffled, wincing, to the Prospectus and did as he said.

'What now, Jennifer?' he said.

I was sure he knew perfectly well, but to learn a thing properly, I knew how helpful it could be to say it aloud. That they had taught me at Park Street Comprehensive, even if I had not understood it also applied in this field of study.

'Thighs: Front,' I read. I looked down at them. They looked quite white and goose-pimply, compared to the blaze I imagined around the back. I fought the impulse to look down over my shoulder and inspect the damage for myself. I had not been told to do that. Perhaps the Professor knew it was worse, having to imagine it.

Of course he knew it was worse.

I had no idea what position Thighs: Front would require, so I stood perfectly still and tried to feel grateful for a moment of rest. I looked at the Professor, who was checking something in a pair of books, running his finger down the index and comparing references. I looked at his wife. She was sitting back in the corner, on her pouffe. She was sitting with her knees apart, facing me. To my astonishment I realised she was silently showing me her crotch.

What was that white thing, peeping slyly out from beneath the black shadow of her pubic hair? Good heavens, was the Professor's wife also squatting on a paper tissue? Was she trying to tell me something?

Speechless, agog, I looked urgently into her face. Her make-up was perfect; her expression alert but quite neutral.

Then perhaps I shivered, or perhaps a microscopic ash flew out of the fire and landed in my eye making me squint for a second; but I would have sworn one of the Professor's wife's eyelids flicked instantaneously down and up.

'There's an interesting variant to the Desk,' said the Professor, rising and rummaging along the bookshelves, taking out a volume, opening and shutting it and thrusting it back with barely a glance. He scratched his head, took out another, scanned the table of contents, and laid it irritably aside.

'I mean, the Desk, conventionally, simply supports the upper body, rather more so than the chair-back, which we really should have put after it.'

He seemed put out at this flaw in the prospectus.

'And the Couch is more accommodating still,' his wife pointed out pleasantly. She was now sitting with her legs crossed, her hands clasped on her upper knee, though I had not been aware of her moving a muscle.

The Professor glared at her. 'Yes, hang it, it is,' he said.

I thought I ought to try to pour oil on troubled waters, so to speak; to smooth out, if I could, this little unpleasantness. Apart from any social consideration of good manners, there seemed to me a possibility he might decide that the entire Initiation was invalid and must be conducted again properly tomorrow, from the beginning.

'The desk doesn't look very comfortable,' I said. 'And the little one isn't comfortable at all.'

'The question of comfort doesn't enter into it,' he barked. At once I discovered I had seized the wrong end of the stick. 'It's a solid horizontal support,' he said argumentatively, slapping the top of the desk with his hand in a way that made me flinch. The rulers had not yet been put away, I noticed; nor had he told me to tick them off.

The Professor's wife stood up. 'I'll show her, shall I?' she volunteered.

The Professor looked at her. Wearily he beckoned her over.

The Professor's wife walked smartly to the Desk, not to the side but to the front, so that she stood at it with her back to me. For a moment she looked over her shoulder, making sure I was paying attention. Then she bent over the desk, pressing her sweet little breasts against it and pillowing her sleek head on her arms. Her bottom was white and succulently round. I could see it might well need spanking quite frequently.

The Professor's wife stretched her legs out backwards, straightening her knees and creasing the toes of her little black shoes, and delicately and precisely in my direction, she parted her thighs.

The paper tissue had vanished.

I was far from sure, however, that the area she had revealed was perfectly dry.

My heart went out to her. How brave she was! What if her husband should decide to examine her? He might even take advantage of her in this vulnerable position. As he had said of me, when I was in a very similar position, how could any disciplinary authority withhold his hand from such a tempting target? If her name was Marion, did she even know the danger she was putting herself in, laying herself down so invitingly?

At that moment the Professor's wife stood up, without being told to. 'That's how,' she said curtly, 'conventionally.' Then, with the merest glance at me, she walked away back towards her corner.

The Professor was back at the bookshelves, his back to us. He held an open volume in one hand, consulting it. Without turning round he lifted his other hand in the general direction of his wife.

'One moment, darling,' he said. 'There is a part for you in this.'

Suddenly he was looking at me. His mood had lightened, the threat of thunder gone from his brow. Whatever it was he had found in his books, it had reduced the problem of procedure to nothing at all.

'If Jennifer will permit,' the Professor went on, 'such an unprecedented departure from common practice.'

My bottom and the backs of my legs were aching with a heat and tenderness that was quite unknown to me. I wasn't sure what common practice was; but whatever it might be, I was certain the perfect pupil would not let herself be limited to it. Not if the invitation came from such an expert and discerning tutor as my Professor.

I lifted my head, tossing my unruly hair out of my face. 'By all means,' I said boldly.

6

An Interesting Departure

'There's nothing to worry about, Jennifer,' said the Professor, which immediately had the effect of making me worried. 'It's nothing terribly elaborate or complicated.'

His wife came over and stood beside him, her raven-black head bending close to his honey- and silver-waved head as he showed her, presumably, some passage or illustration in the book.

'Oh, darling,' she said mildly, in a tone that made it hard to tell whether she was protesting or congratulating him. She squeezed his arm, pressing her sweet breast for a moment against his side. She gave me a brief appraising glance, not now as woman to woman but as expert to novice, measuring me up to see if I was up to whatever he had in mind. 'Hasn't this got some awful name in Arabic or Turkish or some such thing?' she asked, turning the page with an inquisitive finger.

I clasped my poor bottom, rubbing my hands down over the cheeks and down the backs of my thighs. My heart was beating rapidly. What had I let myself in for?

I combed my hair back behind my ears with my fingertips. I looked around among the dim furniture. 'Is there a mirror, please?' I asked my hosts, my voice rather faint and breathless. 'I think I need to pull my stockings up again . . .'

The Professor's wife gave me another look as before. 'I think she might take them off for this, don't you, darling?'

The Professor shut the book, looking at me thoughtfully. Slowly, then with decision, he nodded his head. 'Suspender belt, stockings, shoes: all off,' he said.

Though it would remove a tiresome duty from my mind, I was not sure that that instruction did anything to restore my confidence. Surely, I said to myself, although a young woman needs to bare her bottom if she is to have it properly spanked, there can be no need for her to take off any more of her clothes. On the other hand, the Professor's wife was wearing nothing at all except her sandals and that rather elegant velvet choker; and she had not been spanked, not recently at least, despite all her reminiscences. Desperately I hoped this 'departure' of ours was not leading me astray, away from the strict path I had meant to set myself.

It was ridiculous to feel self-conscious now. I had offered to take my stockings off once already. I had been parading about all afternoon without my skirt or panties. The Professor's wife had as good as wiped my crotch for me. As for her husband, the lower regions of my body held no secrets he had not seen, touched and probed from the most advantageous of angles.

So I obeyed as smartly as I could, rolling down my stockings and placing them neatly, each in its respective shoe, and putting my suspender belt away tidily in the pocket of my skirt. Yet the Professor seemed to sense my hesitation. He spoke to me directly, to buck me up and lift my spirits.

'Rest assured, Jennifer, the letter of the prospectus will be observed,' he said. 'We're merely giving you an opportunity, an insight into arrangements that operate at higher levels.' His voice sounded rather dry and casual, as I had heard it on the radio.

'I'm not sure an arrangement can operate, darling, strictly speaking,' pointed out the Professor's wife, who seemed to have a sharp ear for flaws of grammar.

He took the point without a change of expression. 'Arrangements that can be made,' he said. 'How very dull. Arrangements that may obtain. What would you say, my dear?'

The Professor's wife turned to me and opened her arms.

'Come here, Jenny darling,' she said. 'I think you'll find this quite interesting.'

Her husband snorted contemptuously but without ill humour, and began clearing things from the top of his desk: the blotter, the books, the carafe and water glass, and so on. The rulers he slid into an upper drawer; but left the ends of them sticking out, I noticed.

The Professor's wife did not embrace me, but put her hands lightly on my upper arms and smiled her hospitable smile. I tried to relax and smile too, but as I was too conscious that we were both now completely nude below the waist, I was unwilling to look down. If anything, I felt less at ease with her now than I had before the business with the tissue. I thought she was an ambiguous creature, equally ready to protect or betray me.

She leaned forward and gave me a kiss on the cheek, as light as the brush of a passing moth.

Startled, I looked nervously at her husband, but he had noticed nothing – at least,nothing he might disapprove of. He indicated the top of the desk, swept bare.

His wife let go of me and sat herself up on the desk. She slid backwards with exaggerated movements of her hips and gave a sudden giggle when the cheeks of her bottom made a squeaking noise on the polished wood.

'For goodness' sake,' said her husband, irritably.

'Sorry, darling,' she said.

She had moved back until the whole of her legs were resting on the desk-top, and not even her feet hung over the edge. Sitting upright, she flexed her shoulders and stretched her smooth white arms, making her small breasts stir and lift on her ribcage; and then quite unselfconsciously, she opened her legs and spread them as wide as the surface allowed. She put her hands to either side and slightly behind her, and leaned back on them, smiling in a docile and rather unnerving fashion.

What, I thought, if the Professor's wife was some kind of female exhibitionist, appearing naked at my Initiation not because her lord and master had bidden it, but because she enjoyed appearing naked in front of his unsuspecting pupils; enjoyed disconcerting them and making mischief for them, leading them innocently into more and more serious errors?

But if it was so, her husband would have seen it and taken care of it, I reminded myself. I was becoming very well acquainted with the extent and power of his authority. His wife, however abnormally, was here, at the expense of her duties to him elsewhere, because he commanded it. I had heard him do so; and he commanded it for my sake, because he knew her presence would stiffen my spine and quicken my attention.

How foolish I was being, I thought crossly, pushing my hair back into place once more. I was no longer innocent. I had passed every test that had been set for me; I could have convinced the most sceptical eye of that in a second. Now I had been selected for a yet more searching test, and a greater honour. I smiled obediently at the Professor and at his whitely reclining wife, and then I bowed my head, waiting for instructions.

'Sit up on the desk, Jennifer,' said the Professor.

I understood from the position that the Professor's wife had put herself in that I was to sit between her legs. I turned and lifted myself up and sat on the edge, wincing a little, I am afraid, as I pressed my tender backside against the wood.

'That's the way,' said the Professor's wife behind me. She did not move. I sat between her feet, my legs dangling, and looked inquiringly at my tutor.

He waved his hand, as if brushing away a fly. 'Further back,' he said.

Steeling myself, I slid back into the vee his wife had made with her legs. I was not told when to stop. I slid back until I came to rest in her crotch. I could feel her body through my clothes. I stopped, rigid, my feet stretched out in front of me.

'A little too far,' said the Professor.

Hurriedly I scooted forward, but only a few inches before I felt his wife's hands slide under my arms and wrap themselves around me.

She was sitting up straight again now, and supporting me from behind. I was reclining, neither prone nor upright, with some of my weight on my elbows and the rest on the thighs and chest of the Professor's compliant wife.

She lifted her knees either side of my body.

Her husband beamed down at us. He was clearly gratified to see his idea begin to take shape. I supposed it was a position not commonly used, even in this household. No doubt it was some harem punishment, the secret of which had been discovered in ancient Arabia and passed on from Initiate to Initiate until the scholars learned of it, and recorded it in their books.

I could see now, how this position made the fronts of the thighs particularly accessible.

The Professor stepped back, surveying us as if he was an artist, about to model our tableau in stone. He put his head on one side and rubbed his chin.

I could feel his wise eyes exploring the pale length of my legs, up to the point of their division. I felt a little ashamed of my pubic hair, which was still a little sticky, and so sparse and unkempt compared to the neat bush he was used to contemplating. I had felt that behind me just now, the merest prickle in the cleft of my bottom as I came to rest against the body of his wife. Her body was warm. I was surrounded by her fragrance, as if we had stepped outside in April and embraced in the open air.

Then the Professor gave his head a little shake.

'Forward, I think, you'll have to be,' he said.

For a moment I misunderstood, thinking he was chiding me for presumption and over-eagerness again. His wife, however, moved behind me, pushing us both forward together until my knees reached the edge of the desk and I could lower my feet.

'Splendid,' said the Professor. He gave his wife a quick smile over my head. 'I think I'll take my jacket off!' he said.

'It is quite warm in here,' said his wife, who had made up the fire while we were arranging ourselves for tea. Her voice seemed to purr in my ear. I at any rate was warm; and I was glad to hear she was, less clothed even than I. There would be warmth, I thought distantly, between our bodies, as there is between lovers in bed.

70

How stupid of me! How could I ever learn to discipline my thoughts and concentrate on the matter in hand? We were not in bed, nor were we about to perform an act of love! Spank me, Professor, I wanted to cry, spank me at once! Of if spanking is not the precisely accurate term for punishment taken on Thighs: Front, then scruple not to consult your remarkable dictionary, but let your hand fall, and drive away these girlish fancies! And let me not, I prayed, disgrace myself by oozing on top of your desk.

The Professor took off his jacket and hung it on the peg beside my skirt and panties. He took off his tie and rolled it neatly around his hand, and stowed it in his jacket pocket. He rolled up the sleeves of his white shirt and fastened them with expanding silver arm-bands.

'The front of the thigh,' he announced, 'though less fleshy and one might say cushioned than the back, is supplied with a good many nerve-endings. It may well be decided to include punishment of the front of the thighs when the subject is to be, for any reason, nude, thus obliging her to face the disciplinarian and shamefully display all her female charms – '

'Except her bottom,' said his wife.

Her husband looked irritated but did not deign to recognise her interruption with so much as a pause.

' – in their most eloquent state; which is to say, under stress.'

I was not nude, I reminded myself; that was not what he had planned for me. There was no cause for panic.

'But there we speak of extreme measures,' the Professor went on, as if he had read my mind. 'The most common and convenient use of a smack to the front of the thigh is of course when the subject is seated. Perhaps a sharp reprimand is needed at the dinner

71

table; or a reminder to keep still and not rustle sweet-papers at the opera – '

The Professor's wife gave a merry little laugh, which made me think her husband was speaking now from actual cases.

'When travelling by car, lengthy and quite pointed punishments may be given without the necessity of unfastening her safety belt!'

'Even if she's driving,' said the Professor's wife pleasantly. She rested her chin on the top of my head.

'The skirt is drawn up the thigh, along with any intervening petticoats, slip or so on,' concluded her husband in sudden haste, with a gesture that dismissed the subject; or at least the theoretical part of it. He stood before us. His eyes met mine. 'Are you ready, Jennifer?' he asked.

I was thrown, for a moment, by his queston. Had he ever consulted me before? I could not remember.

'Yes, sir!' I cried quickly. 'Of course!'

And I tensed myself, pressing my knees together and thrusting them towards him. I felt the arms of his wife restrain me, bracing me.

The punishment came at last, swiftly, a flurry of smacks and slaps. Though it stung with a vengeance, I was glad of it, for it seemed my Initiator was spanking me with a new resolve, inspired no doubt by the novelty of my Position. He too seemed to consider that I did not need the gentler, preliminary smacks that he had given me when introducing me to the first Position and the first Device, but spanked me firmly and fully from the outset. I was not sure I preferred the new arrangement, but I was grateful that he thought I had come far enough to deserve it.

The next alteration he made was no surprise.

'Open your legs, my dear,' said the Professor.

Gasping, I opened them, as wide as my hostess's

72

legs allowed. I wondered whether a third subdivision of the second Area ought to be made in future Prospectuses – Prospecti – whatever they were. The inner thigh, with or without capital letters and a little lecture, seemed at that moment to be an Area all on its own, twice as sensitive as either of the other surfaces. I revealed mine, feeling something of the shame that the Professor had mentioned afflicting the nude subject; but feeling reassured, too, by the warmth of the inner thighs of the Professor's wife against my bare legs. Looking down at myself I could see for the first time the clarity of the pink prints left on my flesh by the punishing hand, and now also the blotchy confused red marks between my legs, where the rulers had darted and played.

The Professor laid his left hand on my ankle, pushing my legs as far as he could to the side and leaning into the gap between. He continued to smack the fronts of my thighs, working now inwards and downwards, claiming again that tender skin.

I cried aloud, bucking against my restraint. The Professor's wife held me secure. Beneath my arms her hands slid quietly and deliberately up onto my breasts.

The Professor raised his head. 'Darling,' he said, in a tone of reminder, not stopping work for an instant.

His wife's right hand left my breast. I hardly knew it was gone. I was too concerned with her husband's right hand.

I now saw that he did not spank me with both hands, but only with the right, as he had said before taking me for the first time across his knee. Yet the speed and dexterity of his hand was such that a novice might have been forgiven for thinking she was being spanked by an entire team of disciplinarians. I marvelled at his hand, through a haze of pain. I wanted to take it to my lips and kiss it. As he had wondered how any parent or teacher could have restrained themselves from spanking me, so I now wondered how any young woman could fail to give him her bottom to belabour.

The Professor's wife's right hand reached over my right shoulder, holding something out for him to take. It was the Rulers: the Plastic one and the Wooden one. She had just retrieved them from their drawer without disturbing the Position or putting her husband off his stroke. Her own dexterity was something to marvel at too.

'The Rulers!' he announced, with satisfaction: I will not say greed.

'Professor!' I cried in turn. 'Wait! Wait, please!'

'Darling,' said the Professor's wife, in a tone of mild reproach, 'don't you think Jenny's earned a break?'

'A break,' he echoed shortly. 'Naturally.'

He stood back from the desk, breathing quite hard. I saw that he was rather red in the face. I hoped he was not cross with me for presuming, or for failing to frame my plea in a properly respectful fashion. I hoped a novice might be forgiven for a lapse of manners in the heat of an extraordinary trial.

And it was hot. Sweat stood out all over my chest and shoulders, and seeped from the roots of my hair. My legs throbbed, darkly, making me hiss between my teeth.

'All right, Jenny?' asked the Professor's wife. I felt her breasts against the slippery slickness of my back. 'All right?'

I nodded, exhausted.

'A glass of water, dear,' said the Professor's wife, calmly.

Nodding, the Professor went to the shelf where he

had stood the carafe, balancing it precariously in front of a miscellany of works by Lucretius and Laclos. He half filled the glass and gave it to his wife, who put it to my lips, her hand still underneath my arm.

I drank a sip, another; then lifted my own hand and took the glass from her. 'Thank you,' I croaked.

It was possible to sit upright, I discovered. The new, and recently redeveloped pain in my thighs quite shouted down the tenderness of my bottom. I sat up, clear of my hostess's body, and drank up the glass of water.

The Professor was waiting, carafe in hand.

'Another?' he said.

I wondered if it would be polite to accept, or better to refuse, and not delay the process any further. There were not one but two Rulers waiting to be re-acquainted with my flesh. Then there were a deal of other things to be done afterwards: the Hairbrush and the Strap were to be brought out and exercised, and there were curious unknown Positions involving Couches and Toes to be practised. I wondered what the pentathlon athlete must do when she stops for refreshment: prolong the break in order to rest and recover as much as possible of her depleted energies; or swallow quickly and return at once to the next endeavour, so as not allowing herself to forget her focus or lose her rhythm for an instant.

I gave the glass back to him, nodding. 'On,' I said. I hoped he could not tell that one syllable was all I could manage. I hoped the Professor's wife did not mind me lying back straight away on her bosom, sweaty and heated as I still was.

'Good girl,' said the Professor with an ironical tone.

He returned to stand between my limp and freshly-

75

spanked thighs. He showed me the two Devices in his hands.

'The Plastic stings like the devil but does not mark,' he reminded me. 'The Wooden may mark, but the effect is more contained,' he said. 'Would you say that's the truth of the matter, my love?'

The Professor's wife answered him lazily. 'It depends,' she said.

'Well, well, let us say that it is so,' he resumed testily. 'The point is, Jennifer – ' His face cleared, and his tone grew serious. 'I am sufficiently impressed with your achievement so far, that is to say your obedience, your capacity, your general demeanour – '

'And your considerable beauty,' added his wife, shocking me. 'Under stress,' she finished, delicately with hardly a pause, so that I did not know whether she had paid me a compliment or withdrawn one.

'Indeed,' said her husband, in the tones of a connoisseur; which he evidently was, for he had chosen her. His wife was so pretty, even in repose or at an ordinary task like handing round tea, that I could only think she would excel if our respective positions on top of this desk were to be changed over.

Beware, I told myself sternly. Do not begin that moistening nonsense again.

I was so distracted I had forgotten that the Professor had left off halfway through a sentence. 'Sufficiently impressed, as I say,' he said loudly, 'that I shall offer you a choice, in your fate.'

It sounded very grand. I looked up at him, still panting slightly. I wondered if he would let me choose to take my jumper off, and undo the top button of my blouse.

'I shall let you choose,' he said, 'which Ruler I apply to you now; and I shall trust you for the other one.'

For a moment I feared to understand him. To

choose only one Ruler? And tick the other one off on the board without further ado? And he was asking me to make the decision? I could hardly believe it.

I could see it was the sort of choice *he* might make in a lecture or TV demonstration, where he might include an experiment or leave one out, depending on how time was doing and whether the audience were rapt or shuffling in their seats. But how was I to know which I should take? Both stung, so far as I was aware; and as for marks, I was already so covered in red hand prints it hardly seemed to matter whether a set of orthogonal ones were laid on top.

Could he possibly be asking me my preference? Could he be flattering me so far? To be sure, one Ruler would be less torment than two, and would take less time; and the spectres of Hairbrush and Strap still loomed in the mists of Time Future. For a moment, I weakened. Take the Plastic, I thought, if he claims it is less. More at first, according to him, but afterwards less; and there is every reason to think in the long term here. You are not out of the woods yet, I told myself confusedly, imagining that I was surrounded by a forest of Hundred-Foot Rulers, Bamboo Canes grown to gigantic lengths, and stout Hairbrushes sprouting bristly branches. Take the Plastic, and be free.

'No, no,' I moaned. 'Both. Both.'

'Jenny,' urged the Professor's wife. 'Have the Plastic now, and save the Wooden one for next time. That's what I'd do,' she said, cuddling me.

'No,' I said. She didn't understand. We were barely halfway through the Prospectus. I might yet fail my Initiation and be cast out again, sent back to Kevin and a life of moral confusion and lost opportunities. I could never forgive myself for failing if I had elected to miss one of the tests appointed for me.

'Both, sir,' I said. 'Please.' And I spread my legs wide, pushing my hostess's feet off the sides of the desk.

The Professor smiled. Could I see pride in his eyes, pride in his new pupil? He lifted his hand. His hand held the plastic ruler. 'She has made her choice,' he said gravely.

The waking of the sting in my thighs took no time at all. I flung back my head and rolled it back and forth on the Professor's wife's shoulder, clutching and scrabbling at her hands. The ruler walked up and down, and paid a visit to the crease of my groin. For the first time I gave vent to a shriek.

Then it was the Wooden again. I felt it stripe me from knee to crease, both sides. I bucked my bottom up and down, thumping on the desk-top in a delirium of pain, as if I was trying to fling myself out of my hostess's embrace.

'Sorry!' I gasped, as the Ruler smacked down.

She put up a hand and briefly caressed my damp hair. 'Pet,' she whispered. Thoughtfully she wound her legs around my own, hooking her feet around my ankles, helping me to keep them wide apart and still.

At last the Rulers ceased their measuring, and another phase of my suffering was over. I moaned, as quietly as I could. My thighs felt as if I had been strapped astride a live electric cable. My limbs were trembling with tension and shock, my hands and knees gripping the desk-top as a shipwrecked woman might grip a piece of the wreckage. I was the wreck; powerful shudders jerked through my whole body.

'Darling,' said the Professor's wife, in a voice of indulgent reproach, so I hardly knew which of us she was addressing. Propping my weight on her shoulder, she reached forward and stroked my thighs. I jerked again, yelping. The gentlest touch of this woman's

78

hand felt like a hot iron on my skin. Yet she continued, despite my cries, and soon her caress began to soothe me, to blunt the sharpest teeth of the pain that raged through my nether regions. I allowed her to continue, sinking down to lay my head on the desk as she came up, first squatting on her heels, then leaning forward over me to stroke me everywhere I had been spanked, with infinite refreshing softness. I closed my eyes. The Professor's wife's perfume seemed riper now, more like summer than spring, mixed in with a warmer, headier scent that seemed entirely natural.

I opened my eyes and looked up. I could see nothing but the white breasts of the Professor's wife, moving back and forth above me as she soothed. Now she leaned even further forward. Her sweet flat belly was above my face. I glimpsed the tidy black bush of her pubic hair. The intriguing aroma of her increased in my nostrils. She was wet, all over; my sweat mingled with her own. The desk was so wet beneath us with perspiration, that not even we could have told whether any other of our secretions might be mixed there.

I hoped the Professor would not be able to tell either.

The Professor's wife brought her bottom over my head, a quick flash of a dark cleft between pale cheeks, and then she squatted aside my stomach, rubbing my thighs briskly with both palms. As she rubbed, the cheeks of her bottom jostled my breasts beneath my white angora jumper. Her action was not so gentle now, nor so soothing, and the dull pain stabbed me so I groaned.

'Well,' said the Professor's wife pleasantly, lifting her leg across me and jumping down to the floor. 'That was different, wasn't it? I am glad you thought of it, dearest. Only, I hope you won't mind if I go and get on now, my sweet, please? I haven't even washed up the tea things yet, and if I don't do them now this minute I shall get all behind, as my beloved mother used to say.'

She gave me a sweet grin over her shoulder, and I swear there was a little wiggle of her bottom to go with it.

Then she kissed her husband and received his blessing, delivered in the form of two friendly pats on that same bottom. She stuck it out rather impudently, I thought, to receive them. Then she gathered up the remains of our tea, with the same care and attention that she had so recently devoted to my person.

The Professor regarded me gravely. 'You may stand, Jennifer,' he said.

Smoothing my damp hair back into place, I sat up gingerly. Taking as much of my weight as I could on my hands, I rolled off the desk in what, I'm afraid, must have looked to the spectators a rather graceless and ungainly motion, and stood leaning on it. Seeing as the Professor seemed to have finished with me for the moment, I took the liberty of rubbing my legs, both with my hands and against each other. They felt astonishingly warm, and full of a terrible stinging tenderness that hurt anew with every move I made.

The Professor's wife came back towards the desk, smiling graciously as I stepped aside. She seemed to be carrying her breasts on the tray, like strange albino pomegranates among the tea things. I was pleased to see she also had a cloth of some kind, and as she wiped the top of the desk, the cheeks of her bottom moved vigorously with the wiping motions of her hand. 'There you are, my sweet: all clean and fresh for you,' she told her husband. And she had another word of encouragement for me as she passed the notice-board on her way out, though at that instant I was not so glad to hear it.

'The Slipper next, Jenny, I see. Jolly good! I'll go and get you one.'

'No need, dear,' said her husband. 'I'm going to take our visitor upstairs, and show her what's what up there.'

I looked at him apprehensively.

'Jolly good,' said the Professor's wife again, rather more vaguely, though still with the sweetest of smiles. 'Have a nice time.'

And she went out, closing the study door.

7

A Conducted Tour

'Until then,' said the Professor, inspecting me as I stood there on his carpet in my rather hunched, crab-bed posture, trying to stop rubbing my legs, 'until then, I think we'll have you in the corner, shall we, Jennifer?'

'The corner, sir?'

'Yes,' he said, rolling down his sleeves and fetching his jacket. He pointed. 'The Corner. You know: hands on head, face the wall, that sort of thing. On Display.'

He came close to me again and laid his hand with, I suppose, justifiable pride on the rich and glowing havoc he had made with it. I jumped, then stood trying not to squirm. 'Your bottom, my dear,' said the Professor, as if offering a dowager a compliment on her Adam fireplace, 'is at this moment quite the most beautiful and radiant thing in this room!'

And he gave me two sharp spanks just to brighten it up, driving me into the corner.

Then, while he sat at his desk and wrote in his notebook, I stood with my hands on my head and my feet, as instructed and measured with one of his hateful rulers, eight inches apart. The paper on the walls of the Professor's study was the deep ruby colour of old port wine, and looked expensive. I stared at a few square inches of it and tried to look forward to my trip upstairs.

The little I had seen so far of the Professor's magnificent house had certainly made me curious to see the rest. How lovely it must be to live in a place stuffed full of books, antiques and objects that could be admired for their beauty as well as for their practicality. Within these walls, how many interesting things must be going on all the time! As I myself had witnessed in the short space I had been here, the air rang constantly with intelligent conversation and the shaping of fascinating and challenging ideas.

All the same, now that I had actually been promised a conducted tour, I found myself unaccountably reluctant. My butterfly mind had darted away, alarmed, I suppose, by that word 'bedroom'. Perhaps I wondered why it was necessary for us to go upstairs to find a slipper for me. Was it not rather like the old joke about workmen having to carry a grand piano to the room 'where the hammer was'?

I listened to the scratching of the professorial pen. I wondered, wistfully, if he was writing about me, and whether he would mark me down as a promising pupil.

Not for the quickness of my intelligence, at least, I realised while I stood there, the perspiration drying on my body, my legs aching and trembling and itching for another touch of someone's soothing hand. If the Professor had to take me upstairs for the Slipper, it must be because there was no one to fetch it down for him. His wife had, as she had just told us, lots to do; we had been keeping her from her chores by involving her in our business. And he could obviously not send me, because I was a stranger in the house and wouldn't know where to look – or which particular slipper I required. I wondered whether fetching the Slipper was the sort of task that could be entrusted to the mysterious Marion, whoever and wherever she was; or whether she would mess that up too, as she had evidently messed up the Professor's library.

The sound of the pen ceased for a while, to be replaced by a curious quiet and very repetitive creaking sound. I had noticed during the course of my punishment across the Professor's knee that his chair had a slight creak. Just so it had creaked under the combined motions of his hand and my body, especially when my legs gave a particularly violent jerk. I supposed the Professor must be drumming his fingers or scratching his ear, or doing any of those unconscious little jiggling things that so many of our great minds do while they are thinking; but there was no other sound, only the rapid, rhythmic creaking of the chair-spring.

In a moment, it ceased; and after a slight pause the sound of the pen returned.

There was a typewriter in the room, on another table. Obviously the Professor preferred not to use it. Presumably it was his wife who typed all his articles and scientific papers for him. I wondered if she ever made any typing errors. I supposed it was she who had typed out the Instructions for Young Women about to Receive Initiation for me. There had been no mistakes in that. I made a mental note to find the Professor's wife before I went home, and thank her for sending it.

At that moment the Professor himself put his hand on my shoulder, taking my elbow and lifting my hands off my head. 'Enough of that now, Jennifer,' he said, as if it was a particular whim or perversity of mine to stand in the corner, and he had indulged it for as long as he could. 'It is time for us to make our ascent,' he said.

You might have thought I had had enough of that particular corner, or indeed any corner, in the Professor's house or any other building. Their potential for sensory or intellectual stimulation is extremely limited – which is, as the Professor puts it, the point of the corner as a location for the freshly-spanked pupil; or equally for one waiting her turn for attention. By depriving it of all distractions, the corner concentrates the mind of the erring one upon her bottom; and, if she is well disciplined, upon her error.

Corners being such dreary places, it was a wonder I felt so reluctant to be removed now from mine. Yet I tried to find reasons to linger, if not in the corner, then in the study itself.

'Should I not get dressed first, sir?' I asked.

The Professor shook his head. His wise eyes seemed to understand my ruse. 'It is a most instructive and entertaining spectacle, to follow any bare-bottomed young lady upstairs,' he said, smiling placidly. 'How much more so when she presents a view as gorgeously illuminated as you do. Why,' he said courteously, 'you will positively light our way upstairs!'

Blushing above now as well as below, I said a silent farewell to my knickers and my skirt, and hoped it would not be too long before I was reunited with them. Still I cast about the room. Was there no other opportunity to delay?

My eye lit upon the notice-board. 'Shouldn't we take the Prospectus?' I said, rather loudly.

The Professor rubbed his chin, smiling like a cat. 'I think I shall allow you to keep the subject of the next lesson in your pretty head,' he decided. 'But you may go and tick both Rulers first, if you like.'

I shuffled over to the horrid piece of paper and with great satisfaction and relief, dispatched those two Devices. Three remained. I did not have to read them to remind myself of them.

'And Thighs: Front too, sir?' I asked, massaging that portion of myself discreetly.

'If you like,' he said, and I ticked them off, though the tone of his voice made me quite sure he was reserving the right to make use of that particular Area again today, if he felt the occasion warranted it. I must bow to his wisdom, I thought, or perhaps a curtsey might be a more appropriate gesture. I must not be too eager to rush ahead to the end of our long, dark journey.

I could not in fact have rushed anywhere at all just then, but I was obliged to walk, however the muscles of my hind-quarters shouted in protest against it, with my right elbow in the hand of my attentive tutor, out of the study and into the cooler air of the hall.

Observing the slight difficulty I was under, the Professor asked knowingly: 'Legs seizing up are they, Jennifer?'

I nodded, biting my lip as I crept. 'Yes, sir,' I said.

'That stiffness comes when you don't exercise them immediately afterwards,' he told me. 'The extra blood stays in the Area instead of circulating round the body. It's that that makes the tissues so rigid and painful to move. If you exercise, the blood pumps and the congestion eases. But you have to do it straight away.'

He let go of my elbow and moved in front of me, smiling a little smile of mock apology, as if acknowledging that it was he himself who had prevented me from exercising afterwards, not least by not telling me I should.

'To increase the effectiveness of Smacked Legs,' he said, walking to the foot of the stairs, 'put the subject in a corner. To ensure her endurance, send her out on a bicycle ride.'

Limping up the hall after him I supposed he was

quoting from his own writings. He certainly had a way of putting things. I had made up my mind, as soon as I could, to go into a bookshop and order his complete works.

'You'll see,' the Professor said, standing aside to wait for me. 'We'll go into all that one day.'

I was overjoyed. It was the first hint he had given me that I might expect to pass my Initiation. 'Yes, Professor!' I said, hobbling along faster. 'Thank you, Professor!'

The light in the hall was bright after the dimness of the study. A thick blue carpet, soft as the fur of a Persian cat, ran along the floor and up the broad staircase with its banister of solid oak. My imagination was swept irresistibly away by the thought of all the people who must have stepped along that hall carpet: some of them intimates of the household; others colleagues, friends and guests. Visitors must come here all the time, I thought excitedly, from the wonderful, starry worlds of broadcasting and the press. Publishers; politicians; masters of august colleges and members of Royal Societies – I thought I could see them all, walking up this staircase before me, past the marvellous paintings that hung on the wall. I thought they brushed by me on the landing as I went, admiring their elegant, fashionable clothes, and almost, I swear, scenting their perfume. I wondered if I might one day walk among their company, fully clothed for preference.

Nor was this an empty-headed yearning to bathe in the glitter of High Society. I knew that like all great minds, the Professor must have surrounded himself with an inner circle of peers and admirers: those who had risen with him to eminence, and those who emulated him and worked in hope of one day achieving as much in their own right as he had. They lived for the day when they would stand shoulder to shoulder with him. Perhaps they even dreamed of inheriting his place after he had stepped, as all finally must, down from his podium and into private retirement.

At the moment, however, the Professor was still stepping upwards, close behind me. I could feel with an odd discomfort the power of his gaze upon my bare bottom and the backs of my legs, even as he spoke of the pictures we were passing. 'Odilon Redon,' he said, as I turned my head to see. He was indicating a canvas with the knuckle of his index finger, but looking at me, not at the painting. 'Felicien Rops, that drawing. Aubrey Beardsley you know. These are by the photographer David Hamilton, are you familiar with his work? That lovely sense of calm, even languour – that heady atmosphere of possibility.'

I had never heard of any of these people. I would start to learn at once. I looked eagerly at the next painting we passed and was startled to find it showed a woman in Victorian dress wielding a birch, and a row of docile schoolgirls in various attitudes of disarray and distress. In the corner, two who had already passed along the line appeared to be comforting one another.

Tiring of my limping pace, the Professor passed me, bounding on up the stairs as energetic as a young swain seeking the boudoir of his beloved. His voice came floating down to me. 'There are a hundred essay topics on this one staircase!'

As I tried to hurry after him, my thoughts were not with the Professor's words, I'm sorry to say. That strange painting had put me in mind of a whole set of other people who must frequent the Professor's quarters: his students, my fellow pupils. Though I could hardly call them fellows yet; that was presumption again, not yet thrashed out of me, I noted guiltily. I had met none of that dedicated flock, nor knew anything about them, neither their names nor their faces; though I supposed, in a sense, neither the name nor the face mattered a great deal – only the way they comported themselves, in the corner or across the desk. Who were they all? What were they like?

I seemed to see a crowd of young women, my contemporaries, of all shapes and sizes: tall, short, buxom, slim. There were shy ones, who walked with downcast eyes and hands behind their backs; artistic ones with knitted dresses and clouds of red hair flying; studious ones who brought their own equipment in satchels and bags; laughing ones who departed quieter than when they arrived. Were there older women too, mature in years, who came to lift their ample skirts and offer a broader target to the Ruler? Perhaps there were; and foreign students, women from India and Japan, come to add the Professor's methods to the traditional teachings of their upbringing. Good heavens, I thought: perhaps some of them might be men! But whether they were men or women, I thought, all would strive, to the extent of their more modest talents and vision, to improve themselves and the discipline they studied – to take the great work of the Professor's life and carry it on in the world. What a splendid and inspiring dream, I thought, wincing as I lifted my striped legs up the final stair, to imagine oneself one day joining the ranks of those apostles!

The Professor was standing outside a door.

'This is the bathroom,' he told me.

'Thank you, sir,' I said.

He opened the door, and switched on the light inside, but neither made any move to go in himself, nor directed me to. He stood aside, holding the door open.

89

'I expect you need to avail yourself,' he said.

Suddenly I realised I did, very badly.

'Yes, sir! Thank you, sir!' Could I think of no more intelligent or eloquent reply than that, every time? Well, perhaps later, I told myself, but no more than that was to be expected of me at present, on account of the sudden and urgent pressure I found myself under. I could only hope the Professor's words had constituted a proper granting of permission, as I hurried into the bathroom.

Reaching an automatic hand to close and bolt the door after me, I found the Professor was following me in.

'Sir?' I queried anxiously, beginning to hop up and down again.

The Professor seated himself on a large wooden chair that was placed next to the deep white bath, and adjusted several cushions at his back.

'What's that, Jennifer?' he asked.

'Can't I – can't I go, sir?' I bleated, ungrammatically and far from eloquently.

Plucking the creases of his flannel trousers, the Professor crossed his legs, and laced his formidable hands around his knee.

'Feel free,' he told me, whimsically.

I looked doubtfully at the toilet. It was large and deep and clean, and fitted with a polished wooden seat. There was a capacious white cistern above, with a wooden pull hanging down on a brass chain. There was a full roll of toilet paper, and another to the side, under a coloured glass bell. There seemed no reason why I should not obey both Nature and the Professor.

I lowered myself onto the seat, tightening my lips and narrowing my eyes as I compressed the tender cheeks of my bottom against the wood. I met the

Professor's eye as I parted my knees, grateful that all my earlier oozings seemed to have dried up while I was standing in the corner. I willed myself to use the toilet. Perversely, the sphincter of my bladder stayed tightly clenched. Exert my will as I might, it would not open. I began to blush.

The Professor smiled pleasantly.

I fought a desperate inner struggle; but to no avail.

My companion made a slight throat-clearing noise and looked down at his clasped hands. 'My wife – ' he remarked.

Instantly the long-held waters burst from me and cascaded noisily into the pan.

' – does not approve of me watching my pupils on the lavatory,' said the Professor, too well-mannered to notice my involuntary interruption. He smiled, as if the very notion of his wife's disapproving of anything should amuse me. '*You* don't object to my presence, do you, Jennifer,' he observed.

'No, sir,' I said, not wishing to contradict him. Bravely I added: 'It gives a kind of novelty, sir – to the proceedings.' I was still in full flow as I spoke.

The Professor's brown eyes twinkled. 'My wife,' he said again, 'detests me to watch her on the pot.' He pronounced the colloquial phrase with exaggerated consonants, primly. 'She would rather have the cane before breakfast, every day for a week, than to have me sitting here when she is sitting there.'

'Dear me,' I said lightly, tinkling on. I was feeling a trifle embarrassed myself, and tried to concentrate on what he was telling me.

'In fact,' he said, 'she hates it so much that I have made it into a special punishment, for her most appalling faults.'

'That's very imaginative, sir,' I said, preoccupied now, and a little worried, by my own copiousness.

How could I possibly have held so much in without noticing? I suppose I have been very absorbed, I thought.

'Oh, not really,' said the Professor mildly. 'Only it is an interesting thought, isn't it?'

'Fascinating,' I agreed. My bladder was empty at last, and I thanked all the gods of water for it as I reached for the toilet roll.

'Do you not intend to go any further?' the Professor asked, watching my movement.

'Not – at present,' I said. 'I think that might have seized up too, sir,' I said. 'With the rigid tissue, sir.'

He made a small noise of resignation, but did not speak. I hoped I had not disappointed him. I stood up and took hold of the wooden handle that hung down from the cistern.

'Sir,' I said. 'Please may I have a wash?'

He settled back, without complaint, as if for a long stay. 'By all means, Jennifer.'

I flushed the toilet, feeling I should assure my instructor that I was not succumbing to some trivial whim that women are subject to when they are in bathrooms; and that it was no selfish thought of my own comfort that had prompted me to ask. 'I think I got rather hot, sir,' I said, as the water finished its splashing and gurgling, 'downstairs just now; on the desk I mean, with your wife – '

I found myself colouring up again at that, trying to wrestle the words that came tumbling out of my mouth into some form that would not draw his attention to the special location and nature of some of that heat. Why had I mentioned the Professor's wife, I upbraided myself furiously? She had nothing to do with it at all.

'Exercise makes you hot, doesn't it, sir?' I appealed, and then in horror realised that now I was sounding as if I was hinting that he should wash too. 'Well, it does me,' I hurried on, 'and I think I did get rather sticky, and then dried while I was cooling off, sir, in the corner – I don't want to cause any offence, sir . . .'

The Professor gave me a dry, pained smile. 'I've given my permission,' he pointed out, a trace of iron coming back into his tone.

'Yes, sir. Thank you, sir.'

I crossed my arms and pulled off my jumper, and hung it on the edge of the bath. Then, with a smile of apology, I unbuttoned my blouse and laid it on top.

Though my heart was speeding up again for some reason, the Professor seemed utterly unmoved by this further increase in the area of flesh I had on view. I suppose he had had enough of examining my flesh on the way up the staircase, and I decided not to remove my bra.

'You may use my wife's flannel,' the Professor told me, 'and her towel – there.' He pointed to a matching set in primrose yellow. I hurried to take them up, and ran a basin of water. Cold water, I thought: a cold flannel pressed to my bottom and in between my legs, where my spanking had been particularly sharp. Then warm water and soap, for hygiene. Could I manage to satisfy both needs, without the Professor noticing?

'I trust this will not take long,' he said at that moment, as if hearing the fevered thoughts running through my head.

Hastily I turned on the hot tap, and stirred the mixture with my hand. I squeezed the flannel in the water and wrung it out. A faint scent rose from it as if revived, a scent of soap and clean flesh. I turned the taps off and stooped over the basin.

I passed the flannel across my face, around my ears and the back of my neck. Being watched while I washed myself was a novelty too. Despite his gallantry on the stairs, I could only think that there might be something rather disgusting about watching a young lady wash herself. I must try to be neat, and quick, and keep as much poise as I could. I rinsed out the flannel, soaped it and continued. I washed my shoulders and under my arms, around the straps of my bra. I rinsed the flannel and soaped it, and wiped it carefully over my bottom, from the waist down each sore cheek. The water was very helpful there, as I had thought it would be.

Trying to make a graceful arc of my body, and turning slightly on one heel to give the watching Professor what I hoped might be the most attractive view, I washed my thighs, and down my shins and calves. Then while I dealt with the flannel again, I turned to ask if I might wash my feet too. 'They do get rather dirty walking barefoot, sir – not that your house is dirty, of course, but – '

'Please do, Jennifer,' he said, ignoring my excuses.

I'd been afraid that standing on one foot with the other up in the basin might make the least attractive and in fact most vulgar spectacle of me, even worse than sitting on the toilet; but the Professor was apparently ready to forgive me that, I imagine in consideration of all the other rude presentations of myself that I had to make in the course of my Initiation. I supposed his work must oblige him to put up with a good deal of rude exhibitions of female flesh, especially considering his wife's predilection for naturism.

As if to prove to me that none of this bothered him at all, he rose as I began to delicately wash my crotch. 'I'll do that for you,' he said; and he even held his hand out for the flannel.

Was there no limit to his thoughtfulness and care

for me? Grateful as I was, I thought I must show him that I needed no mollycoddling and was prepared to finish what I had started. Good heavens, I had been washing myself every day since childhood! The skill did not disappear just because I had received my first good spanking.

'It's all right, sir, I can manage,' I said, doing so, and trying to speed up the process as best I could without splashing water about.

There was a peculiar gleam in the Professor's eye as he sat down again in his chair and readjusted its cushions. I was confident I had spotted his little test, and congratulated myself on showing, for once, no trace of a dither.

Though the time was passing, my patient educator permitted me to dry myself on his wife's towel. As I did so I glanced at a white-painted cabinet on the wall, where I supposed patent medicines were kept, as in more conventional homes the length and breadth of the country, and elsewhere. I wondered if there might be something else in there, some balm or ointment that would ease the throbbing that still troubled my bottom and thighs. However, I imagined that in a few minutes it would have become redundant again, so to speak.

Washed and dried, and considerably refreshed, I reached for my discarded clothes. The Professor stayed my hand. 'Not the jumper, I think,' he said.

'It is rather a warm one,' I admitted, stroking my hair.

'You may put the blouse on,' he announced, 'but leave it unbuttoned.'

I wondered if there was some special significance to this unusual arrangement, but I supposed once again the Professor was demonstrating his concern for me: I should not catch cold after my wash, but fiddling

95

with buttons can take time, especially if they are the tiny buttons on a young woman's best white blouse. Slipping my arms into the sleeves, and leaving the blouse hanging loosely about me, I let the Professor turn off the light again and open the bathroom door. My head high, I was determined to show no reluctance as he ushered me on to the next stage of my voyage of discovery.

Along a short corridor we went, passing an unmarked door at each side, and through another door at the end, which led us into the grand master bedroom.

I hardly need tell you it was a gorgeous room, beautifully furnished, and decorated in black and gold. The bed was enormous, quite dominating the other furniture: a tall Jacobean oak cupboard and several chairs that might be even older, upright and hard, without arms. I smiled to see that even in bed the Professor and his wife were not to be parted from the materials of study, for there was a bookcase too, of modest size, but crammed tightly with choice volumes, brochures and glossy magazines. Heavy black floor-length curtains covered the window, shutting out the dark outside. Two doors either side of the bed gave entrance, I supposed, to dressing rooms for the master and mistress. They were closed, so for that time I had to imagine the magnificent clothes that might be stored in there, and content myself with imagining.

The head of the bed was crowned with a wooden canopy that looked more like an ancient altarpiece. It was decorated with what I recognised as implements of the hunt: spurs and riding crops and so forth; even leather collars on stout chains, such as I presumed Masters of Foxhounds must fasten around the necks of their favourite beasts.

'I see you are a hunting man, Professor,' I said.

'What?' he said, following my gaze. 'Oh, yes. It's all a hunt, you know.'

'What is, sir?' I said.

'The whole thing,' he said, rather vaguely. He was wool-gathering – deep in the mysterious cogitations and difficult philosophical problems of the Higher Intellect.

'Life, you mean, sir,' I said, with a nonchalance I hardly felt. I looked at the bed and then at the floor around the bed. That luxurious golden counterpane might be hiding anything behind its elaborately embroidered hem. I fingered the loose cuffs of my blouse, and gave a small shiver.

'Yes,' the Professor agreed, as though he had been thinking of something more down-to-earth after all, but conceded the justness of my reply. 'Shut the door, Jennifer, would you,' he said.

Turning to obey, I saw for the first time the other dominating feature of the room, no less impressive than the bed itself. On the wall behind me there hung a huge and splendid mirror in a golden frame: quite twelve feet high, it was, and almost as broad. It did not hang flush against the wall, but tilted outwards at an angle, its top against the ceiling. When the Professor and his wife were in bed, either of them would be able to look up and see at once the whole bed, and themselves in it; assuming they should ever wish to for any reason.

What I could see as I gazed up admiringly at that remarkable piece of glass was my own unprepossessing self in my crumpled blouse, with pink blotches all over my thighs. And caught as I was, arrested in mid-turn, I could see for the first time since arriving at the house my own poor bottom, and the state it was in.

'Would you like to inspect yourself, Jennifer?' the Professor asked. 'You may find it educational.'

So when I had closed the door I stood in front of the mirror and twisted this way and that, searching out as much of my rear aspect as possible. 'It's not as bad as I thought, sir,' I had to admit. I was surprised and rather embarrassed to hear an almost wistful tone in my voice, as though I had disappointed my own fervid imagination. Our various exertions had indeed left me quite pink across both cheeks of my bottom and right down to my knees; but an unwise sleep in the late spring sunshine could bring on a more dramatic glow than that! Perhaps the exercise of climbing the stairs, not to mention the thorough washing I had given myself, shamefully protracting a little chore that should have taken five minutes at most, had helped me recover from the last Position, just as the Professor had advised.

'There's room for improvement, certainly,' he said, airily.

In the great mirror I saw him sit down on the bed. So my guided tour had already come to its end. In some sadness, not to say trepidation for the events that must now follow, I went dutifully towards him and presented myself at his knee.

8

Behind the Door

'Do you remember my little challenge to you before we left the study, Jennifer?' the Professor asked. It did not seem to diminish his authority one jot that he was sitting down and had to look up to see me.

I was ready for him, however unready I might think I was for what the answer would invite. 'You said I was to memorise the subject of the next lesson,' I said, 'in my pretty head.'

At once I gasped and coloured, looking down at my feet in confusion. I had not meant to repeat the playful little compliment he had popped on top of that command, like a shiny red bow on a Christmas gift, but it had thrilled me so to hear him say it I had obviously memorised it too, and trotted it out along with the rest.

'Sorry, sir,' I said.

'And it is?' said the Professor, once again overlooking my discomfiture.

I took a deep breath. 'The Slipper, Professor.'

If he had hoped I had forgotten, he did not show it. 'Exactly, Jennifer,' he said. 'The Slipper. A traditional implement borrowed, as it were, from the nursery, where for generations little boys and girls – '

My head must have been completely turned by the shock of making such a silly mistake, or I should never have interrupted him. 'Yes, Professor, you told me,' I said.

He gave me a strange look, his head slightly to one side, the concealed lighting of the bedroom throwing the noble form of his nose into relief. 'So, Jennifer,' he said, after a pointed little pause, 'what did I tell you?'

'You said they have conscientious nannies who bend them over the bed for it, sir,' I repeated dutifully, folding my hands. 'It's flexible but firm, and conveniently at hand at bedtime, sir, or first thing in the morning. You might use one of your own slippers, sir – the ones you wear, I mean, because the – the subject will see them all the time and be reminded. Or you might ask her for her own slipper instead, if she's wearing slippers,' I hurried on, terrified of what might happen if I stopped, 'because that might be a bit less frightening but a bit more hu-humiliating, sir.'

The Professor sat back, regarding me quizzically. 'Who told you to say that, Jennifer?' he asked.

I bit my lip. 'No one, sir.'

'Have you ever disciplined anyone with a slipper, Jennifer?' he went on.

I had to admit that I had not.

'Have you ever received it yourself, then? I know you haven't, unless you've been lying to me.'

'Professor!' I cried, shocked.

'Well, then,' he said calmly, 'I hardly think you're in a position to comment, are you?'

I hung my head. My fears had been justified.

'Are you, Jennifer?' he repeated, more sternly.

'No, sir,' I said. 'Only I've thought about it, sir, and I thought I should tell you, and not try to keep anything secret from you, sir.'

'I didn't say you were wrong, Jennifer,' he reminded me, 'only that I don't remember asking for your opinion.'

'No, sir.'

'Or giving you permission to express yourself,' he continued, quietly but crisply.

I did not speak. I had been forward again, and in trouble for it. If only I had remembered to ask permission! Obviously I still had a long way to go before I learned to behave in a properly disciplined manner. I would need a great deal of punishment before then, I told myself severely.

Yet I still managed to be startled when I heard the Professor's next words.

'That means a total of three spankings, my dear – '

'Three!' was my involuntary gasp.

'One on the Prospectus,' continued the Professor. 'Another, once again, for presumption,' he said, with a reproving frown. 'And first, a number of strokes by way of introduction to the Device. It's a little game,' he said, amplifying, 'I play with everyone at her Initiation.'

A game? I was surprised to hear news of anything so frivolous from a gentleman as earnest and grand as the Professor. I knew by a 'game' he must mean another test of some kind: a new challenge, like the Desk Variant, but one that would be suitable for all Initiates. I hoped it would be an opportunity for me to prove myself for once without pushing myself forward. Already I had begun to see the generosity in the Professor's methods: the velvet hand in the iron glove, I said foolishly to myself.

The Professor was still speaking. 'Three spankings,' he repeated, 'in a trio of Positions.'

At once my mind flew back to the Prospectus. What was left? Could I remember? I remembered some of the words in that column had seemed rather cryptic.

The Professor must have observed my brain in flight. 'Any thoughts, Jennifer?' he said casually.

'Yes, sir,' I said. 'Thank you, sir,' I added, to show him I understood he was complimenting me by asking my opinion now. 'A bed is rather like a couch, sir,' I said.

'Yes,' he said, stroking the golden counterpane with an almost sensual motion, 'you're right there, of course. But don't forget the Couch in question is in my wife's sitting room; and we need not pre-empt that, need we?'

'No, sir,' I said immediately. 'I wouldn't like to disappoint your wife, sir.'

The Professor looked me in the eye and for once I held his gaze without trembling, and took advantage of the fact that I was speaking already, with permission, to explain my idea. 'But you said the little boys and girls with the conscientious nannies used to bend over the end of the bed for the Slipper, sir, and I was thinking we might honour tradition, sir, since we're in the bedroom, only we can't use the end of the bed, exactly, because of the footboard.' It was carved of oak, thick and quite high and fancy, to match the elaborate construction that housed the head.

'Not true,' said the Professor, his eyes sparkling. 'An invalid assumption.'

An invalid assumption! I hoped that would not mean extra. Apprehensively I looked at the carving of the footboard, imagining all those knobs and flourishes and spiky bits biting into my middle while the Slipper was performing its horrid work on my bottom.

'It's a compromise between Chair-back and Couch, perfectly serviceable even for a novice,' the Professor told me, standing up and running his hand along a relatively level piece. 'Novices are allowed to put a pillow over it,' he explained serenely. 'In fact you may as well do that now, and we shall use it for the result of our little game. For the second Position,' he continued, while I fetched one of the pillows from the head of the bed and hung it lengthways over the footboard, wondering how on earth I was to get myself up over it, 'we may bring forward Toes. And for the third,' he concluded, while I wondered in trepidation whether he could possibly mean to punish my toes, and if so, wouldn't they be an Area not a Position?

'Well, the third we shall let emerge when the time comes,' he promised. 'You will be aware that you have not yet seen the Slipper, Jennifer,' he said next. 'It is hidden in this room. Your task now,' he said with a merry smile, 'is to find it. You remember the children's party game? Well, in one variant version that some authorities believe to be the original, whoever found the hidden Slipper would bend over for a spanking with it.'

'I don't think – ' I began to myself, speaking aloud without meaning to.

'What?' said the Professor sharply. 'Don't murmur, girl.'

'Please, sir, I was only thinking, I don't think they would look for it, then, sir.'

'It's only a game, for goodness sake,' he replied tartly, consulting his wristwatch. 'For them.' I thought my objection stood. Much good might it do me. 'The longer you take to find my slipper, Jennifer, the more plentiful your prize. Starting now.'

In a flash, I was down on my hands and knees, looking under the bed. How keenly I was aware of my bare bottom sticking up in the air in that undignified posture; but the Professor took no advantage of my pose, obeying the rules he had set and not interfering with my search. Frantically I crawled around the huge bed, sweeping aside the voluminous

103

folds of the heavy counterpane. There were no slippers to be found underneath the bed, so far as I could see without a torch. With a glance of trepidation at its owner I climbed up on the bed itself and looked in the niches of the headboard and among the hunting paraphernalia; but it was not there either.

I ran to the ancient cupboard, and opened it. It was full of the most innocent-looking bed linen, though it was of course of the finest quality.

In the room, the Professor had said. There seemed nowhere else for it to be. Could the dressing rooms possibly be considered, without cheating, as sub-sections of the bedroom itself, rather than rooms in their own right? I made a dash for the nearer of the doors; but as I rounded the corner of the bed something caught my eye. I have no idea how. Swerving gracelessly I ran to the spectacular mirror, reached my arm behind it and pulled out, triumphantly, a leather slipper, old and well worn but not even dusty.

'Thirty-two seconds,' said the Professor to my amazement, as I laid my trophy in his lap. 'That really is quite excellent, Jennifer,' he said with vigorous admiration. 'Please allow me to shake you by the hand!'

Speechless and slightly pink, I gave him that smallest of conceivable honours.

'I have never before known anyone take under a minute,' he enthused, 'and very few under five!'

I smiled, as modestly as I could manage.

'Now normally,' said the Professor, 'I'm obliged to score the game at ten seconds to the spank; but even rounding it up, that would leave you with a derisory and utterly pointless four extra. No, Jennifer,' he explained, as the smile died on my face, 'for you I shall be obliged to pay the full rate of one spank per second, which is an extra thirty-two spanks, beginning now.'

And while I was still gaping at this unheralded and not particularly welcome distinction, the Professor solved the problem of how I could achieve the new Position in a trice, by taking hold of me around the hips, lifting me up bodily and folding me across the footboard of the bed.

Head down again, and a trifle dizzy from my surprise and from all my scurrying around (during which, I suddenly realised, I had not once been troubled by the stiffness of my hind muscles), I still had presence of mind enough to notice that the Professor's pillows were large and thick. I was decidedly glad of it, though still quite sensible of all the carved spikes and knobs, crockets and finials or whatever they are, digging into my midriff. Comfort was not the point of this procedure, I told myself sternly; and then, as if to prove the point, the Slipper landed.

It was a distinct sensation, I noted: smoother and flatter than the hand; and not so sharp and whippy as the Ruler (either kind); more spread out, in a way. But once again it took me a while to work out these details, perhaps half of my prize strokes, which I was required to count aloud as they landed.

'One, sir! Two, sir! Th-three, sir!'

It was remarkable how the simple act of numbering each stroke that fell seemed to stretch the time of punishment. It was as if, in calling the number to mind each time and managing to get it out of my mouth, I had time to incorporate each and every stroke, and dread its successor.

'Eleven, sir! Twe-e-elve, s-sir! Th'-teen, su-uh!'

This effect was something else I did not work out straight away, though I had definitely sensed it, in some wordless and intuitive way, by the time we rounded twenty and came into the last dozen.

'Twenty-four, sir. Twenty-five, sir. Twenty – six – sir.'

By now my voice had lost all tone and sunk to something approaching a murmur; but my diction had become mysteriously clear once more. When thirty-two at last arrived, delivered itself, and departed, I lay shuddering. The house seemed very quiet suddenly. There was no traffic in the road outside; indoors no movement of furniture or footsteps. In my head loud bells of agony were ringing, but I saw no need to try to answer them, nor any way to silence them.

Carefully, without touching my bottom, the Professor lifted my legs, and raised me up until I was clear of the footboard, while my head, arms and the upper half of my body slid gently onto the bed.

He allowed me to rest a moment before summoning me to crawl off it and present myself upright in front of him, my arms at my sides. In a minute I would know what Toes signified on the Prospectus, I thought, panting slightly. Though I had some idea, it did not pay to make assumptions. They might, after all, be invalid.

Feeling my breathing come gradually under control, I was suddenly conscious of a strange stiffness and almost soreness, nothing to do with the Slipper at all, or with any of the other punishments I had been given; for this stiffness was inside my bra. My nipples were erect!

'Well, Jennifer,' the Professor was saying, as he flexed the Device back and forth in his hand, 'now you know something of what the Slipper can do. The next Position you will receive – '

Thinking quickly I said: 'May I put the pillow back first, sir? Before the next Position?'

Pleased by this little show of tidiness and attention to detail, the Professor inclined his head, and I quickly took the pillow off the footboard. It had been really quite squashed by my weight, and I plumped it up, taking advantage of the movement to turn it over, moving the wet patch to the underneath. Was it smaller, I hoped, than the mess the Professor's wife had wiped off the chair-back for me? Was I learning, ever so slightly, to contain myself?

'The next Position on the Prospectus is denoted by what, Jennifer?'

'Toes, sir,' I said.

'Meaning what, do you suppose?'

Well, he had asked me directly, so now I must hazard my guess. 'Touching them, sir. Me, sir, I mean. Bending over, touching my toes.'

'Excellent, Jennifer. Please do. Knees together, on this occasion. It may reduce access but it's a little more taxing.'

I bent over, wishing I didn't need to be taxed. Wishing too my legs were not quite so long. Men like my legs, I know, though I'm sure they haven't considered how inconvenient they can be, in certain situations. Kevin used to like me to wear short skirts, and if I did he would always try to touch my thighs. I wondered what he would think of them now, all bare and still rather pink in front.

I made an attempt to look at myself in the mirror again as I bent over. I wanted to see what colour my bottom was now, and whether my legs looked any paler in comparison. But the Professor took hold of my hips and turned me round to face the mirror, so I couldn't see it without holding my head up, which is quite an effort when you're bent right over. He, on the other hand, could see himself, and every stroke he placed.

I was amazed at the jolt they gave me, and the noise they made. Somehow the footboard of the bed had screened the full effect of the song of the Slipper from me. Now it seemed to explode. Each whack and smack was a burst of sound and bright red pain. I could only stand there and suffer, and struggle to hold my Position.

For this was the first Position I had suffered in which I was given no support at all. There was a second, later, but it is too painful to mention now. One atrocity at a time.

'Touching the Toes,' said the Professor. 'One of the most traditional and practical of all Positions. Terribly undignified for the subject herself, which can be an advantage; at the same time, if the subject's legs are long enough, like yours, my dear, this one and this – it can be quite an attractive Position, both to the disciplinarian and any spectators that may be invited along. But I rather expect you're finding right now, Jennifer, what a difficult posture it is; hard to maintain, hard to absorb the kinetic energy of the spanking without displacing it into lateral or vertical motion – flinching or falling down, that is to say. There, like that, Jennifer, yes. The line of balance is under attack with the force of each stroke, do you see? It can only be sustained by increasing the tension of the spine. All this while the balance organs in the inner ear are upset by being upside down. Which makes it a Position more suitable, in my own opinion, for a lightweight, stinging punishment like the switch or a cane of fine calibre, than for something with the punch of the Slipper. So we'll say that's enough for now, shall we, Jennifer?'

'Yes, sir!' I cried, 'please, sir!' – varying the formula a little. Since the Professor had not so much punctuated his lecture with smacks as underlined one word in four, you may think it was not unfair of me to agree so vehemently with his suggestion.

This time the Professor helped me to stand, lifting

me with his hands under my arms and supporting me. He seemed quite unoffended by how much he necessarily rubbed and squeezed my breasts in the process. I wish I could say I was just as unconcerned, but I must confess how my nipples sparked and tingled, almost as if they were trying to compete with the throbbing of my bottom and the Backs of my Thighs, an Area whose usefulness in Slippering he had hardly needed to mention in his talk, so obvious was it. Tautened by the Position, my thighs seemed to ring out like gunshots each time the Slipper spanked them, until I had almost begun to wish for the softer, sleeker snap of a Ruler; a Ruler in Wood, Plastic, even Whalebone or Stainless Steel, for all I cared.

I was helped over to the mirror and allowed to inspect myself. My face was red as a cherry, my hair a wind-tossed hayrick. My blouse was off one shoulder and had slipped halfway down my arm, while my bottom could have been hung up in the main road to stop traffic. I was horrified, and out of breath, and all I could do was stamp my feet and hug my bottom, jumping up and down.

The Professor stood back, watching me. 'That's the idea, Jennifer,' he said. 'Exercise. Bicycle ride. Lie down on the floor and pedal your legs in the air,' he suggested. 'That's it,' he said, not minding in the slightest that he was standing just in the spot from which my performance would be most obscene. I suppose he wanted to check his handiwork.

'I thought – ' I panted, bicycling away, still patting and rubbing myself, 'you meant a – real – bicycle ride.'

'Oh yes,' he said easily, 'that too. I mean, in good weather. Or bad weather, if it seems like a good idea. You should see what a little cold wind and rain can do to a well-warmed bottom! Do you own a bicycle, my dear?'

'I could b-borrow one,' I said reluctantly.

'Not today,' he said, reaching down and patting my bottom almost affectionately, testing its gradually declining temperature, I felt sure. 'You couldn't have a bicycle ride in the middle of an Initiation. I mean,' he explained, leaning down until his face came quite close to mine, 'you might not come back!'

I stopped pedalling and unsteadily got to my feet, clinging on to the footboard of the bed. I leaned there, massaging myself and saying nothing. I would not meet the Professor's eye.

'What's the matter now?' he demanded, as if my behaviour was an affront.

'You don't think much of me,' I said. I straightened my back, sniffing, and pressed my hands to it where it hurt from bending over. I held my head up, chest out. 'You think I haven't got the will to finish what I start. You think I haven't got any discipline at all.'

'My dear young woman,' said the Professor. 'On the contrary, I am perfectly satisfied with your performance today. Perfectly. You have been a model Initiate. I wish numerous other young women I could name might have been here to see you.'

I tried to compose myself. Not thinking, I began to button up my blouse, as though I had just that minute put it on, and was wearing a skirt I meant to tuck it into.

'Very nice, Jennifer,' said the Professor, politely.

He reached out his hand and stroked the fabric of my blouse, running his hand down my shoulder and slowly over my breast. I don't know why, it was perfectly ordinary cotton poplin, and rather sweaty and unpleasant by now, I should have thought.

'I meant what I said, you know,' he said softly. 'You are doing very well indeed. So far,' he added, inevitably.

110

'So now, next and last, what do you think?' I shook my head. I had no idea. He sat on the side of the bed again. 'Across my knee!' he said.

How clever he was! By now, after the strain of the two most exacting Positions I had held, I was almost grateful to go over, especially on the bed, where I could lay my head down and almost relax beneath his hand. Already I suspected my body was learning to find it the most natural and reassuring place in the world to be, at least until the spanking started. And just to make sure I didn't get lazy, this time the Professor had me reach out my arms over my head, crossed at the wrist, and held them with his left hand while he spanked me with his right. He spanked me slowly, almost casually, without a trace of force or urgency, though there was no doubt of his will. The loosest slap of the Slipper anywhere around my bare bottom and open thighs raised a tongue of flame on the scarlet embers of a now well-established ache. There was something almost juicy in the sound of the Slipper as it fell, as if now that it was well warmed up traces of natural oil had begun to seep and swell inside the leather.

At the same time, an uncommon sleepiness and deep tranquillity had begun to claim me. I seemed to float on the pain, detached from what was happening to my limbs. I could not have kicked if I'd been instructed to.

To my distress, in this fearfully lax and undisciplined state I found I was no longer able to keep silent while punished, but had begun to wail and make horrid mewing sounds at each fall of the Slipper. I was sighing and rolling back and forth on the bed, pressing my pelvis against the Professor's lap with complete abandon.

'We'll take a break now, shall we, Jennifer?' said the Professor unexpectedly.

I struggled for breath. 'Oh, please, sir, no!'

'No, Jennifer?'

'No, sir.'

'No break, Jennifer?'

'Please, sir, no,' I whispered. 'Sin – since you ask. Please let's get it all o-over with, sir!'

'Very well, Jennifer, if you insist,' he said; though I was sure he was not displeased at my reply. In fact I wondered if he might have been testing me once again, at the moment of my least resistance, as he had tested me downstairs with the temptation to waive one of the Rulers; and this test too, I thought, I had passed.

The rest of my spanking speeded up, and proved that a Thigh need not be taut to benefit from the Slipper. The longer the Thigh, the Professor remarked, the more opportunity it allows of demonstrating that point. I think, honestly speaking, that I was past appreciating it. The Professor permitted me to stuff a fold of his rich counterpane into my mouth and bite on it to stifle my involuntary noises. I was grateful he did not have my knickers near at hand for the purpose. I regained a little of my dignity, I think, during that final segment of Slippering, and I was grateful my tutor had organized the event so thoughtfully and so effectively. If I was anything approaching a model pupil, as he had said, flattering me, I was sure it was only because he was a model disciplinarian, and knew exactly how to handle even the most overdue and inexperienced subject.

When the onslaught had come to a stop, and before I had been told to get up, I asked, weakly: 'Am I in a position to comment now, Professor?'

The Professor was amused. 'Certainly, Jennifer,' he said, fondling my raw backside a little roughly.

'The third was not the toughest, or the most horrifying, but I think it was the most educational, sir,' I said.

'Little minx!' marvelled the Professor, and he gave me one final hard smack, right across the underhang so provocatively tilted up by the combined Position of Knee and Bed. I replied with the shrillest of squeals. Then he levered me unceremoniously off his lap, allowing me to lie as I fell, not minding that I crumpled the counterpane now, as well as chewing it. If I had made any mess by oozing onto his grey flannel trousers, I hoped he would forgive that too; or at least not punish me for it at once. I wanted nothing now except to lie there until the furious fire in my rear finished blazing. To be able to feel chilly there again! I thought a hundred years might just do it.

I had meant what I had said about the third Slippering. Some tiny part of my brain that was neither comatose nor hurting was astonished to learn that I was capable of reaching such a state of relaxation and passivity, and all as an effect of what was really the most elementary physical discipline. There had been other lessons too, about rhythm and responsiveness: the extraordinary way a lax bottom can bounce and swing under punishment; the learned reflex of the hips to ride, rising and falling with each stroke, in a way almost reminiscent of the crudest sexual thrust.

I don't know why I should feel called upon to make such a bizarre and wildly inappropriate comparison. I suppose it was because while fingering with utmost caution around the disaster area I must presume my instructor had now made of my whole backside, I made a sad discovery. Educational as the experience had been for me, I still had not learned one crucial lesson, or at least my body had not. For my vulva was as hot and wet, inside and out, and fragrant, I must assume, as a bowl of steaming cockles. All my soaping had been for nothing! I was close to despair.

113

The only aspect of the situation that gave me hope was an observation I had made this time, while I lay over the Professor's knees and bounced up and down on the bed; that even that most expert and resolute of disciplinarians was not immune, from time to time, to the irrelevant reflexes of the flesh. It had not been a well-turned crocket or shapely wooden finial that had poked me in the belly at every stroke of the third Slippering, but what memory told me men call an erection; likening it to a great building, a monument or a skyscraper, I have always supposed.

I was surprised at my tutor, but did not think the worse of him for it. In fact I was charmed, and really rather flattered. All men are flesh, especially, I feel sure, in that part. I only hoped I was not wholly responsible for his suffering what he might consider an incidence of indignity (and, I thought perhaps, discomfort). If it was my fault, I hoped it was not a fault that required specific and immediate punishment. If it was, I thought, in my swoon, we shall be here all night.

I was aware, at that moment, of the Professor getting up from the bed. Lifting my head I saw him moving quietly and very quickly away from me, towards the further of the closed doors, and I wondered why.

In three strides he was there, twisting the knob fiercely and jerking the door open. To my astonishment a red-headed young woman in a black dress and white apron came pitching out, with a high-pitched cry of dismay, and collapsed face down on the carpet at the feet of her discoverer.

'Ah,' the Professor said. 'Marion.'

The Importance of the Alphabet

So this was Marion. A short young woman – so young, barely into her majority by the look of her, that I kept thinking of her as a girl. Her figure was rather plump, I noticed as she scrambled to her feet, and hardly mature. Her costume was an old-fashioned maid's uniform, complete with a little frilly white cap that she was trying to straighten on her tousled russet curls. Her face was freckled, her broad mouth agape in fear and woe.

What had she been doing behind the dressing-room door? Something that involved leaning on it, apparently, for she had lost her balance the instant it was opened. Now it was closed, and she stood in front of her employer, and attempted to make a good account of her presence.

'I was wondering why the lights were on in here,' the Professor said. 'What were you doing in your mistress's dressing room?'

'Cleaning, sir,' Marion said.

I did not expect much of Marion. The circumstances looked bad. If there was a case of innocence to be made, I wished her well, but I doubted whether someone who could not keep a shelf of books in order could possibly prevail under the fearsome intelligence and penetrating eyes of the Professor. She had not made a good start, I thought. During her interview, however, I was permitted to remain where I was, lying on my face; and I was grateful to the maid for providing a suspension of activities.

'In the dark?' said the Professor.

'I heard you and the lady come in and I was scared, sir,' said the maid. I was surprised at her frankness.

'Scared?' said the Professor. 'Why? Were you doing wrong?'

'No, sir!' said the maid. 'I was trying to be quiet, sir!'

I was not sure that followed; and nor was the Professor. 'You failed,' he said tersely.

'Yes, sir,' said Marion, and she looked at her shoes. I was surprised and quite interested to see that they were black with button straps, identical to her mistress's.

'You were hiding,' the Professor said.

The little maid looked up, shaking her head. 'I wasn't, sir!'

'Then what were you doing, Marion?' he asked her in a voice of steel.

'Cleaning, sir!' said Marion again in desperation. 'All it was, was, I was cleaning the mistress's PVC, sir – ' I felt, rather than saw, the philosopher wince at her dissolute grammar. 'And I heard you come in, sir, with the lady, and then I remembered the missus told me I was supposed to do them in the laundry room, sir, instead of up here. So I put the light out and I was going down there when you started with the lady, sir, and then I thought I'd better wait until you finished.'

It was diplomatic, but shaky. I wondered how I would have behaved in her predicament. I hoped I would not have been in the wrong place to start with.

'I think you were looking through the keyhole, Marion,' said the Professor shockingly. 'I think that's what you've been doing all this while.'

The maid shook her head vigorously. 'No, sir!'

Was there any chance that she was telling the truth? I could not suppose so. The keyhole would have been useless for the second spanking, and probably the first; but it would have been excellently placed, I thought, to view the third.

'I was wanting to see you in any case, Marion,' said the Professor. 'Am I right in thinking you've put some books away in my study recently?' His voice touched me with a chill finger between the shoulder-blades.

'Yes, sir,' said the domestic. How eloquent her tone made those two monosyllables! Her conscience was clear, that tone said, while her expectations were profoundly dim.

'In the way I told you?' pursued the Professor.

'Yes, sir. I think so, sir,' she said.

'You think so! What was that way, Marion?'

'Please, sir, in alphabetical order, sir.'

The Professor surveyed her. 'And how well do you know your alphabet, Marion?' he asked.

Clasping her hands behind her back, just beneath the starched white bow of her apron, the girl recited: 'A B C D E F G – G, sir,' she repeated, sucking in her cheeks. 'G.'

'We heard that, Marion,' her employer assured her. 'G, of course. And after G?'

'H, sir,' said Marion bravely. 'H I J K – K M – '

'Wrong!' cried the Professor in a voice like the clang of a bell.

'K O,' hazarded the struggling maid.

'No!'

'K L, K L, sir!' And seeing the tyrant withdraw at this unexpected recovery, she plucked up her courage and rattled on: 'K L M O P Q M R – Q M R – Q M R P, sir,' she asserted, desperately.

'P, you goose?' cried the Professor.

'I mean M, sir!'

'You have had a thousand M's already, girl! M's that stand for Marion, and Mischief, and Much Meddling; and Misfortune, Marion, and Misery . . .' He leaned over her like some workhouse official menacing Oliver Twist.

Bravely the little maid stood her ground. 'V W X Y Z,' she said in a rush.

The Professor hit his forehead with the heel of his hand and gave an inarticulate cry. He sank down again upon the bed, the pedagogue defeated.

'The ignorance of this generation!' he said, appealing to me. 'I tell you, Jennifer, I was convinced by one part of your paper, and that was where you drew the connection between the decline of school discipline and the increase in ignorance.'

I agreed with the Professor instantly and completely, of course; though I was not sure I had properly made that point; or if I had, not sure I'd known I was making it. Certainly I had not made it as succinctly and confidently as he had.

'Marion, that was an exemplary performance,' he said.

Her freckled features brightened. 'Thank you, sir.'

'Exemplary in its incompetence,' he said.

'Yes, sir,' said Marion, her face falling again.

I wondered how much she understood of his sarcasm. Not very much, I was sure. She was like a puppy that judges its state of happiness by the tone of its master's voice. Then again, her fate was already written on the wall in letters of fire. There was no need for her to be able to read to understand that; and no need for her to strain, I thought sadly, to comprehend any more. That was the blessing of discipline: that there was no need to think.

118

'There's only one possible way of rewarding a performance like that, Marion,' said the Professor. 'Only one species of applause could possibly do it justice.' Resignedly, he took the erring young woman by the arm and pulled her in between his knees, looking sorrowfully into her round pink face. 'Which is, Marion?'

Over his shoulder the maid looked at me lying half-naked on the counterpane, my bottom glowing fifty shades of pink.

'Some of what she had, sir,' she said gravely, nodding.

'Which was?'

She looked at him warily, wondering if there was a trap in the question.

'The slipper, sir,' she said.

'So you *were* spying!' cried the Professor, springing up like a lion to devour her.

'No, sir, I wasn't, sir!' Even I believed her that time. 'Only, I know the different sounds, sir,' she cried.

'Eavesdropping, then,' he thundered. 'Spying with a different organ.'

'I couldn't help it, sir! It was loud. Anyway it's there, sir.' Marion pointed inarguably at the Slipper on the floor, where the Professor had flung it when he rose.

The Professor nodded, reigning in his temper. 'And you think it would be easy and convenient to pick it up, do you, Marion?' he asked her, slowly and coolly.

Marion paused, scanning his face. 'Yes, sir,' she said, with a note of caution.

'I expect you do, girl,' he said. 'I expect you do. I am sure you would welcome a mere slippering instead of what you will have.' Marion said nothing now, but stood inspecting her toes again, rather as I might

119

have done in her place, I feared. *Mere* was not a word I would have readily applied to any one of the Slipperings I had just received.

'In any case, you're quite wrong, Marion,' said the Professor. 'My guest hasn't yet had what you're going to have.'

My first thought was that that was a rather unnecessary and tasteless remark. Then I realised that once again, obviously, I had underestimated the Professor. Knowing the torpor I had slipped into during the course of my last spanking, he was speaking in this way to alert me, and remind me not to get too comfortable during this unexpected delay. That was when I learned that the great man could discipline two young women at once, with a single sentence!

'Fetch the Hairbrush,' he commanded the little maid. 'And you, Jennifer,' he said with a demonstrative wave of his arm, 'may stand in the corner – '

'Oh please, Professor,' I said at once, without fear for the consequences of interrupting, 'couldn't I perhaps watch? You know, it would be very educational for me, sir, if I could be allowed to watch your technique.' I knelt up on the bed with my knees apart and my hands clasped modestly upon my bra. 'I'm sure it's not part of a regular Initiation, sir, but you know we have had two Variants already, and I would understand so much more, I think – that is, if the maid doesn't object, sir.'

The Professor gave a fastidious grimace. 'I dare say she does, don't you, Marion?'

Marion had gone back into the darkened dressing room. Now she returned with an attractive, rather masculine hairbrush, made of dark reddish wood. She carried it in her apron, which she held stretched out in front of her, as if it was a thing too precious and delicate for a mere servant to touch.

'Yes, sir,' she said.

The Professor beckoned her impatiently, with a jerk of his arm. 'And she knows it never makes the slightest difference, don't you, Marion?'

Marion made a little bobbing curtsey, and offered her master her cargo. 'Yes, sir,' she said.

He snatched it up with barely a glance. 'Take your knickers down, Marion,' he said in a voice as terrible as a rumbling volcano.

A traditional maid's uniform includes a large number of petticoats, I discovered, and under them, loose old-fashioned drawers. These, when she had excavated her way to that level, she lowered. As the Professor took her over his knee I was charmed to see that Marion had freckles on her bottom too.

Turning slightly towards me as the girl made her last, settling motions, my instructor said: 'There's only one reason I'm allowing you to witness this, Jennifer. So that you can get yourself thoroughly prepared beforehand. I shall expect great things when your turn comes!'

So shall I, I thought, at least inside your grey flannel trousers; and then I was ashamed of that thought. It was puerile and flippant, and proved how necessary and timely these reminders were. Of course I had been starting to feel giddy, enthusiastic about what I was going to see. Now, instantly, I felt apprehensive once more. The Hairbrush was the next Device on our Prospectus, after all.

At the moment, however, it was being lifted two or two and a half feet above Marion's bare bottom, and then smacked down upon it. Marion's bare bottom was one of the plumpest parts of her, or to be accurate, two of them: one on the left and one on the right. On the right the Professor's wife's Hairbrush landed, held in the Professor's right hand. It leapt up again at once, to something like the same height, and landed anew, on the left.

Right, then left, I noted. I wondered if it mattered, on which side one started. I tried to remember how many of my various treatments had begun on my right cheek, as opposed to my left or exactly in between – a region that the Professor favoured, I had noticed, for some of his most emphatic strokes: such as, with Marion now, the fifth, the tenth, the eleventh and the twelfth. The twelfth made her shout.

'Not a childish Device at all, my dear!' I heard the Professor declare.

To my frustration, I was unable to recall the pattern of any one of my punishments with any certainty. The clarity of the first few strokes had soon been overwhelmed by the great quantity that had seemed to follow after. The oppressive sense of time passing to which many men and women are prone, especially amid the hurly-burly of the modern world, can be escaped, I had already discovered, across the knee of a capable disciplinarian. While individual smacks and spanks, like this one and this that Marion was now receiving, might sting and linger in the memory even longer than they lingered in the flesh, the actual sequence of them quickly became blurred. I was interested to notice the same effect was true when one watched another recipient across the knee – was this Marion's fourth or fifth half-dozen that was making her sing out with such a hoarse and mournful cry?

So vocal was she, I thought what a good educational aid it might have been (an even better one, that is), if the Professor had had the young woman recite her alphabet again, repeating it after him like a schoolgirl, one letter to a stroke. I wished I had the courage to suggest it to him, even now; but of course, if I had thought of it he must have too, and already I despaired of it.

It was quite a pretty voice the young maid had, I thought, wondering if it ever rang out so fetchingly in a Christmas carol, or when calling a boyfriend across a busy street. She was quite pretty altogether, I realised, belatedly, even from this disadvantageous angle. Kneeling up, I moved nearer across the bed. Her head was hanging down out of view and some of her upper half was obscured by the Professor's body, especially her left shoulder and arm.

'Unlike the Hand, the Hairbrush never tires,' pronounced the Professor, as if it was some oriental proverb of great wisdom and universal relevance.

Rather shyly, I sat on the edge of the bed alongside the Professor, as near as I dared. I supposed I must be seeing an example of a principle the Professor's wife had mentioned earlier: the beauty of the female form under stress. Marion, at this moment, was a beautiful sight.

Upturned, so full and round and so sweetly divided, framed by a shapeless mass of white petticoats to that side and a shapely region of black stockings to this, the maid's bottom blossomed under the Hairbrush. Her freckles, copious as stars over the ocean, were in danger of being totally eclipsed by the broad red blush of thirty-six sunrises. At least I think it must have been that many by then; judging by Marion's sobbing I could not think it had been very many less; or fewer, as the Professor would say. I wondered how many I had had this afternoon, and was grateful to think I had not broken down myself, although the Wooden Ruler had been sharp enough to put tears in my eyes like any onion, from pure astringency.

The Professor caught sight of me at his side. 'I'm sure you observe, Jennifer, how a plump Bottom absolutely demands the Hairbrush; that is, when the

Hand is no longer sufficient.' He spanked her once more on either cheek, then paused, resting the brush. I was certainly very impressed by the way the Hairbrush, angular as it was, made short work of Marion's generous curves. Considered as an Area for punishment, her Bottom had a succulent breadth to it that must make mine look terribly skinny, and it possessed all the elasticity and sensitivity of youth.

'The Plump Bottom tempts the disciplinarian to spank always by Hand,' the Professor said, regretfully, as the maid's sobs came under control. He fondled the bottom on his lap, as a contented person might fondle a pet animal. 'Well, you have seen what little good that did,' he said, picking up the brush again. 'Hold her legs, please,' he told me.

I reached tentatively for her ankles.

'No,' he said. 'Get down on your knees, on the floor, and put your arms around her feet. Place yourself where no detail will escape you.'

Obeying these instructions, I found the prescribed position and brought my face very close indeed, closer than I had ever thought possible, to the young woman's bottom. Her cleft was a dark valley ending in a tuft of soft hair as dark as a cocker spaniel's coat, around which the two swelling hills of her buttocks seemed to glow with many different shades of red: from shrimp pink to maroon. Marion, in that region, smelt rather noticeably of piss, and I hoped very much that wetting yourself was not the next stage after bursting into tears.

'A library out of order is an invitation to Chaos!' lectured the Professor, somewhere up above my head.

It was alarming how close the Hairbrush now whistled past the end of my nose. Although I could not help blinking as it smacked down, I squeezed Marion's round calves tightly to my breasts and proudly held up my head. It was exhilarating, like going for a ride at the fair, where your body instinctively feels in danger while inside you know perfectly well you are safe, protected by a mechanism of unerring accuracy. The Professor would not mind me thinking of his right arm in that way, I decided; and he would not miss Marion and hit me on the nose with the Hairbrush, no, not if he spanked the poor young woman until he could spank no more.

I hoped he would not have to do that; spank her for that long, I mean. I already felt a little sorry for her. Nasty as the Hairbrush obviously was, I could not wish it on her to keep it off my own bottom. Nor, I thought a little anxiously as Marion's spanking went on and on, would I like the Professor to become unable to fulfil his obligation to me because of having to see to her.

As if he had sensed my moment of doubt, the Professor promptly threw down the brush on the bed and, grabbing the little maid by the hips, lifted her up in the air. I let go of her at once, of course, swaying back out of reflex and grabbing at the bed to hold myself upright.

The Professor set the still wailing young woman down on her knees on the floor next to me, with only his right leg between us. She knelt there facing him between his own knees, which were now spread wide as the cut of his flannels would permit.

Though I was not as close to the site as I had been ten seconds previously, it was obvious to me that the Professor was once again – or more probably still, given the speed with which events had developed – afflicted with a very prominent erection. It became more than prominent a moment later: it became evident. The fly of the Professor's flannels was fastened with a zip, which he had opened, freeing the proud growth itself to breathe the air of its master's bedroom.

I could not restrain a gasp of admiration. How magisterially the phallus jutted from his groin! Uncircumcised, its shaft was as muscular and graceful as the neck of an antelope; while its glans, scarcely peeping yet from its fragrant sleeve, was the very shape and sheen of the helmet of Achilles, or some other hero of ancient renown.

'You may express your gratitude for this correction, Marion,' said the Professor in the most noble tone.

Sniffing only slightly now, the girl raised her curly head, and removed her hands from her vivid bottom, where they had fled. Her cap was hanging down over one ear and she reached up to reposition it. Clearly she had performed this service for her master before. How tenderly my hand itched to reach out and help her as she fumbled with her hair-grip!

The maid now approached her face, opening her mouth, not grossly wide, I noticed, like a child gobbling candy-floss, but in a decorous O just large enough to receive the Professor's swollen member. Yet dutiful as all her movements were, I had been close enough, my face on a level with her own, to notice the grimace of distaste she had to suppress as she received that gift. I was sad then, to think she was unhappy in her duties.

For a servant, especially a young, pretty, female servant, may be called upon to do many things, and must always be cheerful and willing. She must love her employment, since it is hers and no other's, and brighten the dull mops and dish-rags of domestic service with a ready smile. The Professor recommends a certain hymn of George Herbert's to be learned by heart, exulting in housework and the spirit of devotion. Privately I imagine Mr Herbert in a skirt and pinny, trembling as he polishes the mistress's thigh-length boots.

With such a master and mistress, I thought, so eminent and yet so condescending, it should have been easy for Marion too to be devoted; to do at once and gladly all that she was bidden, even while, at this moment or that, she might have preferred to be else-where. To be found wanting and summarily spanked could of course never be pleasant, but discipline must always be taken in the spirit in which it is given, if the subject is to get the benefit of it. And then, after such a discipline, to be granted the sudden and overwhelm-ing benison of the Professor's virile member to suck – should that not assuage all pain? Yet how she la-boured over it, her cheeks red as apples with straining at it. To her it seemed as much of a chore as the spanking itself.

What a marvel the great man was. Was there no end to his resources, I asked myself dizzily. I was impressed beyond measure at the inspiration of his decision to relieve what I could only think must have become a very uncomfortable physical condition – and to relieve it in a way that sealed, so to speak, and reinforced the very discipline that had produced the condition in the first place!

Suddenly the Professor's eyes, which had been closed in dreamy intellectual meditation, opened and fell upon me: upon my eager face so close to the fount of his pleasure.

'Oh, no,' he said lazily. 'That won't do at all. In the corner, girl.'

I went at once obediently and faced the wall, my hands linked on top of my head. I was hardly sorry to be denied sight of such an awesome event. To be granted the opportunity – to be actually required and commanded – to perform such an intimate personal service for the Professor himself! To have his hands – his Hands – resting on your shoulders, caressing the back of your head while you worked! I doubted very much whether Marion appreciated the true honour that was being pressed upon her, into her, within her very lips, even now behind my back. How could she gobble him in such a heavy and ungrateful manner? Did she not know what a great man her master was? Had she never listened to him on the radio?

I heard a small grunt which I recognised immediately as signalling the Professor's delight.

In my mind's eye now, as clearly as though some convenient periscope had suddenly dropped from the bedroom ceiling, I seemed to see Marion's shoulders freeze and her bottom stop bobbing. Her mop of wild red hair would give five little jerks, or six, or more! as though some invisible hand was spanking her still; and now the Professor would be withdrawing, glistening wet and perhaps already shrinking visibly. Silently I thanked him for directing my eyes away, for I could not wish ever to shame him by looking upon his mighty organ in detumescence. Behind me, a rustling sound announced, clear as any commentary, that the little maid had lifted her apron to envelop him and wipe him dry.

There was some shuffling of feet, the rustle of clothing being rearranged, the swift tiny buzz of a zip being fastened. Then I heard the words of Marion's dismissal.

'Now take my compliments to your mistress, girl,' the Professor said, 'and ask her will she please, as a matter of some importance, see that you learn the letters of the English alphabet, in the exact order which it pleased our noble ancestors first to arrange them.'

'Yes, sir,' said Marion uncertainly. She sounded a little subdued now, I thought. Then she asked: 'What about the PVC, sir?'

'Damn the PVC,' replied the philosopher succinctly. 'Attend to the ABC!'

I heard the hard little shoes hurry across the floor, and then the sound of the bedroom door closing. There had been no time for Marion to inspect herself in the giant mirror as she went; nor had she even asked the master's permission to do so. I could not understand how a woman could be so uninterested in the effects of a punishment that had seemed to me quite thorough. With more than a little pity in my heart for her, I thought perhaps young Marion was not altogether suited to her job.

The Professor sat, no doubt, on the bed still, laughing softly. I could almost see him shaking his head over the girl. Beneath his breath, he began to whistle a little tune.

Uncomfortably I realised that at some time in the last five minutes my vagina had began to seep again, all down my leg, while my heart was pounding like a sprinter's. My ears burned hot as match-heads as with shame I understood. I was jealous! So handsome was the Professor, so much already did I admire and wish to please him, I had even begun to envy his household staff! How stupid I must be. No matter how devoted and willing the pupil, no matter how ready to abase herself in the cause of learning, the simple domestic chores poor Marion had to perform would be forever beneath her.

'Jennifer,' called the Professor. 'Come here, please.'

10

The *Ne Plus Ultra*

'She will masturbate now,' said the Professor idly.

'She is young,' I said, instinctively impelled to excuse her.

The Professor snorted good-humouredly. 'She will do it whether she wants to or not,' he said, 'for my wife's pleasure.'

I was unsure how to respond to this. Was it a confidence he was imparting to me? What lesson did he mean me to derive from it?

'If she doesn't come off quickly, to use a suitably Lawrencian phrase, her mistress will do it for her.'

Now that startled me altogether. 'You're both so generous to her!' I exclaimed. Then I blushed slightly. It was wrong of me to make reference to the act he had forbidden me to witness.

'It is important,' the Professor said, toying with the Hairbrush, 'to give servants gifts and favours. That's the way you inspire devotion in them, you see.'

So it was as I'd suspected. The maid had neither the will nor the heart to aspire to discipline for her own sake. For the treatment she'd received, though she had thoroughly deserved it, her employers had to compensate her. She would not be satisfied with the wonderful gift of the Professor's emission, which she obviously didn't treasure, but had to have a clitoral spasm of her own.

'They have ways they use, to reduce the pain,' he said. 'Some go for anaesthetic, would you believe? Drugs and ointments of several kinds. Cold compresses have their adherents, who quote Victorian authorities, governesses' handbooks and the like. The daughters of the upper classes, and, no doubt, many a sly kitchen-maid, were formerly accustomed to rub themselves with butter.' He smiled indulgently at me where I stood before him, my hands still on my head. He knew I would appreciate this shocking extravagance.

'I myself,' he said, 'agree with my wife. She discovered the principle in her early years, and I have found it affirmed in memoirs of more than one brothel-keeper.'

He spoke this surprising phrase with nonchalance, but with his bright inquiring eyes still fixed upon mine as if to gauge the tenor of my response.

'Wisdom and good sense can appear in the strangest of places!' I said, rather faintly.

'It is orgasm that provides the most effective relief,' said the Professor, 'for the pain of corporal punishment.'

I felt my blush deepen. In my energetic and erratic fancies, I had rather missed the point again.

'I suppose it exercises the rigid tissue,' I said, in the rather off-handed way of someone who pretends to knowledge she doesn't actually possess.

'Oh, certainly,' said the Professor, to my gratitude. He put the brush aside and plucked at the knees of his flannel trousers. I was aware of the warm sharp reek of Marion's hind-quarters, perhaps tinged with the whiff of the Professor's own rich and creamy effusion, still lingering in the air.

'Wouldn't it be very wrong, though,' I asked, adopting the Socratic method, 'for a subject who had

131

deserved punishment to try to relieve the pain herself?'

'Oh, doubtless,' said the Professor. For a moment I began to suspect he was making fun of me.

'The pain is the point, surely,' I said, stubbornly.

'Oh no, my dear,' said the Professor pedantically. 'The discipline is the point.'

I felt rather confused. I suppose that since I was still little more than halfway through my Initiation, I could not expect to understand the mystery completely.

One thing, however, was clear in my mind.

'Professor?' I said. 'May I have permission to make a small – ' My blush, so newly cooled and faded, returned in force. ' – exhibition of myself?' I finished.

'By all means, Jennifer,' the Professor said graciously.

'Thank you, sir.'

I took off my blouse again. 'I haven't got an apron,' I said, 'but perhaps this – ' I wrapped the sleeves of the blouse around my waist – 'will be acceptable.'

I tied the sleeves together in the small of my back, then spread the blouse on the bed. I picked up the Hairbrush and put it on the blouse. Holding the blouse stretched out in front of me and curtseying carefully with bowed head, I offered the brush to my tutor.

'What makes you think I'd use that on you?' he asked, jocosely.

Startled again, I looked up.

'That's a junior Hairbrush,' he said, taking it out of my makeshift apron and tossing it on the floor. I thought it looked quite senior enough to me. Then he pulled my blouse itself off me, bundled it up and threw it all the way over to the far side of the bed.

I was surprised that a gentleman who set such store by orderliness could perform such careless and cavalier acts. Then I realised of course that he had done them on purpose, to give Marion an extra task or two when she came to clean the bedroom next: tasks that could not help but remind her sharply of her punishment.

'Come downstairs,' said the Professor. 'That's where we keep the big girls' Hairbrush.' And he raised his eyebrows in a rather arch and unnerving way.

I said a silent, regretful farewell to all the other rooms on the top floor, whose doors had remained closed to me. At the same time, I felt that the study was perhaps where a new pupil more properly belonged; far away from the painful sight of such ignominious domestic mishaps as the bedroom had shown to me. If we had not gone up there in the first place, I reflected, the incident would never have occurred; and whatever its educational value, I felt sure Marion would have been happier to forego it.

I looked again at the paintings hanging on the staircase as we went down, and noticed that yes indeed, sexual arousal and satisfaction was an element of several of them, sometimes featuring in places and on occasions where the innocent spectator might be surprised to see it. I felt no less guilty for oozing as I had, sure that the properly disciplined young woman should aspire to a state of purity and clarity above such sordid bodily reflexes. I was sorry that the punishment of my bottom in particular, and then Marion's in addition, should have caused the Professor his own inconvenience. How calmly and gracefully though, he had dealt with it!

We returned downstairs to the study, where the solemn tick of the grandfather clock welcomed us. The

Professor threw another shovel of coal on the grate, reviving the ailing fire. I lingered by the notice-board in my bra, looking at my skirt and knickers, and wondering how I was to retrieve my blouse before I left the house. Perhaps the Professor's wife would let me pop up and fetch it; she knew what it was like for a woman to have to go around inadequately dressed.

'Sir?' I said, looking next at the Prospectus.

'What's that, Jennifer?'

'May I have permission to tick off Slipper, sir?'

'Oh, yes, girl, of course,' he said expansively.

I looked at the remaining words. 'But not Couch, I suppose, sir.'

The Professor straightened, wiping coal-dust from his hands. 'Couch?' he echoed.

Already I was wishing I hadn't mentioned it. 'Yes, sir,' I said, after a pause.

'Couch: Cushion or Couch: Knees Up?' he asked.

I still was not sure exactly what either of those might mean. 'No, sir,' I said. 'I don't know, sir,' I said.

'You concede that you have not yet experienced either of those Positions?' he asked, holding the palms of his hands to the fire.

'Yes, sir,' I said.

He feigned surprise. 'You have?'

'No, sir,' I said. 'I concede.'

He turned away from me. The dancing firelight gave his face a ruddy glow, and gilded the ends of his hair.

'Put ten more strokes on the list, Jennifer,' he commanded.

'Oh, what for, sir?' I cried, startled and dismayed. 'I'm sorry, sir,' I said, before he could have a chance to reproach me. 'I mean, may I have permission to ask a question, sir, Socratically – ' I found myself playing with my hair, and took my hand away quickly. 'Only I think a well-disciplined subject ought to do her best to understand her punishment, so as not to make the same mistake twice, sir.'

'You said no to me, Jennifer,' said the Professor, lightly.

I was appalled. 'When, sir?'

'In the bathroom,' he reminded me. 'I told you I would finish washing your nether parts with my wife's face flannel, and you refused me. Ten,' he said. 'I should take it, dear girl, and not try to argue about it. Refusals of all kinds can entail penalties much more severe than an extra ten, you know.'

Ten just for saying no! For sparing him trouble and, I had supposed, embarrassment! Of course I had not really been about to argue, but for a moment I could hardly think this punishment was just. Then I recognised that was only my pride speaking; the very pith of the wild, wilful quality in my character that the Professor had consented to subdue.

I took up the pen and drew the horrible strokes, trying not to wonder how they would be applied, and when. This third line of them stuck out beyond both the first two. I wondered how many there would be altogether, in the end. I wondered whether I would have to go on to a second column.

'What a picture you make,' said the Professor gently, 'standing there in your little white bra, dreaming of the future.'

I was not sure I would concede 'little': my bra was a few sizes larger than Marion's; several more than anything the Professor's wife might have needed to wear. But the merest mention of it seemed to make my nipples stir and my breasts swell with longing. It felt much, much worse to be condemned to stand naked except for a pretty little bra than naked except for a pretty little choker and button shoes.

'How is your bottom now?' the Professor asked me.

'Numb, sir,' I replied.

'Numb, Jennifer? Too numb to feel the Hairbrush, do you suppose?'

'I don't think anything could be that numb, sir,' I said.

'My dear,' said the Professor, as if patronising a public-spirited lady on *Any Questions*, 'I think you're right.'

I put the pen back on the small desk, while the Professor stepped behind his own desk and opened a drawer. I supposed it would be the same one where he kept the Rulers; I could not imagine that every drawer in the desk was full of Devices.

The Professor pulled out a wooden object nine or ten inches long and, smacking it down on his pale green blotting pad, slid it over for my inspection. 'What do you think of that, Jennifer?' he asked.

'Is that the Senior Brush, sir?' I asked, wanting to be absolutely sure before I committed myself to an opinion.

'One of them, Jennifer, yes,' said the Professor.

I knew as soon as I looked at it, the next lesson was not going to be easy. Marion's hairbrushing had been sharp and difficult for her, and I feared mine might be just as uncomfortable for me. Though I would approach it with a willing heart, still I knew my flesh would quail. I could feel it quailing already, even through the steady burn planted on it by the Hand and the Rulers and the Slipper.

A Senior Brush, for mature students. It was wooden, naturally: a very dark, dense-looking wood, set with thick clumps of stiffly spreading bristles. The head was oval in shape, no more than three inches across, all of a piece with its handle, which had been thoughtfully shaped in three dimensions to invite the user's hand. The bristles were quite yellow. I was slightly surprised. If the Junior Hairbrush had seemed masculine, the Senior one seemed almost feminine. I wondered if it might be very old too; if the wood had grown dark with time and use. Perhaps it was not unreasonable to imagine generation after generation of women lifting their skirts and lowering their knickers to make its acquaintance.

'I expect it's quite hard, sir,' I said.

'You may pick it up,' he informed me.

Willing my fingers not to shake, I took up the Hairbrush in my right hand, and, as if in unconscious imitation of what was about to happen to me, turned it upside down. I had been half afraid it would have a design in relief on the back: a monogram or family crest of some kind, which the Professor wished to print all over my bottom. To my relief, it was plain. It was heavier than it looked, and when I pressed my fingernail into it I found the wood was very hard indeed, the grain an almost invisible silver shadow, like the first hint of grizzle in a black dog's coat.

My hand started to shake in earnest then, so I had to bring the left one to support it as I laid the brush down carefully on the edge of the blotter. I realised I was handling it as though it was made of glass and likely to crack into a thousand pieces. 'I expect it works quite well, sir,' I said, trying to keep a quaver out of my voice.

'Careful, Jennifer,' the Professor admonished me. 'Levity is no part of a wise young woman's preparation.'

'No, sir,' I said. 'I think I am prepared, though, sir,' I told him.

'Are you indeed,' he said drily. 'And I suppose you are ready to take up a Position, too, are you?'

'No, sir,' I said, touching my hair and then forcing my hands back behind my back. 'Not quite.'

'Why not, pray?' came the relentless voice.

'Because you haven't told me which Position to take up yet, sir,' I said. I felt myself on firmer ground, saying that.

'What do you think, then?' asked the Professor, conversationally.

'Think, sir?'

'What Position do you think would be appropriate?' he elaborated, with menacing patience.

I was flattered to be consulted, but I would have to take a wild guess. 'Please, sir, Marion took her Hairbrush Spanking across your knee.'

'And you think that would be appropriate for you, Jennifer, do you?'

My nerve would not break. 'Yes, sir,' I said.

There was a short pause.

'To begin with,' I added.

The Professor squared the blotting pads on his desk, then set the Hairbrush exactly in the middle of it. 'Excellent, my dear,' he said quietly. 'An excellent answer. Let us put it into practice immediately. First, come and stand here, between my knees.'

He turned his chair and sat forward, his flannelled legs apart. I went to him and stood, with the slightest of shivers, between them. My thighs rested lightly against the edge of the chair-seat. I put my hands on my head.

'Put them down,' the Professor told me. 'Put them behind your back.'

As I stood there, looking into his face, the Professor began to brush my hair with the gentlest of strokes.

'Let's have you looking nice,' he said.

I caught my breath as the bristles swept across my

138

head, and felt my nipples stiffen painfully inside my bra. Thank goodness he could not see them! I did not want him to think I was more feeble than Marion, requiring manual relief before a punishment even began. I did not want him to think I required relief at all.

I was overwhelmed at his unexpected kindness; tears sprang to my eyes. The great man was brushing my hair with the care and attention of a lady's maid, finding my long-lost parting and smoothing my tresses back to each side behind my ears. He turned me around and brushed the back. Soon my scalp felt itchy and uncomfortable no longer, but airy and light. I was amazed at his gentleness. It seemed to penetrate my skin like pain.

'Every hairbrush has two sides,' said the Professor after a while, in a rhetorical, quotational tone of voice. 'Shall we proceed to the other?'

'Yes please, sir,' I said softly, not knowing what else I might legitimately say at that point.

'You may adopt the Position you so artfully suggested,' he said.

Artfully! I was beyond all art, I thought. What did he think I had meant by asking to be put back across his knee? I had meant nothing except to face the inevitable; or rather, to offer my bottom up to it.

The Professor helped me do so, guiding me into position. I found myself gazing once more at the dark brown floorboards.

The Professor's hand moved slowly, exploringly, across the bare cheeks of my bottom.

'Still numb?' he asked.

'A little bit, sir,' I said. 'Except when you touch it. Then it's quite – sore, sir,' I explained, catching my breath.

'Excellent,' he said again. 'You're quite red, you

know. You colour very well: strongly but fleetingly. It must take quite a lot of work to get you up to full brilliance.'

He laid the backside of the Hairbrush to my own. It was quite cool. Helplessly, I felt my buttocks clench, as if they had been tickled. The brush would not stay cool for long, of that much I was sure.

'I want you to pay particular attention to this, Jennifer,' said the Professor. 'The Hand is natural, and extremely personal. The Ruler is scientific and precise. The Slipper is hearty and raises a good dust, and has a fetching symbolism of its own. But the Hairbrush, Jennifer,' he said, moving his arm around, stroking my bottom in circles with the brush 'is the acme, the *ne plus ultra* of Spanking Devices. You might even think of it as the last actual Spanking Device on the Prospectus. Beyond the Hairbrush lies what, Jennifer?'

The blood was already beating dully in my temples from hanging upside down. 'The Strap, sir. Which is the last,' I said, just in case it had slipped his mind.

'Exactly,' he said gravely. 'The Strap: half spanking, half whipping. The Americans would no doubt insist on including their beloved Paddle, of leather or wood. In rural areas, it has sometimes been the whole of their education!'

The Professor moved, tilting me as his knees shifted. My breasts were pressed uncomfortably against his left thigh. My nerves were twisted to such a pitch that I thought I could hear them keening in my head. When would the punishment begin?

'Of course,' my tutor went on, 'we have several paddles here – souvenirs of lecture tours, gifts from exchange students and the like; but in this country we tend to think them too self-conscious, too whimsical for adult use. Matters of personal and domestic discipline do not require commercial, specialised equipment.'

Hearing the way he warmed to it, I recognised that the theme must be something of a favourite of his.

'For centuries, parents spanked their children and employers their servants in private, without the intrusion of industrial manufacturers, and often in extremely primitive conditions. A young lady might very profitably be set to binding her own birches, a young gentleman to carving a paddle of his own, or one for his sisters, but that was a matter of craft, not commerce. The attention of the subject can be wonderfully extended and intensified by making the very Device which he or she will subsequently receive. In addition, there is the value of craft itself: the discipline of producing a useful object. Idle hands these days are more likely to be pressing the buttons on some futile computer game!

'But I digress,' the Professor admitted, patting my back just below my bra and sliding his hand down around my buttocks to caress the region of my anus with a single finger-tip. 'I intended, Jennifer, only to make the minor, semantic point that the Strap and everything beyond are not properly spanking Devices because they are manipulated in an entirely different way from everything you have experienced today. The Strap, the Tawse, Switches of various woods, the Cane, the Birch, the Martinet, Whips of all sizes . . .'

I was dizzy at this catalogue. Perhaps the drawers of the Professor's desk *were* full of Devices after all! Would I be expected to learn them all? How ever long would that take?

'All those, and others, lie beyond Spanking. The Strap marks the upper limit of the Prospectus – a kind of Black Belt, you might say.'

'Yes, sir.'

'And below the Strap, the Hairbrush reigns supreme.'

I felt it coming through the air at me. After that I was not sure what I felt. Sharpness, like the Ruler, but with weight; weight like the Slipper, but rigid! Rigid! Rigid! How it snapped at a poor young woman's bottom, that horrible, hard, rigid piece of wood. This was what Marion had taken forty or fifty with, a lesser version of it for younger women, and it had made her cry. I was determined not to cry, though I shouted loudly and squealed without modesty or restraint.

'A good old-fashioned Hairbrush Spanking,' said the Professor, emphasising alternate syllables with quick whacks on my left cheek and on my right. 'Highly suitable for the lithe and lovely. Picture the scene, Jennifer. Perhaps a disagreement, on a Sunday afternoon walk in the country. The young woman is marched to the next suitable place along the route, where she is confronted with the consequence of her own petulance. Her handbag is demanded of her, her hairbrush taken out. A convenient log or litter bin is designated The Place: then Mother, Father or Fiancé lifts the skirt and Sunday petticoat, and directs that the peach-trimmed knickers be lowered.'

He had paused, in the recollection of this improbable-sounding event. The Hairbrush hung suspended over me. I could feel its baleful shadow like the heat of a hurtling meteor. Now it landed, loudly, and my feet flew up in the air like any startled pony's.

'Your feet are kicking again, my dear,' the Professor pointed out. 'I shall have to spank your legs until they lie down and behave themselves.'

He introduced my left thigh to the Hairbrush, and then my right. Then came three more smacks on my left, closely spaced, followed by one savage one on the right. Then, while I was still sprawling, all hope of dignity fled, an almighty spank on my inner thigh landed, just where the skin is tender as a baby's. I shrieked so loud the Professor returned at once to the cheeks of my bottom, popping and smacking delicately around and about for a while. I could feel him restraining himself, lightening the force and tempo of my punishment out of consideration for my earlier sufferings and inexperience.

'At home the young lady or young wife always keeps a hairbrush on her dressing table: so handy for those private punishments, secure from the eyes of the rest of the family. A hundred years ago a "Conversazione" correspondent in the *Englishwoman's Domestic Magazine* famously suggested the purchase of two hairbrushes,' the Professor told me, 'one for the hair, the other for the purpose of discipline; "for reasons of hygiene", as she expressed it. As I recall,' he said, shifting my weight as though to ease the circulation in his thighs, though I feared it was more to improve the exposure of my lower regions and the accuracy of his aim, 'the correspondent was anonymous. Many of them were, you know. You can check that later,' he said in an aside. 'I have all the volumes for that period. Whether it was her own discipline or her children's, she also unaccountably failed to make clear. Perhaps in her mind there was no distinction.'

Through the delivery of this learned and interesting illustration, the spanking of the Hairbrush on my bottom had become very slow and almost languid, though neither light nor imprecise. The Professor still placed each tap of the brush smartly where it would most make me shiver and quake, and wriggle helplessly across his lap. It became apparent to me that while perhaps it was less cruel, and easier to endure, if handled with such expertise and care, the oval tip of this Device could wreak just as much deft damage among feminine curves as the sharper corners of Marion's model. There might be advantages after all to being granted the Senior Hairbrush.

'Oh, Jennifer!' exulted the Professor in a melodramatic whisper. 'How you shine! How lustrously you shine!'

With those words he slipped his fingers into my crotch. Squirming out of embarrassment as much as tenderness, I knew instantly he had discovered my shame: that I was wet enough there to float a boat. Yet he said nothing but only wiped the mucus smoothly and intimately down the inside of my thighs, as if to soothe the pain the brush had put there.

Wanting to assure him that, even though I couldn't conceal them from him any longer, my mind was still above such accidents of flesh, I tried to speak.

'Surely the Fiancé,' I squeaked tonelessly; and then again, making a bigger effort: 'Surely the young lady's Fiancé would not lift her skirts himself, sir, on a Sunday afternoon walk or any other time, sir? Surely only a Husband would have the right to do that?'

'True, Jennifer, true,' mused my historian; 'or a Parent, wishing to display to her Intended how his Dearly Beloved is accustomed to being punished, to set a good example for their married life. Such things used to happen more often than you would imagine, Jennifer,' he proclaimed, spanking me again.

There came another pause: quite a long and rather welcome one. I was not told to rise or move. Although it is extremely uncomfortable to hang one's head down for so long – and though the burning in one's bottom goes on and on regardless of actual strokes – when a spanking stops, it seems bliss itself. You feel you could lie like that forever, warm lap to warm lap.

'Do you know, Jennifer,' said the Professor in a smooth and even tone, 'I've just realised I'm still spanking you across my knee. And I did promise to vary the Position after a while. How frightfully forgetful of me, I do apologise.'

'It's quite all right, sir,' I answered valiantly, 'though I must say it would be nice if we were still in the bedroom, so I could lie down for a moment or two, sir, and get my breath back.'

'You can lie on the floor if you like,' said the Professor, lifting me in his arms and carrying me over to the yellow carpet in front of the fire. 'You can lie there and be a bare-skin rug!'

And depositing me on the floor face down in a huddle, the Professor stood and laughed at his own pun with sharp barks of laughter like the excited, high-pitched yapping of a happy dog. I was surprised to hear him forsake his customary gravity, and I wondered why it was. Rubbing my bottom slowly and thoughtfully, I remember thinking to myself: I hope he is not behaving oddly because of that new erection of his that has been boring into my belly for the last ten minutes.

11

A Curious Fancy

As I lay there on the yellow carpet in that darkened room, in front of the softly crackling open fire, the deep languour that I have spoken of already claimed me, softening the hard floor under me and drawing a blanket of drowsiness across my nude limbs. I hardly know how I could have been so careless as to give in to it. I suppose all my activity had tired me out, weakening my resolve; and perhaps the grave, measured ticking of the grandfather clock and the gentle, calming tone of the Professor's beautiful voice had soothed my poor bewildered brain even while his hand stimulated the punishment receptors in my well-warmed bottom.

At any rate, while in that sudden and very welcome interval when I lay stretched out on the floor, I seemed to fall into a light doze; and I had a dream. Such a dream! I would not have dared mention it to the Professor or his wife, and I almost blush writing it down here for all to read; but though the dream was so peculiar and fluid and nonsensical, as dreams always are, yet it seemed to be so real; so vivid that it was an adventure in itself – another part of my Initiation, which means I could hardly leave it out. I beg your pardon if you are one of those who are, as so many claim to be, bored by the recital of other people's dreams. If that is the case I urge you to skip

at once to the next chapter, where I promise to continue my narration in a more regular and upright –
if that's the appropriate word – manner.

I dreamt that two young women were standing in
front of the Professor. They were sisters, and had
been sent here together to be punished. Their offence
was not very clear, as, in fact, such things often
aren't, even in waking life.

The younger sister was dressed in school uniform:
green blazer, green skirt, a white shirt with a tie. I
knew her name was Christine, and that she was a
senior girl in her school, some sort of scholarship ent-
rant who had been sent for extra lessons from the
Professor. I remember her very clearly. Sometimes, I
actually was her, in the dream.

Perhaps I was the other one too, though I remember her more vaguely. I think she was older, more
grown-up. When I think of her, I remember her in her
underwear: a black bra, black stockings and suspenders, tight black panties. Her name was Lucy, or
it might have been Felicity. At the beginning of the
dream I think she was more decently dressed, in a
sober suit and high-heeled shoes.

I was there too, at the beginning, though I was
invisible; or perhaps like the eye of a camera, filming
the scene. I was there as some kind of witness, I knew
that; as an observer. I had to see that the punishments
were carried out properly.

I do not know exactly where we were. We were
indoors, I'm sure. Perhaps it was the Professor's study
in the dream, and the sisters were standing where my
sleeping body lay. Only I do not remember either of
the desks being there, or the globe, or even any bookshelves; and I do remember a sort of upholstered
bench, like the back seat of a car. I remember the
Professor standing and confronting his erring pupils.

The women stood together, with their arms at their sides. They were blonde, and quite tall. I think I saw their faces, but I cannot remember them properly. They were pretty, I remember that.

'What you two need is a good spanking,' the Professor said.

I think they agreed, but whether they actually did or not would not have been important, even in a dream.

'Christine, step forward,' said the Professor.

The schoolgirl obeyed smartly; a credit to her uniform.

The Professor told her to touch her toes. I remember seeing her bent over, fingertips extended, touching the toecaps of her brown shoes. Her sister, on instruction, came forward and lifted Christine's skirt, folding it back over her hips. Christine was not pleased to have her underwear exposed by her sister. She seemed fretful, as if she would have preferred to take her skirt up herself. But her sister attended to her, doing what was necessary in a methodical, impersonal manner, like a nurse undressing a patient who was restrained or incapacitated in some way. It was obvious it was not the first time she had had to do it.

Underneath her skirt, Christine wore knickers of regulation bottle green, a much darker colour than her outer clothes. She did not seem to be wearing her blazer any more; in fact I have a memory of her with her breasts quite bare, her brown nipples hanging down like berries on a bush. There was some confused discussion about clothes, which was resolved in a while by Christine's green knickers being pulled down to her knees. It seemed only right. She did not move a muscle as her smooth pink bottom cheeks were bared.

I was quite alarmed to see her sister begin to spank her on the bare bottom, very deliberately; lifting her right hand high and bringing it down on the pink flesh with a loud smack. She did it repeatedly. Then for a while it seemed I could not see. I was talking to the Professor's wife, who had something important to tell me. Her face was made up in a very extreme and dramatic way, with huge half-moons of soft grey eyeshadow and artificial circles of rouge on her cheeks. She held her face very close to mine, yet I could not make out what she was saying. Though her lips were moving in big exaggerated motions as if she was shouting at me, her voice was no more than a murmur, as if she was behind glass. Meanwhile, somewhere in the room, Felicity was still giving her little sister a good bare-bottom spanking.

I remember I was most concerned about this: in fact, I think I was trying to tell the Professor's wife. I thought she should warn her husband or conceal it from him, as she thought best. But I could not speak to her until I had understood what she was trying to say to me, and that was virtually inaudible.

All the while, of course, the Professor was perfectly aware of what was going on. He had no objection to a family dispute being resolved in this way, with one sister taking care of another.

I could see him now that his wife had vanished from my sight. The Professor was wearing a brown leather jacket and standing with his fists on his hips, supervising the proceedings. He was encouraging Felicity to spank her sister well. Suddenly I understood that this was part of his Prospectus for the occasion, that Christine's bottom should be well warmed up, and brought to a perfect state of readiness before he took over.

Now Christine was across the Professor's knee,

149

wearing only her knee socks and school shoes. The Professor had his left arm around her bare back in an embrace of such confident intimacy that I began to feel jealous and sad, almost weepy. I knew I was supposed to be counting the spanks the girl received – perhaps it was to be the same number that her sister had given her. Felicity too had disappeared now, like the Professor's wife. I felt a new compulsion to conceal this fact from him, as if I feared his wrath might be immense and all-consuming if he noticed they were gone.

'Twenty-five, twenty-six, twenty-seven,' I counted loudly. I was relieved to find I knew which number they had got to. The number was obvious, in my dream, from the colouring of Christine's bottom, which was pink tending to red in the middle of each cheek.

Christine was now standing upright, her weight on her left leg, her right knee bent so only the first two toes of her right foot rested on the floor. She had her arms crossed, lifting some sort of brightly coloured sweater or overshirt up to reveal the undersides of her breasts. Her blond head was turned, looking down over her shoulder, watching where the Professor was measuring the heat of her bottom with his hand. I was worried because I did not know where we were.

I had lost count of the smacks, and hoped I would not be in trouble for it. There was a clear, raspberry pink glow all around the underside of her bottom and spilling over slightly onto the tops of her thighs. But it was not complete. I was sure Christine had not had her whole punishment yet.

Lucy stood facing me, legs apart, head up, shoulders back. Her breasts were propped high, squeezed by the glossy fabric of her blouse. She was telling me in a conversational tone that her sister's punishment was more important than her own. I knew what she was challenging me to do, trying to ask of me; but I was paralysed, my body completely absent from the scene.

Now the Professor's wife, naked as I had seen her since my arrival, was tugging at Lucy's skirt and trying to pull it up. Her legs were too far apart, holding it taut: she would have to be peeled out of it, like a soft and tender fruit.

'You must give your sister your full attention now, Christine,' boomed the Professor, as if the room had grown very large and he was right at the other end of it. 'See how she touches her toes.' She was indeed taking that Position now, her bottom outlined clearly by her tight skirt. 'That's the way to bend,' the Professor directed. 'Knees together, hips straight and high. None of this rolling around on the floor like a snake.'

As he spoke these peculiar words, the Professor's hand lashed out and smacked Christine over and over again, driving her across the room towards me. I understood the message that she and his words together conveyed, and I felt rather upset and embarrassed at having caused him to interrupt the proceedings.

Then it was Felicity who was over the Professor's knee, with her tiny black briefs uppermost, and a good deal of creamy white skin between them and her black stocking-tops. Her sister, wearing some sort of short, flimsy nightgown, was asking me if she should go and fetch a hairbrush. It was obvious that that was what Felicity needed; in fact it was the reason she had come. I urged the Professor to agree, to let Christine go and fetch it, though somehow I seemed to do it without speaking.

Somehow the Professor heard, or at least he

agreed. He would keep Felicity warm in the meantime, he said, and then I was giving the partly-dressed woman a hand-spanking. It was a precise, almost prim hand-spanking. I was giving it to her; though in some way, with the absurd self-aggrandisement that so often happens in dreams, I had become the Professor myself.

It was my lap Felicity was stretched out across. She was still wearing her panties, stockings and suspenders. Her back and thighs were smooth and alive, though I do not remember feeling any warmth. Felicity was slim; her spine stood out like a fence under snow. I knew the punishment I was giving her was in some way preliminary to something else. I knew this because she still had her panties on.

I felt nothing as my palm met her flesh. Dreams have defects like that. My fingerprints were clear on the beautiful soft mounds of her bottom, as if I had been spanking her for a while already. I don't remember hearing anything now either, although there was some music at one point.

Christine was standing next to me, very close, with her hands clasped behind her back. She was fully dressed again, I think – she was possibly not wearing her blazer though. She was watching her big sister's punishment so intently that I felt self-conscious. What if I made a mistake and she reported it to the Professor? Even now he was approaching, coming up the stairs. I reached out a long arm and shut the door to gain some time.

'Christine, you must go round behind the couch!' I whispered; and obediently as if I had been the headmistress's secretary with a line of miscreants waiting, the sixth-former hurried into place. With a placid smile she slipped her knickers down to her knees. Then she bent over the back of the bench which

turned out to be high enough to support her hips, and
laid her fine blonde head on the seat. Now the Professor himself was standing behind her, pressing himself against her, rubbing her hips in big circles with
hungry hands. Christine looked up and caught my
eye. She gave me a wink.

'Poor prep!' announced the Professor. 'Hard work
never hurt anybody.' His wife was standing to one
side, lifting her arms and rubbing deodorant into her
armpits, then putting more rouge on her face, and
some on her nipples. She stood thrusting her hips
backwards and forwards in a rude, uncharacteristic
way, until my groin grew hot and melted, and I had
to look away.

Christine was still over the back of the couch,
which now seemed to be a sitting room sofa, which
lace doilies on the arms and embroidered antimacas-
sars on the back. 'Lucy,' the Professor's wife was calling, 'you can take your knickers down now, and
come and join your sister.'

To my astonishment and chagrin, the elder sister
was fully dressed again. She was standing in the corner pretending to face the wall, but actually looking
out of the window across the fields. It was as if she
had managed, by evading my attention, to undo the
punishment I had already given her. I knew if she was
not taken firmly in hand this instant, she would be
out of the room and running away, scot free.

The Professor's wife came to me dangling a little
silver key in a coy, playful manner, holding it up between finger and thumb and letting it swing back and
forth in front of my nose. She kissed me, in the
dream, though I felt and tasted nothing.

'Houdini couldn't do better,' she told me.

Lucy was struggling with a hundred petticoats,
calling me for help. I had to help her take down her

knickers to be spanked, though that was no part of my job. I might even get into trouble for doing it! Still I strove to help. Her body was warm now, her legs slippery, always sliding out of my grasp; though whenever I looked up she was holding perfectly still.

'Two bottoms are better than one,' the Professor told me.

He was leading Lucy over to the seat, conducting her into place beside her sister who was bending over the back. Their hands hung down and the tips of their outstretched fingers brushed the rush matting on the floor. The Hairbrush was still missing, and I thought I would have to find it. But the Professor was ready to begin.

I do not know what put into my dream that sweet vision of two bare bottoms tilted up and raised for punishment. The spanking of two women in tandem or side by side I know now, though I did not then, to be a fine, poignant way to proceed. The Professor is decidedly in favour of it, whenever circumstances make it convenient. When you smack one of them, the other flinches at her strokes; feeling them, as it were, in sympathy. Each of the pair wants to appear the bravest. Each strives to last longer and take more without calling out, without trying to protect herself with her hands, without starting to cry. And while they compete, each gains courage because she knows she is not the only one being spanked. Her punishment is shared with another, equally deserving. If the two are close relations, each shows better in company.

None of this was conscious (if I may use that word) in this dream of mine about a girl called Christine and her elder sister. I thought I was Christine, over the couch, having my bottom smacked repeatedly by an unseen tutor; I was worried because I was sure I

154

still had my knickers on and I knew that was wrong. Should I ask permission to take them down, or would that be inviting worse punishment than remaining silent?

While my sister was being spanked I struggled to reach my hands up behind me to slip my knickers down while our persecutor was busy. I say struggled, but I could not move. Only when a spank fell on my bare bottom or the tops of my legs was I able to move, and then only to kick out in the most untrained and ignominious fashion. I felt my feet seized, my calves smacked and the soles of my feet spanked repeatedly with a ruler.

I was running away then, half naked, running over moorland under a dark and threatening sky. There were people all around me, keeping pace with me, though whenever I swerved or turned my head to see, they deftly avoided my eye, keeping always just behind me, or over to one side where I could not see them. I had a collar on, a leather one. I knew I would get caught any moment and dragged back to face my punishment. Still I ran, and no hand fell on me to take me.

On a high cliff Felicity tried to detain me, wanting me to put my hands on her breasts, tweaking suggestively at the elastic of her own suspenders. I saw blurred red marks, blotches on her thighs, and I knew I had been the one who had put them there. She swivelled at the hip, and showed me her bottom, taking my hand with her own and pressing it to the place. I knew if I stayed I would be in terrible danger. I kept running, wondering where I had left my shoes and hoping I would come across them soon.

Instead I came across the Professor's wife, who smilingly opened the door to me and showed me in to a room where her husband sat with a nude woman

155

over his knees. Another stood in the corner, her face hidden in her hair, her hands on her head, waiting tensely for her turn. They were everywhere, I saw, the Professor's pupils: one over the back of a chair; two more side by side over the back of a settee; one crouching on a low table on her hands and knees, her bottom stuck up in the air. There were women behind the curtains, their clothes in terrible disarray; women toasting their bottoms unwillingly in front of the fire; women stripping off behind the open doors of cupboards, hanging their lingerie on the branches of a large potted shrub. They all looked hatefully at me as if by my very entrance I was somehow skipping the queue.

'Come to me, Jennifer!' the Professor's wife cried, sitting down hard on an upright chair and spreading her legs. 'We'll have some Kleenex!' she cried, laughing as if this was the best joke in the history of the world. She repeated it again and again, while her husband's tireless arm rose and fell in time, playing a sharp tattoo on the blushing plump bottom of a novice. How prettily she squealed!

'Fat as a pig, my dear,' called the Professor to his wife, pausing for a moment's rest in his labour. He rubbed his subject affectionately with his hand. 'Lard might make you more receptive,' he recommended.

'Tomorrow, doctor!' was all the poor girl could cry. 'Not until tomorrow!'

Hesitantly I looked back at the two sisters side by side across the back of the bench. Their bottoms were bare and glowed like moons over rooftops. Though Lucy was so adult, her clothes so immaculate and sophisticated, I could tell it was a relief to her to come here and be reminded that she was not too old for a sore bottom. While for Christine, the sore bottom was still very much a fact of life. I reached out to stroke them both, but my hand could not find them.

156

Then I saw them, with the Professor. They were two bare bottoms, I did not know whose. To my utter astonishment, the Professor had now also dropped his trousers and his underpants, and was busily pushing his erect penis into one of the women, working it in and out for a while as he leaned forward over her back, resting his hands on her hips, then sliding it out and moving to the other.

Even in my dream I knew this was not a convenient and appropriate way of relieving a physical congestion, but an actual part of the treatment itself! How could it be, I asked myself as I stood in the doorway watching the Professor thrust himself into each of them, turn and turn about, skewering them and making them wriggle like that. How could it be that the Professor's wife was watching with a pleased smile on her face?

All dreams are foolish. In our unconscious minds we are quite without regard for social laws, the probabilities of everyday life, or the rules of time and space. We commit ourselves to search for impossible things, in places that seem to flow like water – now outdoors, now indoors, now halfway over the moon. People are not who they seem to be, though you recognise them without any doubt at all. You feel perfectly sure of facts and motives that in waking life are not only unlikely but often incomprehensible. I now seemed to be lying down beside the sisters, quite nude, and trying to entice the Professor to my cleft.

I did not mind how sore I was – being asleep, I probably did not even know that I was sore. I would have been willing to take all my punishments over again, if it had earned me the right to be subjected to that personal indignity, that violation, that penetrating shaft. I was certain that whatever I still had to learn could be injected into me with one spasm of that wonderful organ. After that, everything in the universe would make perfect sense!

It was going to happen. I felt a hand on my bare shoulder and heard a voice saying: 'Are you still with us, Jennifer?' It was the Professor, rousing me from my doze in front of the fire.

12

Support and Stability

'Shall we continue?'

I rolled over. The Professor was showing me his wristwatch. 'Time's getting on, you know, Jennifer.'

I was amazed to realise my entire dream of Felicity and Christine had lasted no more than a single minute!

Taking the Professor's hand and rising to my feet I blushed to remember how the dream had ended. How could I have imagined that so suave and prominent a man as the Professor could ever be seduced by the bare, red bottoms of his students? Why, he had not taken advantage of Marion's exposed genitals, let alone mine.

'I think it might be a good idea, sir,' I said, rubbing my eyes and tugging my hair into order. I did not know if he realised I had actually dropped off for a moment; and I was afraid he might be very cross if I told him. He might even throw me out of his house for falling asleep during a lesson! He would have had every right to.

I thought it was best to accept the next phase of my punishment and try to make it help me remember that there was nothing at all thrilling or romantic about what was happening to me, for all that my unconscious had now joined forces with my body to betray me.

I trusted he would keep to the decision that I had had long enough over his Knee. The incidental stimulus of our genitals by friction and surface heat, even through a layer of grey flannel, was threatening to become a serious distraction. I was glad now that his wife was not in the room, for her presence too seemed to confuse the issue.

Looking down it was not possible to tell, the grey flannels being so roomy, whether the Professor's penis was still erect. I thought it might be.

'What Position may I do, please, Professor?' Asking my question I looked him in the face, and saw that he had understood my glance at his crotch. How rude of me! I bowed my head in shame. What was needed was some pure, concentrated discipline, I decided, to bring me back to earth.

That was not to say I was looking forward to it. Discipline, like medicine, is never pleasant to the person who needs it.

'The back of the chair,' said the Professor.

Stiffly I rose on my toes and winced my way over to the chair. I picked it up in both hands by the seat and carried it to where the Professor was indicating: three feet in front of the fire, facing into the room. I placed myself behind it and bent over. At once the effect of the coals began to compete with the warmth already kindled in my bottom and all down the backs of my legs.

The Professor brought the Hairbrush and laid it on me.

Feeling its shape pressed against my bare bottom, I asked: 'What's the difference between a junior brush and a senior one, sir?'

'A junior one will give you a good enough spanking,' the Professor said, 'for most purposes. Even a very skinny subject will be all right with a junior

160

Hairbrush. But a junior Hairbrushing is a simple, and often very quick punishment. You just whack her until she turns purple and stops breathing, and then you let her go.'

The Professor chuckled, to let me know he was making a joke. I thought that in the last few seconds I might have turned white rather than purple, despite being upside down, for it seemed to me that Marion's punishment had not been terribly quick, nor, in the end, simple. I smiled uncertainly at the Professor's pleasantry, and then made a little appreciative noise: because, after all, he could not quite see my expression at present.

'Kiss the upholstery,' said the Professor, and he started to spank me.

It was a rather sloppy, sideways kiss, to tell you the truth; quite unlike the kiss of the Senior Hairbrush on my upturned bottom. That was a kiss with teeth in it.

I was still not sure I understood the difference between the Senior brush and the Junior. The Junior was rectangular, I thought as the Senior had its way with me and the chair started rocking and bumping on the floor. I tried to imagine how the oval shape of this brush might be concentrating the force more, driving my punishment more compactly into the place where it had to go. Perhaps the brush upstairs looked nastier, with its heavy corners; but might it not do more damage to less effect?

I cannot conceal that this conviction was only in my head. My other end was feeling thoroughly damaged already. As the brush rose and fell I tried to chew the seat-cushion, which seemed to have a lot of toothmarks on it, as if many other subjects had had the same idea in the same Position. A particularly sharp shot made my hands start waving around on their own until I thought I would tip over completely.

161

I grabbed the rungs of the chair and held on for dear life.

'Not so comfortable now, is it, Jennifer?' the Professor asked, as though everything so far had been rose petals.

'No, s-s-sir!' I panted.

Other girls had stood it. So would I. In a minute it would stop, this bitter rhythm; in a minute or two. Meanwhile I must concentrate on how much good it was doing me: making me strong and sure, honest and decisive and pure. No more of the old muddle-headed, muddle-hearted Jennifer. No more of my lazy, thoughtless ways; no more helplessness in the face of life's many challenges. I would waste no more time; I would cram every minute – every second of the day – with virtue and charity, and reading great works of literature, if only it would stop.

It stopped.

'Now the Desk,' said the Professor, while I was still groaning and shaking my hips.

The Professor's Desk! Once again he might have detected the very way my mind was turning. That was the very altar of learning, the sacred island of study. It was on his desk that the Professor wrote his brilliant essays, his inspiring speeches, the witty and devastating correspondence that enlivens all our learned journals, not to mention our daily newspapers. A Desk was the one true shrine and symbol of Discipline, even if its drawers were not full of Rulers and Hairbrushes and Martinets and whatever else it was that he had told me lay beyond the Strap.

On that Desk, a student might place an essay on, say, The Modern Woman and the Decline of Discipline. On that Desk, her essay could be read and marked. On that Desk it could be annotated and criticised. From that Desk it might be praised, denounced, embraced, dismissed. To that Desk then would come, inevitably, the student herself, with her skirt lifted and her panties lowered, to receive whatever corrections, minor or major, her essay required.

And then, wonder of wonders: even after and beyond spanking as an instrument of scholarship, the Desk could provide a platform for the kind of scientific, callisthenic exercise the Professor's wife and I had performed there earlier. My thighs still tingled from the callibrations of the Professor's Rulers. I almost believed, as I approached the sacrificial table, that it beckoned me with the ghost fragrance of our mingled scents, the Professor's wife's and mine.

I glanced at the hairbrush in the Professor's hands. There seemed no reason why, with such a Device, we might not go on all night. I felt weak and rather poorly. It seemed a long time since I had been told to tick off anything on the Prospectus. 'Please, Professor, how would you like me?' I said.

'Face down, bottom up,' he said.

Resignedly, I lay down, my head and body on the desk, my hips over the edge.

'Tuck yourself in, please,' the Professor said softly but sternly. I was to learn this meant lifting my knees up to touch the underside of the desk and wriggling until my groin met the edge and I could wriggle no further.

'Pulling the knees up like that rounds the bottom superbly,' the Professor told me. 'But you'll find it a hard Position to hold. I think you'll appreciate the effect, though, if you can just hold it for six. Hands on the other edge, Jennifer, and keep your back down as much as you can.'

I pressed my breasts and belly to the wood.

The first two strokes were slightly sparing, as if he was testing my balance, daring me to lose the pose. I didn't stir. I jumped at the third and fourth, because they came so much more swiftly than the first two; but I clung on tight. I arched my back deliberately, to see if I had gone askew; and then the fifth landed, on the left, and the sixth, on the right.

I had held the Position for six.

I held it for eight. Now I could hear the blood pulsing in my head, and my back felt like an overstretched rubber band.

For the first time I was wondering if the difference between this Senior Brush and the Junior might, in fact, be a difference not in severity, but in refinement. What the Professor had said suggested this brush would be wasted on an undiscriminating bottom, like the poor maid's. She would squeal at anything, and even shed tears, I thought unkindly. I held the Position for ten.

'Jennifer!' scolded the Professor, as my feet slipped to the floor, and he stepped closer and gave me a running series of little short spanks, vertical, like raindrops pelting on tarmac. The brush seemed to knead my bottom like dough, and I gasped and snorted with the pricking of it.

I wondered how much it would take for me to shed tears.

I supposed a Real Woman, a feminine, sensitive soul, would be blinking back tears after the first three or four good smacks. Six bare and she'd be weeping in earnest. Bawling, in Marion's case.

I couldn't imagine a woman like the Professor's wife would ever burst into tears; not from being spanked, anyway.

And I was not sure I would either. This was not another incidence of my famous arrogance. Being face down over a desk with a hairbrush redecorating your bottom is not a good place for feeling unwarrantably pleased with yourself. What I meant, when I realised I would be unlikely to cry, was that the effect of a spanking, any spanking (so far), was not at all to reduce me to misery. It did not depress me – it was, on the contrary, a stimulant, to blood and nerves. It made me want to shout and dance and jump up and down. And obviously it was tickling my libido too. What was difficult was accepting enough of that stimulant, and channelling it in ways that would do myself the maximum of good, when actually it hurt rather a lot.

Now the Professor turned his attention to the backs of my legs. He patted and tapped them lightly with the brush-back, running up and down and switching from one leg to the other. At irregular, unpredictable intervals, he included a proper spank. Now he returned to my bottom, with single, well-planned, well-placed strokes.

What am I saying, 'well-planned'? How could they be anything else from that superb practitioner? I really began to believe I could recognise the crisp, smart attack of a highly-finished brush-back. I was sure the brush upstairs had been dull and lustreless in comparison, as I supposed all the Professor's wife's things would be as long as Marion looked after them.

Dull was how I had begun to feel too. Under the pitiless continuation of that attack, however stimulating, I felt my body beginning to relax again. I thought about hairbrushes, and wondered why the one in my handbag was a different and unsuitable shape: cylindrical with bristles that radiated from it, meant for curls, which I do not possess. What's more, it was made of nylon. Was this the reason why no one who was cross with me had ever ordered me to open my bag and hand over my hairbrush, I vaguely wondered. Was it one of those things that always happened to other girls?

In the distance, the snapping of the Professor's hairbrush slowed, and finally stopped. I became conscious of an urgent sensation clamouring for attention in my brain. Since it was the same urgent sensation that had been making itself felt ever since I had begun to be spanked, my brain was no longer interested. The desktop was not uncomfortable: it was, in fact, the least uncomfortable Position I had taken, in terms of support and stability.

My mind was wandering. I might even have fallen asleep again if the Professor hadn't suddenly caught me another crafty whack just where a girl likes it least.

'Aa-aahh!'

'Up, Jennifer,' he ordered. 'Hands on head. Ah-ah, no touching, no touching! That's the way . . .'

I stood facing him again, my bottom throbbing so hard I could almost hear it. It sounded like a deep bass pulse, a grating hum. My eyes were watering. I linked my hands and pressed them fiercely down on the top of my head. Sweat trickled from my armpits. My bra was already soaking wet.

The Professor inspected me closely: my face, my belly, the surfaces of my thighs. He touched me on the back of the neck, making me shudder and gulp. Then he touched the bristles of the Hairbrush gently to the cleft of my bottom.

I hissed like water on an iron.

'Some authorities,' the Professor said quietly, 're-commend that the other side of the Hairbrush be used, in conjunction with the more customary back.'

I was clenching my buttocks tight, stiffening my knees in a desperate attempt to get away from the brush, which felt as coarse as a doormat.

'I think that would be a really beastly one,' the Professor remarked. 'Don't you, Jennifer?'

He was so close I could feel his breath on my face. 'Yes sir!' I gasped.

He took the brush away. I was grateful. That kind of treatment, though it certainly focused your mind completely on what was happening to you, seemed as though it belonged in the same category as whips with metal tips, and having your panties stuffed with nettles.

He hadn't actually said that he would never do it, I reflected. I must be on my guard constantly, never to deserve any of those horrifying things.

Now that I knew what it was like, or some of it at least, I was determined that I would always be contained by a spanking. The Professor had talked already about the limits to spanking, saying the Strap went across the boundary. The Prospectus included the Strap, I could see over the Professor's shoulder. It was the only remaining Device, after this one. I would be Initiated into the procedure of Strapping, as a way of concluding my introduction. I would accept that, of course; and then I made up my mind I would never afterwards incur it. I would be obedient to the Hairbrush, and let that draw the line.

Across the Knee, preferably, I thought, and blushed to realise I was already thinking about returning to that primary human Position, so soon after bidding it a determined farewell. It was not a place I positively wished to go, I reminded myself; but if I let myself get so far as to need the Hairbrush, I would rather bend over the warm and accommodating Knee than over the hard-edged Chair-back or the shiny, sticky Desk.

There turned out to be another option, which I had not thought of.

The Professor lifted the chair aside. 'Touch your Toes, Jennifer,' he said.

I suppose I grimaced.

He put his hand on my chin. 'Reluctance, Jennifer?' he asked.

'No, sir!'

'Then what are you doing standing up, child? That's better.'

Straight down from the best support to the most taxing, least stable Position of all. I had to acknowledge the Professor's cunning. A woman could scarcely miss the point of that manoeuvre.

By now the agony of stiff muscles was cramping my style completely. My lips were drawn back in a silent snarl as I stretched the million miles to my bare toes. Rigid tissue syndrome had definitely set in.

My feet were apart. The Ruler was produced. I had estimated eight inches exactly. That made me soar in my tutor's estimation.

'Excellent, my dear,' he said. 'Eight inches is a very useful distance to have by heart. There are many applications of it.'

So saying, he began to show me one.

I suppose the concave curve of the Chair-back had compressed my bottom, and the Desk had relaxed it. Now, with the cheeks braced apart by the position of my feet, the valley of tenderness between them became much more available to the brush. I confess I shouted and squealed. I had to struggle not to lose my posture. My fingers jumped off my toes and waved around in circles, and my knees tried to contract.

How difficult and unforgiving that Position is. I wondered when the Professor would ever need it – for the Cane, of course, and Birches and so on; and perhaps for the Strap, I thought glumly. To my mind, I thought crossly while the Hairbrush continued to spank down on my bottom, it made more sense to

168

make a young lady who was about to receive a long and arduous punishment lie on her face somewhere, where she could best receive it, without creating difficulties.

That was when I created my own greatest difficulty of the entire performance.

I found that my right hand, instead of touching my right foot as it was supposed to, was touching my right buttock. It was open, fingers spread, vainly trying to shield the maximum area of peril.

The spanking had stopped at once.

I quickly put my hand back where it belonged. 'What are you doing, Jennifer?' asked a lofty, scornful voice.

'N-nothing, sir,' I quavered.

'Was that a hand I saw just now?' asked the Professor, a little more pleasantly.

'I don't know, sir,' I said.

A hard spank landed.

'Ow-ow! I mean yes, sir, it was a hand sir, but I didn't mean it to be there.'

There was a long and rather frightening pause.

I knew I had disgraced myself completely. I deserved to be thrown out into the night without my clothes and left to limp home in the nude.

'We don't do that sort of thing here, Jennifer,' said the Professor at last, in an antiseptic-sounding voice.

I tried to say something, but nothing came out. I wrestled with my vocal chords. 'No, sir.' I said.

Another hard spank. 'No, sir!' snapped the Professor, imitating me.

I waited, chest heaving, eyes wide, staring at the carpet.

The Professor's fingers suddenly arrived in my crotch, making me cry out with surprise. I felt them paddle indiscriminately about. He had my full attention.

'That's the sort of thing little girls do,' he said.

'S'sir . . .'

'You're a big girl, Jennifer,' said the Professor, as if he had just satisfied himself of the fact; and he withdrew his hand.

After that he spanked me undisturbed by any motion or protest of mine, for what felt like several years.

My fingertips stayed on my shoes as if they were stuck to the polish. I remembered polishing them, a lifetime ago, to wear this evening. While polishing them I had thought, as I always do, of a film I had once seen, in which an American girl at a high-school hop had polished her Mary Janes so brightly that her date could see her knickers reflected in them. I had wondered if the Professor ever got the opportunity to Inspect his students' underwear before their skirts were even lifted.

I started to yelp. Eventually I was yelping helplessly, as though overcome by hiccoughs.

The Professor made a fast change, dancing the brush in a sparkling run of darts and hops down the outside curves of my body, from hips to knees. He rediscovered, or at least I did, how much flesh there is on my flanks. I began to burn, both sides, like a neglected chop.

Through the arch of my legs I caught sight of the front of his trousers. It was clearly distended again. Stopping rubbing his penis with my belly was obviously not going to make any difference if I immediately started thrusting my gaping vagina at him. Faintly, though, I was surprised at his own indiscipline; that he allowed it to happen so often. And without, now, seeking any relief. Was there no comfort a mere new girl could offer him? Did he think she would be too proud, too nice to allow a gentleman to

170

come in her hand? It might be a shock, I thought, but I was sure it would be one I could stand. Other gentlemen had ejaculated in several areas of my person, over the years.

It would not do to complicate our arrangement, though, I told myself, as my spanking continued. My Instructions and the Prospectus said nothing about orgasms, neither giving nor receiving. I would not like to presume. Presumption got you into trouble.

Perhaps it would be better if he called for Marion again, I thought. Or perhaps his wife would not mind coming in now, just for a few moments of conjugal duty. While I would stand in the corner, or perhaps outside the door, waiting for calm and order to be restored and my Initiation to resume.

The Professor put his left hand on my left shoulder and leaned in to give me a driving blow, with the brush held vertically downwards. It made me cry out unhappily. I lost my balance and went down on the floor on one knee, very inelegantly.

The Professor stood looking down at me. He touched the tip of the brush to the tips of the fingers on his other hand. 'You may clasp your ankles,' he said considerately.

Sniffing, I obeyed.

It made it easier, but not much. My knuckles grew very white as the brush whacked judiciously on, and I thought my feet were going red with interrupted circulation.

'You may thank me,' the Professor said after a while.

I did, but it sounded more like a whimper.

'Forgetting your manners, Jennifer?' he asked, pleasantly.

'Forgetting – everything, sir,' I managed to say. It was true. My head had been completely blank for a while. The blessed relief of that oblivion! I think a young woman today can never get enough of it.

'Up, then,' he said; and it was over.

He lifted me by the left arm and brought me upright. He stood very close behind my left shoulder, breathing just above my ear.

In agony I clutched myself. My legs were trembling so hard that if I didn't give in to them soon I would simply keel over.

The Professor supported me, his arm around my back.

'Jogging,' he said. 'Up and down on the spot.'

I pushed the sweaty hair from my face. For a moment I had thought I was about to be sent out to run around the block. How that would have perplexed the Professor's neighbours!

'Begin,' he said.

I jogged until my bra began to hurt. Then I touched my toes a dozen times and straightened. Then I bent from side to side, touching the floor each side, a dozen times. The close presence of the Professor, Hairbrush in hand, made me think how unpleasant a session of p.t. combined with punishment must be, if anyone should ever have to endure one.

'Sore?' asked the Professor unnecessarily. I was still rubbing my bottom and legs for all I was worth.

'Yes, sir,' I said.

'Would you care for some cold cream?' he asked.

'I'm all right sir,' I said at once.

'No,' said the Professor. 'I mean it.'

I looked at him and stared, without being able to help it, at the brush in his hand.

He smiled mirthlessly, and went and put it away in his desk, closing the drawer with a loud shove. He looked hot himself, and sat down hard in his chair, as if he could not stay on his feet a moment longer.

The chair squeaked. The Professor lifted his hands, as though to show me they were empty.

'A little cold cream is perfectly permissible,' he said, 'during a long spanking. At suitable intervals. Especially for a novice.'

'Thank you, sir,' I said huskily, still rubbing.

'My wife looks after all that sort of thing,' he said, waving me towards the door. 'She'll be in her sitting room, last door on the right. You can tick off Hairbrush before you go,' he added. 'Also Knee, Chairback and Desk,' he said. Bliss!

I looked at my clothes hanging on the peg and thought of my blouse, upstairs on the Professor's bedroom floor. 'Should I get dressed first, sir?' I said.

The Professor looked up at me from under his eyebrows. 'She won't give you any trouble,' he told me.

I tore one hand away from my bottom long enough to turn the door handle.

'Tell her I'll be along in a little while,' he said. 'Oh, and Jennifer – '

I looked back over my shoulder. The Professor was combing his hair and straightening his collar.

'Be so good as to ask her if we might use her Couch next,' he said.

13

Pictures at an Exhibition

The door was closed. I knocked.

'Come in,' called the Professor's wife.

I went in, and closed the door behind me.

The Professor's wife's sitting room was well lit. It was a small intimate room. The walls were eau-de-nil, rather cool, but the air in the room was warm, and faintly scented with cedar. The furnishings were lustrous, in deep turquoise and soft rose, with an accent of black lacquer. Black paper silhouettes of unusual subjects hung on the chimney breast.

I stood there like a schoolgirl, hands clamped rigidly to my pulsating bottom: one to each cheek, fingers turned in, thumbs out. I nodded to the Professor's wife, who was reclining with her feet up on a day-bed, reading the evening newspaper.

The Professor's wife was dressed, I was surprised and slightly disappointed to discover, in a short dressing gown of navy blue silk, over a pair of pyjamas. She had taken off her velvet choker, however, and her feet were bare.

'He hasn't taken your brassière off!' she said.

I felt the need to apologise. I felt I should be sorry for coming into this beautiful civilized room improperly dressed. I was sure my face was a mess too, and my hair; not to mention my bottom. 'We have been quite busy,' I said. 'Perhaps he forgot.'

174

'Forgot?' echoed the Professor's wife, with a peal of laughter. Her hair was perfect, black, shiny and supple. She had repaired her make-up. 'What charming ideas you do have, Jenny!'

She swung her legs to the floor and sat on the edge of the couch, ready to get up now that a visitor, however humble, had come into the room. 'He always has to expose new girls completely, you know. Certainly anyone who lasts this long,' she added, glancing at a little gilt clock on the mantelpiece.

The clock was too far away for me to read. I wondered what time it was. Surely dinner time must have come and gone. Personally, I was not very hungry; but I didn't want to keep the Professor and his wife from their meal. I wondered if they kept a cook, or whether they had to put up with Marion's cooking.

'Come. Come here,' said my hostess, and patted her knee with some enthusiasm.

I approached, slightly wary. I was very sore.

'Do some people give up?' I asked, standing directly in front of her. 'You mean they leave before their punishments are over?' It was a strange idea; almost appealing.

'Mm, or get sent away, mostly,' the Professor's wife said, running her hand up my side.

Of course. I dropped my eyes, trying to keep a check on my wayward thoughts. It was not the students' wishes that counted, why could I not remember that?

The Professor's wife ran the palm of her hand slowly up across my bare tummy. The tips of her fingers lingered against the underside of my brassière. 'He must be saving it for a special moment,' she said, with a contented smile. 'Well, come on, then. Turn round.'

I turned my back, stood with my feet apart, my hands on my head.

175

Without touching, the Professor's wife inspected my bottom.

'He has made a splendid job of you, hasn't he?' she said.

'I hope so,' I said.

'You hope so!' she murmured, and then briefly she caressed my left thigh.

'Forgive me,' she said, before I could react; and then she touched me, lightly but with all four fingers, in the cleft, low down. I yelped and clenched my bottocks tight, squeezing her fingers.

She drew them out, after a moment. She let me catch my breath, and square my shoulders, and then she touched the inside of my left thigh, high up. 'There's one I would *not* have liked,' she remarked.

'It's all quite painful, actually,' I admitted.

'There's no getting away from that, my dear!' said the Professor's wife.

As her fingers probed, with infinite delicacy and tact, I began to wonder if I might be walking around with bruises tomorrow. I would not mind a bruise or two, I thought. I would think of them as badges of merit: tangible souvenirs of Initiation Day. Each time I sat down, I would be inescapably reminded of the need to behave and lead a disciplined life.

The Professor's wife moved me a little away from her. 'Could you bend over for me, my poppet?' she asked, sweetly. 'Hands on knees – oh yes, that's heavenly.'

I wondered how she could apply such an adjective to such an indecent and undignified view of myself as I presented to her at that moment. Once again, I marvelled at her breeding, her wonderful manners.

'My goodness,' said the Professor's wife; and her fingers traced the bright contours of my agony.

'The Professor said I could have cold cream,' I said, upside down.

176

'By all means, dear,' she said. 'The very least I can do.'

She went away, out of my view. She had not told me to get up. I held the position. It felt no worse than standing upright; it was moving that was so hellish.

Behind me I heard a drawer open.

Then there came a swift flash, blue as lightning. Startled, I looked round, and straight into another. The Professor's wife was taking photos.

'Oh yes, Jenny, that's brilliant,' she cried. 'Just the half of your face with your eyes and mouth so wide . . .'

But she did not take another picture. Through the dazzle I saw her take the camera back to the bureau, and come back with a glass jar in her hands.

'Lie down,' she said. 'On the couch, on your tummy.'

I could not remember when I had been given a more welcome instruction.

So this was the Couch, this sumptuous mound of warmth and softness. I lay with my face in the fold of a quilt, my hands up beside my shoulders. 'Here,' said the Professor's wife, lifting me by the hips and easing a fat pillow under my bottom.

'Your husband said please may we come and use this next,' I said, 'your couch.' It seemed a blessedly good idea to me just then. I was hoping never to have to move again.

'I don't see why not,' said the Professor's wife. I heard the snick as she unscrewed the lid of her jar. Idly I remembered noticing there were straps hanging down from the corners of the couch, black leather ones with buckles, and I wondered what they were for. Then the Professor's wife began to smear something moist and chilly on my bottom. It made me shiver and dig my nails into the quilt. It felt wonderful, truly wonderful.

177

'How's that now, Jennifer?'

'It feels more like ice cream than cold cream,' I said, as my burning skin drank it in.

My bottom was being massaged by an expert, too, I realised. Years of experience with well-spanked bottoms, her own and no doubt many others, had taught her how to handle me. Her fingers knew precisely how to move and sidle and sweep, painfully, oh, very painfully at first; but in a little while easingly, gratifyingly.

This treatment was better than any bike ride, I decided.

The Professor's wife put one knee up on the couch beside me. I turned my head and looked up at her, sidelong. Her pyjamas were silk too, like her gown; but a beautiful, dark, almost metallic grey. I wanted to kiss the hands that were rubbing me.

She leaned down over me. I smelt her perfume. 'Better?' she said.

'Your husband,' I said dreamily. 'Said he'd be in. In a minute.'

'He'll be ages yet,' she assured me. 'You have to let this soak in.' She put her face down to mine. I closed my eyes.

'Please,' I said. 'Don't stop.'

She didn't. It can be quite dangerous, she told me, to spank again too soon after applying oil or any kind of ointment, especially if any kind of Device is to be used. 'What's next?' she asked me.

'The Strap,' I said. 'Please don't stop . . .'

'Well, there you are, then. The Strap can be very nasty,' said the Professor's wife, 'on a wet or greasy bottom.' She kneaded me thoughtfully as she spoke.

Her words were music to my ears. I only hoped the Professor would not think that was a good reason to include it at Initiation. I supposed he would not. I supposed his wife spoke now with his authority.

178

At any rate he was not here yet. I started to writhe, happily for once, as his wife's hands rolled and roved in ever-widening circles around my bottom.

'You're glistening now, Jenny,' she breathed, 'really shining – oh, I must take another photo.'

She ran to get the camera.

'You're so beautiful, touching your toes,' she said, remaining over by the bureau. 'Would you do that again for me, please?'

Less quickly and readily than a properly disciplined young lady really ought to move when her tutor's wife asks her to, I slithered from the couch to my knees; then, after an instant leaning on my hands, head bowed, summoning my will, I pushed myself up into the Position.

The camera flashed.

I wondered what it was about that very unflattering pose that she could possibly find to admire. The Professor once made me read the last chapter of James Joyce's *Ulysses*, which is fifty pages long without any punctuation, and find the bit where Molly Bloom considers women's bottoms, 'where we havent 1 atom of any kind of expression in us all of us the same 2 lumps of lard'. Molly Bloom thinks quite a lot about women's bottoms, as it turns out. So did James Joyce, the Professor told me. 'It's quite wrong, of course,' he said. 'A well-spanked bottom can be very expressive of a certain sorrowful state of mind.'

'You can get up now, Jenny,' said the Professor's wife, putting away her camera.

I stood, rubbing my bottom. It was very sore still, but not so sore I couldn't think about anything else. It was quite greasy, I was glad to discover, though the cream had all soaked in.

'Do you always take pictures?' I asked her.

'Sometimes,' she said, coming back to me. 'If someone's particularly interesting,' she said, 'or particularly pretty.'

I blushed, and tried to keep a smile from my lips.

The Professor's wife put her hand on my neck, caressingly. Her eyes were the pale cold blue of a clear December sky. 'It's always useful to have a subject's picture,' she said, 'for her record.'

A tiny chill of uncertainty ran through me. 'You keep records?' I said.

'Oh, no, you keep the record,' she said, poking me gently in the midriff with her index finger. 'You bring it every time you come. It tells the Professor how your behaviour improves, as times goes by. And it shows him how much punishment you need, to keep it improving.'

She brought her lips so close to my ear they almost touched.

'And how much more you need, if it doesn't improve at all.'

Unnerved, I turned my head to face her. 'I might not even pass,' I blurted out.

'Sweet child!' purred the Professor's wife, caressing my back and patting me gently on the bottom.

She moved away from me, aimlessly.

'If I pass,' I said, 'will you give me one of those pictures, to put in my record?'

The Professor's wife laughed. 'Oh, no, Jenny, not one of them. You wouldn't want to go through the rest of your life with your Initiation photo on your record, would you? That would be as bad as trying to go around with a school photo in your passport!'

'You could change it,' I suggested cautiously. 'If a better one happened to come along.'

She laughed again, amused. 'Actually, my pet,' she said drily, 'he often sends the novices out and tells them to come back with a suitable photo of their own.'

I was horrified. 'But that would mean asking some-body to come and take a picture of you, when you were – '

'Exactly,' she said.

I was thinking fast. I didn't know anything about photography, but I was sure there must be remote controls you could use, or timers or something, to let you take pictures of yourself. I put this point to the Professor's wife.

'Well, Jenny,' she said tartly, 'that would be entire-ly up to you. And the consequences, should there be any, would be entirely on your own head.'

I have often heard the Professor's wife use that phrase, *on your own head*. I must ask her one day why she says *your own head*, when it's the other end that always turns out to be the one that receives the con-sequences.

'Would you like to see my album?' offered the Pro-fessor's wife. When I said I would, very much indeed, she went and got one from a shelf that held half a dozen similar albums, bound in dark red leather.

The Professor's wife sat upright on the couch, the album unopened on her knee. I stood beside her, looking over her shoulder.

'You can sit down,' she said, 'if you want to.'

'I don't think I do,' I replied, 'just at the moment.'

The album was made of pages of traditional stiff black card. The Professor's wife opened it in the middle.

On the left-hand page was nothing but a white label, right in the middle. On the label, in beautiful, vigorous handwriting, was written the name 'Camilla'.

Facing it was a colour print, about five inches tall by four wide, with a trim white border. It showed a woman of my own age, possibly younger, with snow blonde hair and the fairest white skin, at the end of a table. I could not see enough of the table to tell whether it was the Professor's Desk. The camera was a little above Camilla, for that was presumably who it was, and she was in the act of bending over, smiling gravely back at the photographer. Her lips were generous and her forehead so sweetly rounded that it seemed she was smiling straight out of the picture at you.

Camilla was dressed in a white blouse, maroon school skirt, white knee socks and black shoes. She was holding her skirt up behind her in both hands, showing you her bottom. Her knickers were a deeper shade of red, like a dark red plum. They were already stretched between her accommodating thighs, turned inside out.

The light was very full and clear in the picture, and the detail was astonishingly good. The folds of Camilla's most intimate parts were perfectly visible, and every little tuft of hair involved in them. At the same time, it was obvious that her bottom was still untouched. Willing and unafraid as she looked, the first stroke had yet to fall.

'Here,' said the Professor's wife, lifting the edge of a quilt and offering it to me. 'Wrap yourself up,' she said. 'Keep warm.'

'Please, no,' I said. The room was quite warm enough. In fact, I was longing to take off my bra, which was itchy as hell with the salts of my drying sweat. Of course I wouldn't have dared, after the discussion we'd already had on the subject; though it had crossed my mind that I could take it off now and put it back on for the Professor when he came in. But I didn't know how to put this to the Professor's wife, and I knew it would be quite wrong and very rude for a subject, especially a novice, to reveal her breasts without permission.

I was wondering if there were more pictures of Camilla on the next pages, showing what happened to her – Before and After, as it were. Instead the Professor's wife turned a clump of pages over together, and showed me a picture of an entirely different woman.

On the left-hand page was another label, this one smaller, with only a date written on it. It was a date of some years previously.

The picture, on the right-hand page, was another colour photograph of the same size, but turned round the other way. It showed a red-headed woman in a basque and black stockings. She was lying across the Professor's knees, which were instantly recognisable in their grey flannels, though their owner's head and shoulders were out of the picture. His left hand lay on the woman's right shoulder, which was bare. He had just given her a smack with a Hairbrush – the latest of many, to judge by the state of her bottom.

The woman's back was arched in a beautiful curve of tension, like a fine bow or an antique musical instrument. Her front had risen up in the air, above the Professor's left knee; her long hair was flying out in a dramatic swirl. Her right hand was raised, curled up on itself like the paw of a wild cat. Her right nipple was clearly visible, straining against the shiny material of her costume.

The brush was neither of the two I had seen that day. 'Is that a junior hairbrush or a senior?' I asked.

'Darling!' exclaimed the Professor's wife fondly. She put her arm round my waist, but she did not answer my question.

I knelt down beside her, resting my tender behind cautiously on my calves as she flipped the pages of her album. There was a picture of a woman in a tight suit jacket, white suspender belt and white stockings, bending over to touch her toes while an unseen hand measured her bottom with a clear plastic ruler. Her panties hung loose around her knees. They looked soft and shiny as silk.

'Joanna,' said the Professor's wife reminiscently, though there was no label and you could not see the subject's face. She leafed back several pages. I thought I glimpsed some nuns, black habits kilted up; then a bare bottom upside down, rather pink, but with a smeary quality to the colouring. Before I could examine any of these mysterious things, the Professor's wife had stopped at another page. 'Oh look,' she said.

It was a picture of this room, the Professor's wife's sitting room, furnished in an older style. A tightly-permed woman in her forties bent over with her hands on the seat of the couch. Her full, pleated skirt was folded up over her back, her pants were lying on the couch. The Professor was spanking her by hand. In the corner stood a younger woman, perhaps a teenager, wearing only a bra and self-support stockings. Her bottom was rather pink, and her hands were on her head.

'Mrs Spender and her daughter,' said the Professor's wife. 'They come four times a year, regular as clockwork.' She opened her dressing gown and held the hem of it around my shoulders, but it was too short to stay there.

The Professor's wife turned the pages. A chubby black woman in a blue brassière lay over an unseen lap or table. I was surprised how much colouring even that very dark skin permitted, on the crown of each buttock and on her thighs.

A woman in black underwear crouched on all fours, her head raised, smiling at someone or something out of the picture. Behind her another woman, unknown, stunningly beautiful, nursed a round-backed hairbrush, with a sly smile of anticipation. She was wearing a short-sleeved blouse, summery but quite severe, and a slate blue pencil skirt. I suddenly remembered my dream of Felicity and Christine; but the picture was gone.

A very young-looking woman in a ponytail, white ankle socks, black and white saddle shoes, and nothing else at all stood smiling triumphantly at the camera with her hands clamped tightly to her bottom. Her breasts were small, with broad pink areolae. The cheeks of her face were flushed, as if she had just been exercising.

'One of our celebrities,' said the Professor's wife, but though I thought there had been something familiar about the girl, the left-hand page was hanging down out of my sight, and she had turned over again before I could see if there was a caption.

'And another one,' she said.

That one, I did recognise. 'Isn't that –'

'It is,' said the Professor's wife.

A television personality. Perhaps I should describe her as a newsreader, though she has presented many other kinds of programme too. Over the back of a chair in black stockings, having her bare bottom soundly spanked with a wooden spoon, was not, I imagined, a position in which her adoring public had ever seen her. In another smaller picture below, she was seen kissing the Professor on the cheek. The Professor was looking stern but benevolent. The newsreader was blushing.

The last picture I remember was also of two people, a man and a woman. Once again the man was obviously the Professor, though neither of their faces were visible. The picture had been taken very close up, to reveal him only from his elbows to his knees; but you could tell who it was by his tweed jacket, grey trousers and white shirt – and by his right hand, for those of us who know the Professor's hands well.

We were looking at the woman from behind too. She looked my age, or younger, as far as you could tell. All you could see of her body was from her hips to her knees, but most of that was bare. She was bending over a tall wooden stool with four legs. Her skirt was blue and white candy stripe, and it had been pulled up to her waist. At the bottom of the picture you could see a twist of something dark behind her knees: her knickers, almost certainly. Most of the light was falling on her bottom, which rested on the top of the stool, and on the backs of her legs, which were pointing towards the photographer. The Professor's hand was holding what looked like quite a powerful piece of bamboo. The bamboo was bent in a way that showed he must be holding the other end in the other hand, and flexing it.

'There,' said the Professor's wife, kissing me fondly on the side of the neck. 'Isn't that lovely?'

I found I was leaning now against the Professor's wife's thigh. It was warm and soft through the pyjama silk.

Lovely. I could not imagine any picture which featured a cane being considered that. Not much of the cane was visible in the picture because of the way the Professor was standing; but it was right in the middle of the picture and there was no mistaking what it was. I wanted to tell the Professor's wife about the cold feeling it gave me in my tummy. I was very scared of even the slightest thought of a cane.

But even with the cane, I had to admit there was something very peaceful about that picture. As in the first picture the Professor's wife had shown me, nothing had happened yet. A woman was bending over, perfectly calmly, and a man was holding a cane quite motionless, bent in a half-circle. In a moment, I thought, the picture would took very different.

The Professor's wife cuddled me again. 'Don't they look a happy couple?' she asked, like any proud mother showing off her children's wedding photos.

I had doubts. I expected the Professor was happy. I was sure the woman was not. She might not have liked having the camera there: knowing other people would be able to look at her, ever afterwards, having her punishment. I was equally sure that if she had to be punished, she would rather not have had the cane. On the other hand, bent over a stool with your knickers down is a very strange position for anyone to be in unless they're happy – in the wider sense – to be there. She was perfectly positioned and not struggling at all. I didn't suppose it was her first time.

'I expect so,' I said, hoping there wasn't a catch.

The Professor's wife asked me: 'Which of them would you rather be?'

I looked at the caption which said rather mysteriously, *Francesca III*; and then at the picture again. I wouldn't have liked to be him, I knew that at once. I was sure it would be quite hard to cane someone properly, and I wouldn't have liked to have to. But would I have wanted to be her? Not if it meant being caned, not for anything – but if it wasn't for that cane – if the cane was a ruler, say – well, it could even have been me in the picture. I'd have been quite pleased with my presentation, if it had been me.

The Professor's wife had been watching my face while all that went running through my head. She gave me another hug. 'Her,' she said, as if she thought I had had enough time to reach the right answer, but needed a prompt to say it aloud.

'She does look nice,' I admitted. I bit my lip. 'I

187

wish he didn't have to give her the cane,' I said brave-ly.

'Why ever not, child?' asked the Professor's wife.

'I don't think her bottom's really big enough,' I said. It was a leap in the dark, completely without reason to back it up. Anatomical criteria, like the question of whether or not a subject's panties came down, might be altogether too trivial to consider. Then again, Francesca might have been writing to the Professor weekly from her finishing school in the Alps, begging him to see her the moment she returned and giving him all the reasons she would need to be attended to swiftly, with a pliable cane. Despite this, I boldly said: 'I don't see why he couldn't just take her over his knee and spank her.'

The Professor's wife leaned back amongst the pillows, amused. 'A spanking instead of a caning?' she said, as if she couldn't believe her ears.

'I don't see anything wrong with the Ruler,' I said stubbornly.

'Why, bless your heart!' exclaimed the Professor's wife.

14

A Novel Tartan

The Professor's wife closed her album. 'I expect he'll be in soon,' she said.

She got up, drawing her dressing gown closed, tying the belt with firm, economical movements.

'How are you now?' she asked, looking down at me with the impersonal sympathy of the professional nurse.

'Still sore,' I said.

She laid her hand on my bottom, high up on the right. 'No better at all?' she said.

I stiffened, closing my legs, lying very still. 'Oh, yes, a bit better, thank you,' I said.

The Professor's wife took away her hand. 'That's good,' she said. 'Because you've got a bit more to come yet, haven't you?'

I said I had. I wished she hadn't reminded me so directly.

'Do you need to pee?' she asked me.

'No, thank you,' I said.

'No?' she said, hovering over me. 'After all that tea? And stimulus?'

I buried my face, wishing she would move a bit further away.

'Your husband saw to it already,' I said. I remembered not to say how closely he had seen to it, knowing how she disapproved.

She stroked my right flank with a stiff, warning hand. Her fingers told me she had noticed how clenched I was holding my cheeks.

'You wouldn't like to freshen up?' she said.

I bit my lip. What I was trying to conceal from her eyes must have been obvious to her nose all along.

Apprehensively I opened my legs. In between was warm and damp.

'Quite a little pool,' remarked the Professor's wife, dabbing the quilt there with her finger.

'I'm sorry,' I said.

She took hold of my left elbow and pulled me to my feet, not roughly, but not fondly either. I thought she might be displeased with me; but she turned me to face her and brought me close, still holding my left arm behind my back. She put her right hand between my thighs and drew it out again, wiping my vulva with her palm. Then she wafted that hand up between us, past my nose.

'Quite a sticky little girl,' she said, in the same tone as before.

I was flooded with shame. 'A tissue would do,' I said, looking around.

The Professor's wife's sitting room was far too elegant to contain anything so mundane as a box of paper tissues; or if it did, she denied it, and led me up a narrow back staircase to a small, unlighted space. I thought we must be in her dressing room, where Marion had hidden to hear me having the Slipper.

The Professor's wife opened a door and pulling a light-cord propelled me into a white bathroom. I had assumed she would not come in after me; but apparently she did not apply her censure of her husband's habit to her own conduct. She locked the door behind us, sat on the edge of the bath and folded her arms. 'Now then,' she said.

190

I put the plug in the hand-basin and ran hot water, mixing it with cold. I looked round for a flannel and saw a pale tan sponge, suggestively shaped, lying on a special dish behind the bath-taps. Inquiringly, I picked it up.

The Professor's wife nodded.

She was giving no sign of wanting to do anything but supervise; but I was not going to be caught out a second time. When I had submerged the sponge and squeezed it out, I offered it to the Professor's wife.

She arched her perfect eyebrows. 'You want me to do it, do you?'

She stood up and untying her dressing gown again, shrugged it off and let it fall across the edge of the bath behind her. 'You can see better than I can,' I suggested.

Not replying, she rolled up her pyjama sleeves and took the sponge. It was not easy to tell whether she was pleased or displeased by my gesture.

The Professor's wife sat down on her dressing gown, her legs spread. She batted her eyelids. 'You'd better take your bra off, hadn't you?'

I was not sure, but I hurried to unhook it and flick the straps off my shoulders. I would put it back on, I promised myself, before facing her husband again.

With a wavering, placatory, slightly nervous smile, I bared my breasts.

Her expression did not change. Though they are soft and round and (Kevin once told me) attractive to men, she hardly seemed to notice my breasts, let alone examine them, as I'd rather feared she would want to. How her moods seemed to change.

'Lift your arms,' she said.

Gracefully as any ballerina I lifted them up over my head, linking my fingers. The room was so small the Professor's wife hardly had to lean forward to sponge the underside of my arms and my armpits, down each side to the waist. Then she gave me the sponge to squeeze out, and took it back and watched while I soaped myself in all the places she'd moistened with her sponge.

I stood between her legs, hands on the back of my head, letting her wipe away the soap. I rinsed the sponge out and let her wipe me down again. The bathroom was beginning to seem quite hot and rather steamy.

The Professor's wife smiled for the first time since we had come upstairs. She made a comprehensive motion with both hands, cupping them and lifting them up, briskly, as though there was a weight in each; and she accompanied the gesture with a quick, lithe arching of her back.

Obediently I imitated her, arching my own back, offering her my breasts.

'Good girl,' she said pleasantly, and began rubbing them with the sponge.

In an instant I had begun to regret how thorough she was being. Each time the sponge rubbed across a nipple, shock bubbles rippled and burst in my womb and in my head. I bit my tongue to keep from gasping aloud, and rolled my head helplessly up and back.

She ran the sponge across the underside of my breasts, and down the valley in between them. 'Did you like my pictures?' she asked.

'They were very good,' I said. 'You're good at taking photographs.'

The Professor's wife reached down and pressed me between the legs with her sponge, making me catch my breath.

'I thought you'd like them,' she said.

She dried my breasts and under my arms with a soft white towel. Then she made me bend over with my feet apart –

'How many inches?'

'Just spread them, Jenny.'

– my hands against the bottom of the empty bath.

She took my bottom lightly between her damp palms. 'A well-whipped young lady,' she observed. She pressed the tip of one finger to my right cheek, then hissed between her teeth, pretending I had burnt her.

'I can't still be that red, can I?' I moaned.

'Red as a cherry, dear.'

She showed me, bringing a mirror from the dressing room and letting me look back between my legs.

It was astounding. Still shiny from the cold cream, my whole bottom and the backs of my legs down to my knees formed one red glow, like a universal sunset. There was no longer any differentiation between punished and unpunished skin: every available inch had been made use of; all the different levels of punishment, and the various Devices and Positions, had together inflamed one vast Area.

Well, perhaps it is not that vast, compared to some women's. But it seemed vast enough to me, bending over the bath in the Professor's wife's private bathroom. Was it really necessary to punish that poor bewildered bottom even more today? Could I not rest it for a while?

The Professor's wife passed the sponge between my thighs, making me groan and breathe deeply, reflecting that this was my rest, and my recuperation, this little interlude in the care of my tutor's wife. I must do my best to derive the maximum of benefit from her kindness and attention, and try to learn her nursing skills in my turn.

The sponge drew its spongy, slippery length over the hot lips of my vagina, over my perineum, making itself familiar with the intricacies of my anal sphincter. My breasts hurt, throbbing as they hung down over the white enamel.

'I'm not sure – ' I panted, after a moment or two of this treatment.

'What, Jenny?' asked the Professor's wife in a deep, sympathetic voice, as she rinsed out the sponge and began mopping me out with it.

'– not sure I'm getting very c-clean,' I said, trembling.

The Professor's wife squatted down on the floor behind me. She took her sponge away and sniffed, delicately but audibly, at my crotch. Then I gave a little shiver. The Professor's wife had put out her tongue and touched me gently on the perineum.

'I think we're doing rather nicely, actually,' she said, very precisely.

I sighed. My knees were turning to jelly and there was no saying how much longer my arms would support my weight. By the time my ablutioner pulled me up and slipped a handful of towel through my crotch, pulling me gently towards her and wrapping the rest of the towel around me like a toga, I could not stand upright but had to lean on her in a rather intimate and undignified manner.

Reproachfully, she squeezed my left breast through the towel like a Spanish housewife choosing grapefruit. Unerringly the ball of her thumb found my nipple and rolled it around and around.

'We have to get you in trim, Jenny dear,' she told me.

I knew our brief time together was drawing to its end. At any minute I would be taken – or even more lamentably, sent, alone – back downstairs to await the pleasure of my instructor, who was coming to test the quality of my bottom with his belt.

In fact, I was feeling far from recovered. While the

Professor's wife pampered me, dabbing my crotch dry and puffing my crevices with talcum powder, I was growing weaker and weaker. The more she looked after me, the more I longed for her to go on doing so, putting me in a nightie and brushing my hair, pehaps, before tucking me up in bed and cuddling me until I fell asleep. At the first sign of softness and indulgence my hard-won state of disciplined regularity was beginning to unravel!

I drew my shoulders back and my chin up. I closed my eyes and breathed deeply, forcing myself to pay no attention to the delicate sly hands of the Professor's wife as they cossetted and teased me. If only I could have another interview with her – another Initiation perhaps, of some different kind even – what wonders she might teach me! But already I could tell the terms of that interview would necessarily conflict with the sterner, less ambiguous lessons I was already undertaking at the hands of her husband.

'I think you are a terribly pure young woman,' said the Professor's wife. Perhaps she had sensed my inner withdrawal from concentration on the matters of purely physical hygiene which had brought us upstairs. Her tone was complimentary; but her meaning was as elusive as ever. I looked into her dark, lustrous eyes. Could she be so cruel as to make fun of me?

I looked down at myself, nude in her bathroom, draped in her own towel. 'I don't think so,' I said. Bravely I admitted the truth. 'I still feel slightly indecent,' I said.

To my absolute astonishment, the Professor's wife advanced her face and kissed me, gently but slowly, on the lips.

She said: ' "To the pure," as a great writer once said, "all things are slightly indecent." '

When I did not respond she looked at me gravely.

'It's a joke, Jennifer,' she explained, pulling on her dressing gown. 'You have to know the reference to St Paul's Epistle to Titus.'

'I have a lot to learn,' I confessed.

'You certainly do,' she agreed, and opened the bathroom door for me.

I hesitated. 'My bra,' I said.

The Professor's wife gave the back of my hand a tiny slap. 'Pish tush,' she said, and switched out the light.

I led the way back downstairs thinking, as the treads creaked beneath my bare feet, about my clothes lying scattered around, as it seemed to me in the extremity of my imagination, all over the house. How should I ever manage to collect them before it was time to leave?

I have never, ordinarily, been in the habit of walking around without any clothes on, not even alone in my home. Perhaps it was that that was really worrying me. Total exposure, it seemed, was a punishment in itself. I felt much more awkward about going downstairs in nothing than I had going from room to room in the Professor's lovely home wearing only my brassière.

That may be hard to understand. It's not easy to explain, either, but I shall try.

I admit, in almost all cases, that for a really thorough and effective spanking, you're going to have to take your knickers down – eventually, if not from the word go. Because you're going to get quite hot, clothing above the waist, which should in any case be light, may need to be loosened and perhaps even laid aside. That seems far enough to me.

Anyone would assume that a woman nude only from the waist down has been stripped for punishment. A woman undressing for bed, for a shower, or a bath, or a suntan, does not leave her brassière on. While I still had mine, I was aware at all times that if there was not a punishment in progress, there was one in prospect. Without it, there was the possibility of getting confused. That in itself was alarming.

In any case, my brassière was the first thing I had taken off without being specifically told to by the Professor. I deferred to his wife, of course, out of obedience and politeness; but I did not know whether her will and the Professor's were always absolutely identical. How insecure a silly little thing like an ordinary chainstore bra can make you, if you are suddenly deprived of it!

As the Professor's wife and I came back into the sitting room, I told myself that I was worrying about nothing. The Professor's wife, now so decently and beautifully dressed, had been walking around with her breasts on display, and she had come to no harm.

'She exposed herself to me, in the bathroom,' said the Professor's wife to her husband, who was sitting waiting for us in his jacket and tie.

'Did she?' he said meaningly, finishing the crossword as he spoke.

'She did,' said the Professor's wife, coming up on one toe behind me. She lifted her knee, brushing the outside of my leg with the inside of hers, as she put her hands over my shoulders. She swept her hands up quickly and none too gently over my breasts. 'Pretty, aren't they?' she said.

I noticed that the Professor did not remark on the fact that his wife was now dressed, completely if casually. Instead he asked pleasantly, 'Why did you take your bra off, Jennifer?'

'I needed a wash, sir,' I said.

He frowned like the straight man in a variety act. 'I don't remember telling you that,' he said.

Helplessly I looked at the Professor's wife.

'It's not too soon,' she said. 'It's not too soon at all.'

'Nevertheless,' he said.

The Professor took a piece of paper out of his pocket and smoothed it on his knee. I saw it was our Prospectus. He merely glanced at it before giving it to me. 'Twelve more extras,' he said.

'Twelve?' I echoed, horrified.

Behind me the Professor's wife drew in her breath sharply. I thought I heard her tutting softly.

The Professor himself looked down at his hands.

'Eighteen,' he said calmly. 'You will learn not to question me, Jennifer.'

Bewildered, stung, I blurted out, 'But Socrates, sir —'

'Penalties are not negotiable,' he said, with ice now in his charming, calming voice. 'Twenty-eight,' he said.

'Yes, sir,' I said miserably.

'There,' he said, pointing to the bureau. I thought he was directing me to a pen, of which there were several, so I took one and made a row of twelve strokes, one of six and one of ten, all under the first three rows representing the extras I had earned. The paper was now full. I was nearly in tears. Who would have thought that such a promising student should slip so badly so close to the end? I must take it as a lesson to pay more attention, I said, scolding myself, and not drift off into unlikely daydreams all the time.

The total of extras amounted to fifty. Fifty strokes! In despair, I lay down the pen and paper and surreptitiously wiped moisture from my eye. Then I noticed what the Professor had really been pointing to.

It was a belt, a man's belt, broad, of worn black leather.

'The Strap, Jennifer,' said the Professor. 'Bring it over, would you?'

I reached for the buckle, which was made of metal and shaped in a way that seemed to invite the fingers. The buckle had no prong and the belt no holes. I began to get the impression that no one had ever worn this belt in the conventional fashion, to hold up a pair of trousers. Every tiny crease and crack of its battered leather had been put there by the same use it was about to receive.

'The Strap is especially suitable for the larger bottom,' said the Professor as I gave it to him, 'to take advantage of the expanse of flesh available for treatment. But it can be perfectly effective on a form like yours, my dear, which we might call full but not overflowing.'

He put the buckle in his right palm and wound the belt once around his fingers to make a good grip.

'This we shall call the last occasion of Touching the Toes,' he told me, 'though because of the lateness of the hour and the considerable amount of punishment already received and still to come, we shall permit you to hold your ankles.'

Gratefully, already aware that any support at all in that Position would be more than welcome, I obeyed. Then the Professor made me almost faint with gratitude by saying, as he got to his feet: 'Take her shoulders, darling, would you?'

The Professor's wife stood before me, legs apart, hands lightly clasping my bare shoulders, fingers pressing up on them. I felt encouraged then, and inspired to straighten my legs and hollow my back as deep as I could. I would lift my bottom up and damn the consequences!

Nor did my adjustment escape the Professor. 'Good, Jennifer, good. Now hold it like that,' he reminded me; and then he swung the Strap across my bare bottom with a loud, moist crack.

I cried out like the greenest and most sensitive of novices. I had never had the Strap before, or anything like it. It was not snappy, like the Ruler, or rigid, like the Hairbrush. More than anything it was like the Slipper, but it reached so far, punishing, when the Professor chose, the whole double arc of the bottom at one flick.

Then again I was receiving this first strapping on top of spankings of several different kinds. Being strapped on a pre-sensitised bottom was a fiendish punishment, I thought, my fingers setting in place like concrete while the Professor's wife's seemed to grip me just as tightly. When my eyes were open I was aware of her feet, bare on the thick warm carpet beneath me. She was wiggling her toes.

I leaned into her, pressing my head into her lap. I swear, if the Professor had not stationed her there, I would have fallen over, no question about it.

'The Strap needs space,' the Professor remarked, taking advantage of it, 'and it needs thought,' he went on, demonstrating by giving me exactly the same stroke, at the same angle, from the other side. 'But it makes quite an impressive noise,' he said, impressing me with it, 'and produces a fine high-coloured pattern very quickly,' he said, speeding up.

Strange choking noises had begun to emerge from my mouth, so that I hardly heard him say, as something of an aside: 'The McTannery Tartan, some of my more vulgar colleagues call it. Right, Jennifer, I think you get the idea,' he said, stopping.

I agreed with him absolutely.

The Professor's wife lifted me upright. As I came, whining with unconcealed self-pity, she took hold of both my wrists in one hand, lifting my hands between our bodies and holding on to them when they tried to fly to the reawakened fire in my behind. She pressed me to her, squeezing my hands into her shallow cleavage.

'Bear up, sweetie,' she murmured, archly; though I thought in my daze she was saying 'Bare up', and I would have automatically tried to touch my toes again if the Professor had not, at that moment, ordered: 'Tick off Toes, Jennifer.'

Still burning, I walked stiff-legged to where I had left the Prospectus and did as he said.

'And now what we came in for,' he said. 'The Couch.'

With as much relief as I had felt dismay when the Professor had said 'Twenty-eight', I lay down full length on the Couch and discovered that Cushion merely meant what I had unwittingly rehearsed with the Professor's wife, when she was putting cold cream on me. I lifted my hips and a Cushion, perhaps even the same one, was tucked under me. It felt almost as restful as before: the only difference being, I suppose, an extra soreness in my bottom, and the apprehension that it was about to be increased rather than assuaged.

Without being asked, the Professor's wife sat at the head and took my hands in hers.

'Legs apart,' said her husband. I did not like that nearly as much. I opened my legs, and began to learn the wonderful power the Strap has of punishing inwards, if you will forgive the indelicacy, when it is left short to spank one cheek at a time.

'The tip, which is cut to a simple right-angled point, can arrive a full quarter of a second after the main impact,' the Professor announced, demonstrating two or three times. 'One day I'll show you how to calculate the extra acceleration!'

'Tha-ank you, sir,' I faltered.

'Tips can be cut square, rounded, or split into fingers, as in the Scots tawse, which you mentioned in your letter, Jennifer,' the Professor said, giving me one crisp whack in honour of each of these styles. 'A tawse can have two fingers,' he said, smacking me twice on the left thigh, 'or three,' he said, with three strokes to the right. 'This is interesting too,' he said, and laid the Strap in rapid succession across my back, across my calves, and across the soles of my feet.

Curiously, the effect of those shocks in three completely unexpected and unscheduled Areas was more bracing than demoralising. While the shocks were still blazing through the thinner flesh there, less cushioned by Nature than the traditional seat of punishment, I felt as if someone had emptied a bucket of cold water over my head. In such desperation was I, four strokes later, I almost wished someone would do just that; though I wished they might fling one over my bottom first. The Strap had fallen each time diagonally, taking in one buttock and finishing long on the opposite thigh, not once failing to include my anus in its path. I was sure, as I bucked and whimpered over my Cushion, that the Professor had swapped the innocent plain belt for one with steel teeth.

'Poor dear,' said the Professor's wife as her husband paused once more in his work; and she stroked my hair.

'Jennifer!' said the Professor encouragingly. 'It is time for the Ultimate Position!'

15

First, Last and Always

In my ignorance, I felt that the Position I was in, on the Couch, over a Cushion, was Ultimate enough. Nude, face down, with my bottom raised, my hands held and my legs parted, I could hardly be more exposed, or more incapacitated; unless they were to fasten me with the straps that dangled from the corners of the Couch. That was one possibility I did not want to think about.

Having your hands held is quite enough in the way of restraint, it seems to me. Of course, your feet can still kick, and you may well find they do, as a punishment goes on and the strokes become keener and more telling. The Professor, like all experienced disciplinarians, makes allowances for a subject's natural reflexes. If her jerks and gyrations become inconvenient or if they interrupt things too much, then it becomes a matter of discipline for her to hold them still; and if she fails, extra penalties may be awarded.

Then, of course, when my hands were held at my Initiation, it was the Professor's wife who held them. That too had made a difference, perhaps. She had sat down beside me and taken hold of my hands without any specific instruction. Her husband had not objected any more than he had objected to her putting her pyjamas on. Perhaps it was bedtime already. Perhaps I was keeping them up. I told myself I really must try, for politeness's sake, to leave before too long and go home. With the Ultimate Position to do, and then fifty extras, I was afraid I would still be there at midnight.

Fifty extras, all for being presumptuous again. Eighteen of them for the primary offence, which was showing my breasts without permission. I should have told the Professor I had had permission from his wife: I knew that now. I had been so shocked by the number, and the way it kept on rising, that I had been unable to express myself properly. Obviously the Professor's wife had been setting me a test by making me take my bra off, and telling me not to put it back on. Whatever I was supposed to do in reply, I had failed. No doubt that was why she was helping her husband punish me, and why she thought it necessary to hold my hands for me.

'The Ultimate Position,' the Professor said. 'What is it, Jennifer?'

My hands were free now, I was clutching my bottom. 'Couch, Knees Up,' I whispered. I could hardly speak.

'By which you understand what?' he asked.

I rolled wearily onto my back, lifting my aching legs clear of the couch and higher. I spread them, bending my knees and raising them up, curling my back until my knees squashed my breasts against my ribs.

The Professor exchanged a glance of pleasure with his wife. 'Excellent, Jennifer,' he said. 'Well discovered. And very nicely expressed.' I felt a wonderful warm glow in my heart to think even an Initiate with fifty black marks on her record could earn such praise from his lips.

I did not know what to do with my hands. I put them down at my sides. Between my knees I looked up at the Professor, displaying all my most intimate secrets to him in the most trusting and obedient way possible. I could scarcely have revealed myself to him any further, unless I had stretched open my labia with my fingers, and that was not something that was likely to happen. In fact, it was only another of those irrelevant thoughts I had been having ever since I arrived, and which, as I say, had been even worse since I'd been completely nude.

'Other Positions are more decorous, more picturesque, one might say,' commented the Professor. 'None is more beautifully acquiescent.'

The Professor's wife walked by, going to the bureau for her camera.

'It is an excellent Position for boys as well as girls,' said the Professor, sliding the strap between his fingers, squeezing and rubbing at the leather here and there with his thumb. 'The genitals are menaced, you see, whatever their particular construction. That adds salt.'

'Metaphorically, he means, Jenny,' said the Professor's wife, seeing my alarmed expression.

Her husband continued. 'At different heights the Position is convenient for different Devices – higher for the Hairbrush, lower for the Cane. You, my dear, will continue to receive the Strap.'

I did. Once. Twice. Three times. Four.

After four I swayed badly. 'We shall pause for a moment,' said the Professor, 'until you learn to hold yourself properly.' He stood back. The belt dangled from his hand.

'Couldn't she hold her knees, dearest, do you think?' the Professor's wife suggested thoughtfully.

He exhaled, a trifle testily. 'If it's absolutely necessary, I suppose so,' he said.

Engulfed by shame, I steadied my body, my toes

205

pointing stiffly at the ceiling, my whole revealed back-side aflame once more. I was determined it was not yet necessary to take any extra concessions.

'Knees Up is a good Position for humility,' the Professor said as he resumed work on me. 'Whether she has earned it or not, the subject is given the privilege of watching her own punishment. The Position allows her to contemplate the face of the disciplinarian ministering to her, to experience the full force of his displeasure,' said the Professor, spanking me heartily. 'And by the same token it permits the practitioner to time and temper his delivery in accordance with the expressions that pass across his subject's face. Your own are most eloquent, my dear.' I was not surprised. I was, after all, receiving the most provocative and forceful attention I had ever incurred from a man.

'There is no mistaking the face of a young lady who is having her McTannery Tartan put on,' said the Professor's wife, in a terrible fake Scots accent.

The Professor gave me four strokes longitudinally. The Strap inscribed its length along the back of each leg from my knee up to my thigh, curving around my bottom almost to my hip. My muscles spasmed and my feet inscribed rapid and uneven circles in the air. I had my eyes shut, and was groaning incoherently through clenched teeth.

After that four, I did need to clasp my hands behind my knees, to hold my legs still and stop from thrashing about. It was getting extraordinarily hard to stay upright, for some reason, and not to roll over sideways and tip myself off the couch.

'It's a very pretty position for a beginning as well,' the Professor said, whacking me emphatically. 'When the subject's still fully dressed. The legs come *up* – the skirt falls *back* – the seat of the panties tautens and

206

stretches wide as the *bare thighs* part.' He underlined the words 'bare thighs' with two tight little licks to the inside of each thigh, with the tip of the belt. I whined in earnest now, the sinews of my knees standing out like wire.

'When you tell her the panties have to come off too,' the Professor went on, 'she has to peel them for you, pulling them up onto her thighs.' Almost lazily but absolutely accurately he slapped me on the flanks with his Strap, making me squeal and snort. '*Quomodo haec velamen detrahet bella puella*,' he chanted, waxing rhythmical in my punishment.

'I don't suppose Jennifer knows any of your old Latin,' scoffed the Professor's wife. I supposed she was trying to spare me the embarrassment of my own ignorance. I hoped she would not get into trouble for her own presumption.

I was beyond caring about Latin. The Strap had lit such a fire in my flesh I thought nothing would ever put it out. I lay there feeling like a very well punished young woman – so well punished indeed, that I began to feel a little sorry for myself. As the Strap licked down across my taut undercurves and stung my exposed anus, tears came to my eyes and ran, because of the position I was in, down the back of my throat. I gulped, in a rude, convulsive way, and sniffed noisily.

The Professor's wife knelt at my side with tissues. Her perfume restored me, and the sight of her calm, immaculate face revived me. In my delirium I thought she was deliberately brushing her silk-wrapped breasts against the side of my arm where it rose from the couch to the crook of my knees – almost as if she would have rubbed her breasts on mine, if my arm had not been in the way. Her husband stood braced with his feet apart, framed between the red and white columns of my own well-whipped thighs. I could see that his erection had returned.

Another finely judged stroke sent my legs out of my grip and set them flailing.

'Knees *and* Cushion, I think, dear,' said the Professor to his wife considerately.

Still kneeling, she pushed pillows under my left side and my right, then one beneath my straining hips. Sorry as I was to require such artificial props, I could only feel grateful to her.

'Cheer up, Jenny. You are doing terrifically well,' she said brightly, squeezing my shoulder and sliding her hand down lingeringly over my breast.

As my tutor leaned in to give me the last, vigorous, concentrated strokes of my first Strapping, in a virtuoso pattern of tight diagonals that left no available inch of my lower quarters unpunished, I reflected that the Ultimate Position was very suitable indeed for the serious student, or anyone dedicated to the perfection of her own discipline. The very difficulty of maintaining it under the onslaught of a magisterial Strapping spoke volumes for the desirability of imposing it on the ambitious pupil. I wondered about the value of making her expose herself in such an ungainly and humiliating fashion. Certainly the consciousness of putting my helpless vulva in the way of any stroke that erred a degree or two from true helped me concentrate, as the Professor himself had warned me it would. Then again I had a superb view of my disciplinarian each time he lifted the black belt and brought it down, and I knew he could smack me a thousand times and never miss. Through the vee of my quivering legs I could watch the way a stray lock of his sandy hair bounced above his noble forehead with each swing, and the small smile of satisfaction he could not help revealing every time I bucked and shouted out loud. There was a direct feedback relationship between us with me in the prone, Knees Up Position. No other method came close.

Reflecting on all these things, I put my hands down on the couch again, level with my hips. Holding my breath now, trembling, taut, I discovered that by pressing down on the seat I could add leverage to the Position and raise my bottom even higher.

There was an audible intake of breath from the Professor's wife, who was stroking my hair. 'Dear me, Jenny,' she said. 'That is impressive.' She stood up, and her camera flashed.

Her husband was taking off his jacket and tie, and opening the collar of his shirt.

'That fulfils the terms of the Prospectus and concludes the main body of the Initation,' he said formally, with a smile and a little bow of acknowledgement, and he tossed his jacket with an energetic carelessness across the back of a chair. 'Now there is only the small matter of fifty extra to clear up, Jennifer, and under the circumstances, considering the somewhat higher Position you have now assumed, perhaps for the first twelve we might reintroduce the Hairbrush – which I'm sure my beloved wife will be happy to supply.'

That good lady murmured zestful agreement, and going across to one of the armchairs, she reached down beside it and fetched up a patent leather handbag, in which she began to rummage. I wondered if a Hairbrush, as supplied by the Professor's wife, would be a Junior model and therefore less severe. Ashamed of that moment of mental weakness, I reminded myself of poor Marion and her sufferings under the Junior Brush. I was sure that by her mere attitude and posture, an Initiate would be able to derive the necessary lesson, even from an inferior Device. An Initiate, I thought to myself, and marvelled. What an astonishing prospect! I could not think how I had been the ignorant young woman who came to the house only that afternoon.

I had not yet heard the Professor repeat his favourite proverb from the sages of Zen Buddhism: 'Before enlightenment: gathering wood and drawing water. After enlightenment: gathering wood and drawing water.' Still I was beginning to understand that simply being spanked, even spanked a good deal, as I supposed in truth I had been today, did not in itself change your life. Afterwards there would be putting your stockings back on and pulling up your knickers, and going out again from this place of warmth and precious civilisation into the harsh, tense, confusing world. Determined as I was not to outstay my welcome, I was already beginning to feel despondency, even dread, at the thought of my bus ride home. To do myself credit, it was not the soreness of a freshly-spanked bottom when pressed against the prickly moquette of public transport upholstery that was distressing, but the sense of anticlimax, of a fall back from grace into dullness. I looked at the Professor's firm right hand as his wife put something into it. How could I live, I asked myself anxiously, away from the care and ample reach of it?

The Professor's wife had given her husband a hairbrush. He had not rejected it. It was slender and black, and quite small. My strokes were numbered now. The formal part of my Initiation was over, and unless I misbehaved in some significant and unforeseeable way, the whole purpose of my presence here would be achieved in fifty strokes' time. I stopped massaging my poor bottom and positioned myself anew. This time I propped my elbows on the Couch and pressed my hands to the small of my back, levering myself up almost vertically.

The Professor took hold of my right leg at the shin; his wife went around the back of the Couch and took hold of my left. After my earlier thoughts about restraint, I suddenly began to feel rather foolish. Together they drew me up, relieving my elbows of some of the weight I had ventured to put upon them.

'It looks to me,' the Professor remarked, 'as if we could do with a bit of mopping up here.'

'Here we are, dear,' said his wife pleasantly, swabbing my unruly crotch once more with a handful of paper tissues. 'What a very juicy young girl you are, Jenny,' she said, to my chagrin; but she did not sound as if this distressed her now any more than it had earlier.

'How many of these, Jennifer?' the Professor asked.

'The first twelve, please, sir,' I replied.

I need have had no fears about the adequacy of this improvised Device.

The bite of even the smallest Hairbrush on a bottom well conditioned by the Strap is quite distinctive, especially when you are being held upside down.

'Six for squealing during Examination,' said the Professor, and he aimed the first two spanks into the cleft of my bottom, striking left and right and stinging the inner quadrant of each cheek. As I yelped he was already moving outwards, planting another stroke on the same diagonal, pointing up to the crown each side. He used this brush in a rapid, popping style, barely touching my flesh with it before flicking it away each time. The sting was no less barbed. He gave me two on the backs of my legs to assure me that those Areas were no more exempt now than they had been when we had a Prospectus to fulfil.

There was a small pause, long enough for the new line of anguish to burn itself into my consciousness.

If I was ever so thoughtless as to disturb an Examination with silly noises, I reflected dismally, I would have only myself to thank for the consequences.

'A second six for what, Jennifer?' came the Professor's voice above me, calm and imperious.

'Being f-forward, sir,' I panted.

'Oh yes,' called the lady who was holding my left leg. 'Bending over without being told.' She sounded almost amused by my folly, and I felt my face begin to burn with shame. How stupid I had been, and how short a time ago!

The next two spanks halved the distance between the last pair and the first. The Professor was joining up the dots. I hope you will not object to me saying something so frivolous: such measures are not my fancy alone. The Professor has been known to draw felt-tip dots on the bare bottom of a bending girl and connect them with his cane. He also takes pleasure in writing or drawing a simple design with chalk on the taut seat of a pair of regulation knickers, then dusting them vigorously with the sole of a slipper until the drawing disappears.

The next two spanks cut my stretched thighs, and the last cracked down where the first had, between my anus and my groin. My body leapt and floundered and struggled, but the two of them held me fast.

They smiled down indulgently between my legs. 'Getting on, my sweet,' the Professor's wife reminded me. 'You have a really healthy glow now,' she said, and patting me gently on the bottom, let her fingertips graze for an instant across my swollen red labia.

'Now ten,' the Professor said, gazing across the room in a distracted kind of way. He was obviously trying to see the Prospectus lying on the bureau, and call to mind the reason for my next ten penalty strokes.

'For Refusal, sir,' I said, hoping he would not think it forward of me to prompt him. I thought it best also not to say what it was I had refused, remembering that it was not to the Professor's wife's taste.

But with her quick wits, she spotted my evasion. 'Refusing, Jenny?' she asked, and now she placed her hand squarely on my vulva. 'Naughty girl. I'm most surprised to hear that. What was it you refused?'

Considering where her hand was, I rather suspected she knew, or guessed; but still I held firm. 'Treatment,' I said.

She tutted, and removed her hand.

To my surprise, they began to lower me down and rearrange the cushions around me.

'Ten to be taken on the Front of the Thighs,' the Professor announced, 'with the Strap, seeing that we have it handy.'

The Front of the Thighs! Irresistibly my eyes turned to the Professor's wife.

Her own eyes were cool and her perfect eyebrows arched. 'Dear poppet,' she murmured. 'Do you think I ought to hold you again?'

Of course this was exactly what had been crossing my mind; and though neither of us mentioned it, I saw her hands move deliberately to her pyjama jacket where it buttoned just above her tiny breasts, so that I knew she remembered as well as I did what state she had been in when she had held me on the Desk between her legs and opened my thighs to the precision of the Rulers.

'Don't tease the child,' said the Professor, rather coolly.

His wife dropped her head. 'I'm sorry, my love,' she whispered. She lifted her eyes to him, her head still bowed. 'Will you forgive me?' she said softly.

He pointed curtly to me, lying sprawled and abandoned on his wife's day-bed. 'You should ask Jennifer's pardon, not mine,' he said.

She stood with her shoulders drawn in, her hands crossed in front of her, and bowed her head to me. 'Sorry, Jenny,' she said. 'I was just being silly. You do forgive me, don't you?'

'Of course I do,' I said huskily; though it did occur to me to wonder what would have happened if I hadn't.

'May I kiss her, dearest?' she asked.

Brusquely he nodded, and stood watching with folded arms as her bright red lips met mine. Her mouth was sweet and tasted of violets. Her breath seemed to soothe away my pain.

She stood up, and I braced myself for the Strap.

It swung up and down. Lights exploded in my eyes. Such force from such a slow, gentle curve! The muscles in my thighs bunched and jumped over and over as the Strap burned its broad black shape into the most sensitive areas of my skin. Tears filled my eyes. I screwed them tightly shut, thinking of the kiss the Professor's wife had given me. Holding on to the warmth and sweetness of her face, her delicately questing tongue, I rode the ascending waves of pain. And when I opened my eyes, there was her face above me in actuality, looking down on me in sympathy and care. I took strength from her smile, knowing she was watching.

The Professor counted out the last strokes. Then he sent his wife to fetch a wet cloth and lay it across my flaming thighs. She gave me her hand to clutch as she soothed me, and took the opportunity to mop my crotch once more, discreetly.

The cool moistness had hardly begun to dampen the fires when my instructor called me to rise. I stood up, leaning on his wife's arm. My legs felt swollen to ten times their natural size. They would not obey me. The Professor allowed me to sit for a while, recovering. 'Don't clutch yourself like that, Jennifer,' he said in a lordly manner. 'Think about your misdeeds, not your sufferings! Prepare yourself for the punishment that is yet to come . . .'

The Professor's wife took her cloth away and wiped my thighs with a thoughtful hand. She draped a shawl around my shoulders. I looked up, half hoping her arm would brush my trembling breasts again; but I was unlucky. Sternly I forced myself to concentrate, as her husband had directed. Twenty-eight still to come! How could I take them in a way that would do me the most good, while demonstrating to the Professor how grateful I was for all his teaching today?

To my surprise he sat down beside me on the couch. His brown eyes smiled at me, the wrinkles creasing in an almost paternal way.

'Twenty-eight extras,' he reminded me. 'Where shall we put them, Jennifer, do you think?'

I was amazed at his words. I wondered if he could possibly be giving me a choice. I tried not to look at his wife, sitting across from me in an armchair. I could hardly admit that if the Position really was up to me, among the ones I had learned today I would surely choose to be held between the bare legs of the Professor's wife, pressed close to her chest, suffused in the rich aura of her perfume. I blushed at my thoughts, and tried once again to apply my feeble intelligence to the question.

It is possible to retain some dignity, I had already discovered, when touching the toes. Even lying across cushions maintains a modest distance between the punisher and the punished. Should I bend or stand or kneel? Should I offer him my bottom or my thighs?

How often among the twenty-eight would he require to place that wicked little implement in the throbbing valley between?

The Professor fingered his chin. 'What lies beyond the Ultimate Position?' he asked me.

So it was a test after all, not a choice. Looking at him sitting beside me, easing the creases of his grey flannel trousers, at once I knew the answer to his paradox.

'Across the Knee, sir,' I said.

His smile returned. 'Very good, Jennifer; and with what Device, do you suppose?'

I smiled myself now, happy and confident as only the successful examinee can be.

'With the Hand, sir,' I said.

'Excellent,' he said gently. 'Do you remember the first thing I said about that particular Device? It's all right,' he added. 'There are no penalties attached, if you've forgotten.'

Of course I had not forgotten a word. 'The Hand: first, last and always, sir.'

He sat back, flexing his fingers. 'And the Area,' he said.

My blush deepened and my mouth dried. Embarrassed, I swallowed, and licked my lips. 'On my bottom, please, sir,' I said shyly.

For the last time that day he turned me over his knee. He gave me twelve for exposing my breasts without permission. He gave me six for questioning a direct order. And when we came to the final ten, he announced that those were for Bargaining. I could hear the capital letter he gave the word; the way his tone deepened with the offence I had given. Bargaining sounded like a dreadful crime, I thought, and with each of that last implacable ten I held my feet up and my head too. I made no outward sound, but inside

216

promised myself that I would learn this lesson, and never again attempt to influence the course or duration of a punishment; if only I could be fortunate enough to be taken on as his student, and visit him from time to time, whenever he summoned me.

It was over. The Professor congratulated me and praised my fortitude; then he set me on my feet and with one last resounding spank drove me into the corner, to stand with my hands on my head and my nose against the wallpaper while my pride and my bottom cooled.

I heard the Professor's wife suggest we celebrate my Initiation with a glass of sherry.

'Champagne would be more like it!' he growled cheerfully, and strode over to the door. He flung it open and shouted into the hallway. 'Marion! Marion!'

There was no reply; no answering sound of hurrying footsteps.

'Oh dear, my love, didn't I tell you?' I heard the Professor's wife say. 'Marion's gone.'

16

An Ideal Position

'*Gone?*' thundered the Professor.

'Marion gave notice a couple of hours ago,' I heard her reply. Her tone was even but not, I thought, complacent. 'I suppose she's packed and gone by now.'

I heard the firm, deliberate click of the latch as the Professor shut the door. 'Perhaps you could be so good as to tell me why,' he said. Though he was not speaking to me, I thrilled to the force he could master with the quietest command.

'I gave her a spanking,' his wife announced.

'When?'

'I told you, a couple of hours ago,' said his wife. 'Just before she gave in her notice.'

Her husband reined in his impatience. 'Why did you give her a spanking?' he demanded.

'For moving your books,' said the Professor's wife, in a tone of righteousness and justification.

I felt the air in the room become very still. In my suspense, I almost forgot my aching bottom, and the tight bands of fire around my upper thighs.

'But *I* gave her a spanking for moving my books,' the Professor replied.

'Oh, so she said,' admitted his wife dismissively, 'but you know what she's like. And you've been so busy.' I could almost feel her eyes turn to rest on me. 'I didn't think you could possibly have found time to

218

deal with the maid. That's usually my job, after all, dear, isn't it?'

'Well, didn't you inspect her?' asked the Professor, baffled by all this.

'Of course I did,' said his wife. 'I made her turn round and pull her knickers down for me, and it was so pretty – you know how sweet she looks with her knickers down, especially when her bottom's all hot and red – and then I simply had to spank her too,' she confessed.

'On what grounds?' he asked, sounding like a prosecuting counsel.

The reply came so quietly I could only just hear it. 'I said you hadn't finished.'

'What?' bellowed her husband.

'I didn't say it like that, darling,' answered the Professor's wife, with something of a return to her previous self-assurance. 'I told her a Quick Reminder would do her the world of good, and after I gave her one, she asked me for her wages owing and said she knew a girl needed seeing to now and then, but she didn't see why she should be spanked twice in one day.'

'Twice?' echoed the Professor, as if he could see nothing in that to object to; and at the same moment in my corner I was thinking, Only twice? How hopelessly feeble the poor girl must be. I remembered her squalling across the Professor's lap under the most elementary Hairbrushing. I tried not to remember her kneeling afterwards between the Professor's legs, her round face bright red as she engulfed his penis.

'Twice for the same offence,' clarified the Professor's wife. 'And she said she didn't see why she should learn the alphabet either, and now she's gone,' she finished, unhappily.

Something unexpected happened then. The Professor called me out of the corner.

'Jennifer?'

I turned. 'Yes, sir?'

'Come here,' he said, with an imperious beckoning wave. 'I want you to witness this.'

My heart beating quickly, I came to the side of the couch where he sat. His wife sat in her chair with her feet drawn up to one side, her dressing gown still belted around her waist. I could not look at her.

'You may sit down, Jennifer,' said the Professor.

'Thank you, sir, I'd rather stand, sir, please,' I said.

The Professor gestured to his wife. 'Stand up,' he told her.

Elegantly, gracefully, she unfolded her legs and rose from her seat. With her hands at her sides she stood before us, her head tilted very slightly forward, her luminous blue eyes turned up a fraction and fixed patiently on her husband's face. Was there the merest hint of a smile at the corners of her mouth? Surely not. She, I thought with a shiver, could have nothing to smile about.

The Professor sat back, looking at her. He folded his hands precisely on his stomach and looked down at his thumbnails, as if he wanted to make sure that something in the world was still in order.

'Perhaps you'd like to tell our visitor,' said the Professor, 'how many maids have left our employment this year.'

'I'm sure Jennifer doesn't want to hear about that, darling,' she said. 'We were going to have champagne.'

'All right,' he said. 'Why don't you go and get it?' He gave me a charming smile. 'We can drink while we listen,' he said to me, though he was saying it for her benefit. 'To the story of the four maids.'

The Professor's wife went out.

The Professor looked at me again. He said, 'I wish you'd sit down,' and he raised his eyebrows slightly.

'Thank you, sir,' I said. But I still didn't want my skin to come into contact with anything, not even the soft and luxurious fabrics of the Professor's wife's sitting room. 'I'll kneel,' I said.

I knelt down beside him, my legs spread wide, and carefully, tenderly, sat back on my heels. It was not too bad.

I looked at my thighs. I was rather afraid that as they were now, they clashed with the furnishings.

'I think you'll find this very instructive,' said the Professor, in a tone of mild satisfaction, as of a man who finds things working out neatly, and to advantage.

I tried to straighten my hair, and wipe the perspiration from the tops of my breasts. 'I'm sorry about Marion, sir,' I said.

'Quite,' he said, non-committally.

His wife came back in with a tray, on which sat three glasses and an ice bucket.

'Here we are!' she sang out merrily, bending neatly from the hips as she put the tray down on the coffee table. In the bucket was a green bottle, which she took out and wrapped in a starched white napkin. 'Do you like champagne, Jenny?' she asked me, looking down at me as she handed her husband the bottle in both hands, the bottom towards him. 'I think it's fun,' she said girlishly, and silkily she wriggled her shoulders.

The Professor loosened the wire. He thrust his thumbs beneath the bulbous head of the long, smooth cork and let it fly in a jet of white foam to cannon off one of the remarkable pictures. Squeaking and flapping, 'Oh, oh, oh!' the Professor's wife rushed to gather the bounty into the glasses. I noticed for all her fuss she collected it with ease and perfect precision.

221

The Professor lifted his glass. 'To a new disciple on the Road to Knowledge,' he pronounced. 'May her feet never falter, and her back never tire.' I wondered why he did not say anything about the regions in between, which I suppose were more on my mind at that moment.

'Jennifer!' affirmed the Professor's wife, gladly, and I had to stand up then and thank them as they drank, and propose their health in turn, which they graciously accepted.

I knelt down again, ready to hear the Professor's wife's story. Four maids this year! I wondered how they could possibly have had such bad luck. I supposed young girls nowadays probably thought themselves above a life as a domestic servant, and would rather not work at all, some of them.

'You can leave yours there,' said the Professor to his wife, gesturing to her to put her glass down before she drank any more.

'Oh,' she said regretfully, but she set it down without complaining, only looking at it with regret in her bright blue eyes.

'Who was the first?' asked the Professor.

'Norma,' she said.

'Yes, Norma,' he said. 'Tell Jennifer what happened to Norma. You can get undressed while you talk,' he told her, as an afterthought.

The Professor's wife unfastened the sash of her gown. With the sides of her thumbs she slipped the facings back, thrusting forward her almost imaginary bosom.

'Norma left,' she said.

'Why?' said her husband, with more than a touch of iron in his prompting.

The Professor's wife pulled back her shoulders and slipped the gown off both at once, hooking it as it slid

222

down her back, bringing her elbows forward and moving her hands behind her to catch it by the collar.

'Because I punished her,' she said, trailing the gown behind her.

'What with?' asked the Professor shortly. I noticed his lapse of grammar with surprise. Nervously I hoped it did not mean he was losing his temper.

'It was only a carpet beater,' she said, almost pouting; and she swished the dressing gown up off the floor and folded it over the arm of a chair.

'Do you recall anywhere, in the standard regimen for household staff, that it is specified that the housemaid may be chastised with a carpet beater?' He made it sound ridiculous, though I was not yet experienced enough to be able to tell whether that was on grounds of severity or style.

'No, dear,' said his wife pleasantly.

The Professor drank champagne. 'What may a housemaid be chastised with?' he continued.

The Professor's wife stood with her hands behind her back, like a schoolgirl reciting. 'The Hand; the Slipper; the Hairbrush; the Cane by you, dear . . .' She waved one hand, in conclusion. 'Several other things, I forget.'

The Professor put his chin down. 'Several other things,' he growled; but he did not make her remember what they might be.

He took another drink, and so did I, a little hesitantly. Though I do like champagne, very much, it always goes straight to my head; and I had never drunk it straight after a spanking before, so I wondered what effect that might have.

'I'm not seeing very much undressing,' commented the Professor; then, when his wife's fingers went obediently to the top button of her pyjama jacket, he said: 'Who came after Norma?'

'Irma,' said his wife.

I glanced at the Professor, wondering if that was true. He made no objection.

'She made a mess in the bedroom,' said the Professor's wife obscurely. She undid the button.

'I think you can manage a bit more than that,' her husband said, chiding her.

'She weed in the corner,' she said. 'She wet herself, and all down the wallpaper.'

The Professor's wife undid the second button. 'Well, she cleaned it up afterwards,' she said, speaking directly to me, and opening the third and last button. 'But after that she was so embarrassed, poor thing, that her heart just wasn't in her work, really, and we had to let her go.'

She flipped the pyjama top casually off one shoulder, wriggling her arm and one breast out, then the other.

'I don't think that's much of an explanation,' observed her husband.

'I'd given her a spanking, a perfectly ordinary spanking,' said the Professor's wife. She was turned slightly to one side, folding her pyjama top carefully. 'I put her in the corner, and came downstairs, and I just forgot about her. She just went clean out of my head,' she said, with a pretty gesture of her hand like a flower unfolding beside her head.

'She didn't dare move,' she said. 'Apparently.'

I thought Irma must have been a pretty silly young woman not to work out that the punishment for leaving the corner without permission would surely not be as bad as for wetting the wallpaper.

'And after Irma?' said the Professor.

His wife unbuttoned the waistband of her pyjama trousers. 'Myra,' she said calmly. She leaned forward from the hips, a slightly truculent expression on her face as she slid the trousers down. It looked as though she would have contested the blame for Myra's departure, if she had not already done so several times in vain.

The Professor turned to me. 'She bit her nipple,' he remarked.

Startled, I almost choked on a mouthful of champagne.

'Myra bit your wife's nipple?' I yelped.

He waved this away. 'No, no,' he said irritably. 'My wife,' he said gesturing, 'bit Myra's nipple.'

Nude, the Professor's wife stood there, her trousers like a shimmering grey puddle around her feet. 'It didn't bleed or anything,' she pointed out. 'I mean, she didn't have to be taken to hospital or anything like that. We were just exercising,' she said, looking straight at me. Her face was as blank as a mask. 'Wrestling,' she said, even more implausibly. 'It got caught in my teeth.'

The Professor drained his glass and took his jacket off. 'You'd been spanking her too,' he commented, unfastening his tie, 'if I remember rightly.'

Almost lazily his wife picked up her trousers. 'Of course I had,' she replied. 'I was always having to spank Myra for one thing or another.' As she spoke she was putting the trousers over the chair arm with the rest of her things. Her bottom was turned towards me. She was very white and clear as fine china.

'And Marion makes four,' said her husband.

The Professor's wife looked at me again, with an expression that said she was going to regret Marion's departure, along with all the others. Yet she seemed calm, almost complacent. I supposed she was saving her repentance until after her punishment, and I envied her sense of tranquillity, her self-control.

'Why is it, do you suppose, that we can never keep staff?' Her husband got to his feet.

225

His wife stood straight, facing him now, her hands clasped modestly in front of her pubis. 'I don't know, darling.'

'Well, you will know in a minute!' he barked, so suddenly and ferociously I almost spilled my champagne. 'I shouldn't have to waste my time on things like this,' he said. 'I'm going to have to teach you to pay attention. I'm going to give you something now to keep your mind on what you're doing.'

'My champagne will be flat,' said the Professor's wife.

'Damn the champagne!' he shouted. 'Bend over and touch your toes.'

Turning face about, she obeyed.

I had never yet seen the Professor's wife, or indeed anyone's wife at all, bending over for punishment, and certainly not in the nude. I thought she had never looked lovelier. Her bottom and the backs of her legs were quite white, as I had said, with just a tinge of rosy pink behind the knees and a deeper, browner hue in the central cleft, between her high, tight little cheeks. Her feet were eight inches apart.

I thought then how lucky I was to be seeing this – how amazing that it should chance to happen on the very day of my Initiation, and while I was still on the premises – and how wonderful and generous of both the Professor and his wife to let me stay and witness so intimate a scene. With that in mind, eagerly I took a great swallow of champagne. The bubbles ran up my nose and made me sneeze, and sneeze so violently and suddenly that I almost overbalanced in surprise, and started to choke and splutter.

The Professor turned to me, frowning. 'Are you all right, my dear?' he asked, sternly.

Clinging to one of the hanging straps, which I had grasped instinctively, I contained myself. I assured

226

the Professor I was all right, apologised for the disturbance and thanked him for his concern.

He turned back to contemplate his wife, who despite my ill-mannered outburst had not moved.

'Please, sir,' I said then, 'I'd like to apply for the job.'

The Professor regarded me again. 'What job?' he said. He was in the middle of rolling up his sleeves.

'Marion's job, sir,' I said.

He turned to look me full in the face, raising those distinguished eyebows. '*You*, Geraldine?'

I got to my feet. 'Jennifer, sir,' I said.

'Yes, of course,' he said swiftly, but with a slight sharpness that indicated how trivial the difference was. 'You are applying for the post of our housemaid?' He sounded frankly astonished.

I stuck to my guns. 'Yes, Professor, please,' I said. 'I'm free at the moment, and I'm not doing anything that really interests me – I mean, I haven't any prior obligations or anything. I can cook and clean and deal with people who come to the door, and I know my alphabet perfectly and love having beautiful books to take care of, and I promise I won't ever wet the wallpaper.' I caught myself up short. I was babbling, and that would not create a good impression. 'I'm sure I'd be quite suitable, sir,' I said, more humbly. 'Madam,' I added, belatedly.

The upturned white bottom did not shift.

'Well, Jennifer,' said the Professor genially, 'it's a most unusual proposition. We'll have to give it some thought, won't we, my love?' he added, addressing his wife.

'I think she'd be splendid, dearest,' she said, her voice perfectly calm and assured despite her inconvenient position.

'Let's not be too hasty about making a decision,'

her husband replied, chiding her. 'I mean to say, we don't want any more abrupt departures, do we?'

'I wouldn't put myself forward if I didn't feel sure I could do the job, sir,' I said. 'I wouldn't presume,' I averred, bravely.

'No, well – you've certainly proved yourself able and dedicated today,' he conceded.

'And obedient,' said his wife, still bent over.

'And obedient,' he repeated. He smoothed the roll he had made of his right sleeve, tucking the edge of a fold in place. 'But have you any experience of domestic work, Jennifer?' he asked doubtfully.

'I do all my own, sir,' I told him.

'Oh, yes, true enough, I suppose,' he concurred. 'But domestic service – the arrangement of a household not according to your own needs and preferences but my wife's and mine – that's a very different proposition, you know.'

I put my champagne glass down on the tray and squared my shoulders. 'I can't think of a more noble and worthwhile cause,' I said frankly. 'It would be an honour to dedicate myself to it.'

The Professor seemed pleased. He folded his arms and stood regarding me with a wry little smile. 'Well, Jennifer,' he said, 'if we do take you on, your training will have to be thorough – very thorough indeed,' he said quietly. 'You do understand that, my dear, don't you?'

'Yes, sir!' I said smartly.

'And since you'll be a household servant as well as a pupil, you'll be subject to my wife as well as me,' the Professor went on. 'Despite the one or two lapses you've heard discussed this evening – '

'Four,' said the Professor's wife, simply.

'Four, yes,' said the Professor, laying his hand on her bare back. 'My wife, as you know, normally looks after the servants, and that arrangement will continue, if anything more scrupulously than before,' he added, in a warning tone meant for her ears. 'Though of course in your case, Jennifer, I shall continue your tuition and may supervise you from time to time myself, when my other responsibilities do not prevent it.'

At once my butterfly mind leapt away to the thousand and one chores I might be required to perform for my master. I imagined myself dusting the study, polishing the top of the Desk, straightening the Rulers, waxing the broad black Strap ready for the bottom of that morning's pupil. I already knew how particular he could be: how very little room I should have in my life for error. What a wonderful way to learn the finer points of discipline, in service to such a prominent authority!

And his wife – what extra little tasks might she have for me, behind the scenes: trivial, domestic things, beneath the concern of the master of the house? I was sure there must be dozens of them. Perhaps it had been Marion's duty to assist her mistress at her bath: to lay out clothes for her and help her dress and undress. I could imagine a well behaved girl might be sent upstairs first at nights to warm the marital bed; perhaps it might even be her place to keep her mistress company, on nights when the Professor was absent.

So rapt was I in my fancies, I almost missed what the Professor had to say to me next.

'You would also be required,' he said, lowering his voice as if to speak of more delicate matters, 'to assist me on the occasion of my dear wife's own punishments.' Graciously overlooking my little gasp, he laid his hand again on his wife's body, touching her pure white bottom, stroking it with his fingertips like a connoisseur admiring the texture of a marble statue.

229

'Occasions such as this,' he said, reflectively, 'when I might, for example, send you to my study, to the middle drawer in my desk, to fetch me my Cane.'

My head was spinning with excitement and delight. 'May I, sir?' I whispered, unable to speak aloud for apprehension of joy.

'As your first duty in your new employment, Jennifer?' he said. 'Yes; you may.'

'Thank you, sir!' I cried; and with my best approximation of a nude curtsey, I hurried from the room as fast as my aching legs would allow.

Padding along the hallway, I simply couldn't believe my luck. In a sudden instant of spontaneous decision, my whole life had at last been transformed. Once more I seemed to feel myself surrounded by a great invisible throng of students and servants, foreign visitors and intimate associates of my distinguished employer, all congratulating me and acclaiming me as I passed by. How I would strive to be worthy of this good, wise, illustrious couple's trust and generosity!

Of course, inexperienced as I was, I could not expect to succeed in every respect at once and forever. No doubt there would be occasions, during the weeks and months and years ahead when a moment of misunderstanding or inattention, forgetfulness or sheer bad luck would put me in the position of deserving punishment from one or other of them. I might not be a Norma or an Irma, another Myra or, least of all, a second Marion; but no, I was level-headed enough to imagine my future might include the odd painful episode behind closed doors: lifting my skirt for the Ruler across my bare thighs; or, good Heavens, could it be possible – taking a Hand-spanking over the Knee of the Professor's wife herself!

In the study I greeted the books, the globe, the

desks large and small, with silent, rapturous gladness. Not wasting another second on idle thoughts of my own, I hastened around to open the wide central drawer of the Professor's Desk and took from among the jumble of surprising oddments within a long, flexible stem of fine bamboo with one end curled into a handle. It made me shiver just to touch its sleek yellow surface; and I felt a moment of sorrow for the Professor's wife, that the same chance incident that had granted me my great opportunity and advancement should have earned her a thrashing with this fearsome Device.

Closing the desk drawer, I happened to look up and notice that the study fire was dying, looking dull red now and darkening, like the traces of my Initiation. There was a poker in the hearth, and a scuttle of coal. Well, I thought, in a flash of inspiration, here was a supreme opportunity to begin work at once in the spirit of duty I was determined to assume!

Hanging the Cane by its handle on the mantelpiece, I stooped and poked the dwindling fire, rousing its embers to a more hopeful glow. Then I dug out a shovelful of coal from the scuttle, and slid it with a satisfying crash into the grate; and I poked it again for good measure. Now my master's room would not grow cold while he was busy elsewhere in the house.

Laying down the shovel I discovered to my dismay that either it or the poker, or both, had left its sooty mark on my fingers and palm. Foolishly perhaps and automatically, I hurriedly wiped my hands, and not stopping to inspect the result, snatched up the dangling Cane and sped back to the Professor's wife's sitting room – taking care to close the study door behind me to keep the warmth in.

At the sitting room I knocked, entered, curtseyed with slightly more confidence than before, and handed the Professor his Cane. He took it without a word, flexing it lightly and stepping away from his wife's bottom, which I rather thought he had been caressing during my absence. I was pleased to think she could not be in such disgrace as to forfeit all her rights to tokens of his affection more gentle than the stern correction she was about to receive.

But it was at me that the Professor was looking now, not at her, and with a frown of censure.

'What's that?' he demanded.

'What, sir?' I replied, in all innocence.

'That black mark on the side of your leg,' he said.

My heart suddenly felt a degree or two more chilly.

'Turn around,' the Professor directed.

There was one the other side too, I saw. I had obviously wiped my hands more carelessly than I realised.

'Looks like coal,' the Professor said fastidiously. 'What is it?'

'It is coal, sir,' I said, and lowered my head. 'I made up the fire in your study, sir,' I explained, not, I admit, without a touch of pride.

The Professor did not seem glad. 'Did I tell you to make up the fire in my study?' he asked.

Now I hung my head indeed. 'No, sir,' I admitted.

The Professor took a step to the side, turning to glance at his wife, still bent in her uncomfortable posture. 'Perhaps your mistress told you to make up the fire in my study,' he suggested.

'No, sir,' I said quickly. 'It was going out. I thought – '

The Professor's sandy eyebrows drew together. 'Your duties do not include thinking, Jennifer,' he said, mildly but gravely.

What could I say? 'No, sir.'

'Your duty is one thing and one thing only,' he said. 'To obey.'

232

How simple he made it sound. I said nothing, but stood with my head still bowed.

'Show me your hands,' he commanded.

I did. They were black.

My master stood back surveying me. He held the Cane horizontally before him and ran his fingers and thumbs the length of it. I thought how thin it looked, how painfully sharp.

'I'm not impressed with your presentation, Jennifer,' the Professor said. 'What was it Marion wore, did you notice?'

I strove to recollect. Fortunately I had seen Marion from quite close to when she was at least partially clothed, and I was able to call the sight to mind. 'A black dress, sir,' I said, 'with quite a lot of petticoats underneath – a good half-dozen, I should think, sir, though I didn't have the chance to count them – and loose drawers, sir: I don't know what you call them, but they were gathered at the waist. Black stockings with elasticated tops,' I recalled next, 'and black shoes with buttoned straps; and a starched white cap and apron, sir.'

Though his wife seemed to be making a curious little shaking movement, almost as though she was suppressing laughter at something amusing, the Professor himself regarded me with sober patience during the recital of this catalogue. 'A traditional house-maid's uniform, then,' he said by way of summary. 'Is that right?'

I gave him a sunny, hopeful smile. 'Yes, sir,' I said.

'Why aren't you wearing such a uniform, Jennifer?'

I was taken aback by this question, and looked down at my be-smutted self. 'I haven't got one, sir,' I said feebly.

'Why not?' returned my employer, crisply.

My eyes strayed to his wife, at least to as much of

233

her as I could see. I jerked them away again quickly. 'There hasn't been time, sir,' I essayed.

This was patently not good enough. 'I didn't ask for an excuse, Jennifer, I asked for a reason.'

He pressed the tip of his Cane against the toe of his shoe and pressed down until the Cane began to bend. 'I shall not usually ask you things twice,' he told me, 'but since this is your first day at work I shall be lenient with you, Jennifer.' He lifted his splendid nose and regarded me with a firm gaze. 'I shall ask you again. Why haven't you got a uniform?'

I felt very light and trembly inside. 'Because I didn't make sure I had one, sir,' I said.

'And whose fault is that, pray?'

'Mine, sir,' I said, as clearly and decisively as I could.

The Professor gave a slight oblique nod of his head. 'What should you have done, child?'

'Asked your wife, sir,' I hazarded, my eyes sliding once more in her general direction.

'I'll have to measure you up,' said the Professor's wife, still in her Position. 'In the morning, Jenny,' she said. 'I'll bring my tape measure and pins,' she said, in a strange, dreamy voice.

The Professor ignored this, while looking at her frankly. 'My wife has been busy,' he announced. 'Too busy to see to your needs.' He returned his searching gaze to me. 'What should you have done in that case?'

'Asked you, sir?'

'Likewise,' he said shortly, meaning he had been busy too, and still was; and still would be for some time to come. In his unblinking brown eyes I saw the question still remained.

I looked down at my bare skin. I thought the red decorations I wore below the waist uniform enough:

234

badges of servitude and discipline. 'Asked to be excused, sir?' I ventured.

This recourse did not seem to meet with his approval. He leaned on the Cane, bending it the other way. 'Young women in this house are not normally excused duties of any kind, Jennifer,' he observed.

'No, sir,' I said.

'I suppose you'll ask to be excused punishment too, mm?'

'No, sir,' I said resolutely. 'Never, sir.'

He pointed with the tip of his Cane. 'Then perhaps you'd be so good as to take a Position there beside your mistress,' he said languidly, 'and you can both learn to accept the consequences of your various actions and inactions.'

My heart beating like a tiny animal's, I hurried over to my new place. Beside the Professor's wife I touched my toes, my nude flanks brushing lightly against her own as I lowered myself into the Position. She did not speak, or turn her head, or acknowledge my arrival in any way; but even as he measured the cane across our bottoms, she slipped her hand into mine, and squeezed me tight.

In my scatter-brained way, I wondered which of us he would have to pleasure him afterwards, or whether both our services would be required – and then the cane came slicing down through the air, and the world exploded in light.

NEW BOOKS

Coming up from Nexus and Black Lace

Wanton by Andrea Arven
April 1994   Price: £4.99   ISBN: 0 352 32916 5
First she was *Wicked*, then she was *Wild*; now she's *Wanton*.
This is the third in the series of the salacious adventures of Fee
Cambridge, the stunning green-eyed socialite of the twenty-
first century.

Jennifer's Instruction by Cyrian Amberlake
April 1994   Price: £4.99   ISBN: 0 352 32915 7
This is Jennifer's personal account of her initiation into the
delights of discipline in the experienced hands of the Professor
and his wife. An exhaustive education in punishment from the
author of the highly successful *Domino* series.

The Palace of Eros by Delver Maddingley
May 1994   Price: £4.99   ISBN: 0 352 32921 1
In this, the fourth in the popular *Palace* series, the wily, randy
Captain ventures into the world of erotic publishing. Once his
licentious editorial team is assembled, their activities make the
books seem tame by comparison.

Emma Enslaved by Hilary James
May 1994   Price: £4.99   ISBN: 0 352 3293 X
Emma's apprenticeship in servitude continues. Taken by her
cruel but beautiful mistress to a North African harem, Emma
discovers the sweet torment of being denied her own pleasure
while forced to attend to the needs of her superiors.

BLACK
lace

Fiona's Fate by Fredrica Alleyn
April 1994   Price: £4.99   ISBN: 0 352 32913 0
The writer of the immensely popular *Cassandra's Conflict*
brings us a tale of two pretty young hostages – a wife and a
mistress – awaiting the ransom from their mutual lover. Their
captors, a group of ruthless Italian kidnappers, come up with
some very original ideas to pass the time.

Moon of Desire by Sophie Danson
April 1994   Price: £4.99   ISBN: 0 352 32911 4
Soraya is in Eastern Europe on Foreign Office business when
she is overcome by wild sexual impulses. As her behaviour
grows more and more lubricious, it becomes clear that the
answer may lie in her ancestors' dark past.

Outlaw Fantasy by Saskia Hope
May 1994   Price: £4.99   ISBN: 0 352 32920 3
Recovering from the sexually hypercharged events of *Outlaw
Lover*, Fiona suffers a setback – the disappearance of a valuable
sexual fantasy disc. The trouble is, the disc is so good that it
will take some powerful persuasion to get it back.

Handmaiden of Palmyra by Fleur Reynolds
May 1994   Price: £4.99   ISBN: 0 352 32919 X
The author of the successful *Odalisque* brings us a third-
century tale of lust and ambition. Samoya has been chosen to
be the wife of the Palmyrene chief, Prince Alif: but the marriage seems endangered when she meets a man who awakens
her innermost desires . . .

THE BEST IN EROTIC READING – BY POST

The Nexus Library of Erotica – almost one hundred and fifty volumes – is available from many booksellers and newsagents. If you have any difficulty obtaining the books you require, you can order them by post. Photocopy the list below, or tear the list out of the book; then tick the titles you want and fill in the form at the end of the list. Titles with a month in the box will not be available until that month in 1994.

CONTEMPORARY EROTICA

AMAZONS	Erin Caine	£3.99	
COCKTAILS	Stanley Carten	£3.99	
CITY OF ONE-NIGHT STANDS	Stanley Carten	£4.50	
CONTOURS OF DARKNESS	Marco Vassi	£4.99	
THE GENTLE DEGENERATES	Marco Vassi	£4.99	
MIND BLOWER	Marco Vassi	£4.99	
THE SALINE SOLUTION	Marco Vassi	£4.99	
DARK FANTASIES	Nigel Anthony	£4.99	
THE DAYS AND NIGHTS OF MIGUMI	P.M.	£4.50	
THE LATIN LOVER	P.M.	£3.99	
THE DEVIL'S ADVOCATE	Anonymous	£4.50	
DIPLOMATIC SECRETS	Antoine Lelouche	£3.50	
DIPLOMATIC PLEASURES	Antoine Lelouche	£3.50	
DIPLOMATIC DIVERSIONS	Antoine Lelouche	£4.50	
ELAINE	Stephen Ferris	£4.99	Mar
EMMA ENSLAVED	Hilary James	£4.99	May
EMMA'S SECRET WORLD	Hilary James	£4.99	
ENGINE OF DESIRE	Alexis Arven	£3.99	
DIRTY WORK	Alexis Arven	£3.99	
THE FANTASIES OF JOSEPHINE SCOTT	Josephine Scott	£4.99	

Title	Author	Price	Month
FALLEN ANGELS	Kendall Grahame	£4.99	Jul
THE FANTASY HUNTERS	Celeste Arden	£3.99	
HEART OF DESIRE	Maria del Rey	£4.99	
HELEN – A MODERN ODALISQUE	James Stern	£4.99	
HOT HOLLYWOOD NIGHTS	Nigel Anthony	£4.50	
THE INSTITUTE	Maria del Rey	£4.99	
JENNIFER'S INSTRUCTION	Cyrian Amberlake	£4.99	Apr
LAURE-ANNE TOUJOURS	Laure-Anne	£4.99	
MELINDA AND ESMERALDA	Susanna Hughes	£4.99	Jun
MELINDA AND THE MASTER	Susanna Hughes	£4.99	
Ms DEEDES AT HOME	Carole Andrews	£4.50	
Ms DEEDES ON A MISSION	Carole Andrews	£4.99	
Ms DEEDES ON PARADISE ISLAND	Carole Andrews	£4.99	
OBSESSION	Maria del Rey	£4.99	
THE PALACE OF EROS	Delver Maddingley	£4.99	May
THE PALACE OF FANTASIES	Delver Maddingley	£4.99	
THE PALACE OF SWEETHEARTS	Delver Maddingley	£4.99	
THE PALACE OF HONEYMOONS	Delver Maddingley	£4.99	
THE PASSIVE VOICE	G. C. Scott	£4.99	
QUEENIE AND CO	Francesca Jones	£4.99	
QUEENIE AND CO IN JAPAN	Francesca Jones	£4.99	
QUEENIE AND CO IN ARGENTINA	Francesca Jones	£4.99	
SECRETS LIE ON PILLOWS	James Arbroath	£4.50	
STEPHANIE	Susanna Hughes	£4.50	
STEPHANIE'S CASTLE	Susanna Hughes	£4.50	
STEPHANIE'S DOMAIN	Susanna Hughes	£4.99	
STEPHANIE'S REVENGE	Susanna Hughes	£4.99	
STEPHANIE'S TRIAL	Susanna Hughes	£4.99	Feb
THE TEACHING OF FAITH	Elizabeth Bruce	£4.99	Jul
THE DOMINO TATTOO	Cyrian Amberlake	£4.50	
THE DOMINO QUEEN	Cyrian Amberlake	£4.99	

EROTIC SCIENCE FICTION

Title	Author	Price	Month
ADVENTURES IN THE PLEASUREZONE	Delaney Silver	£4.99	

RETURN TO THE PLEASUREZONE	Delaney Silver	£4.99	
EROGINA	Christopher Denham	£4.50	
HARD DRIVE	Stanley Garten	£4.99	
PLEASUREHOUSE 13	Agnetha Anders	£3.99	
LAST DAYS OF THE PLEASUREHOUSE	Agnetha Anders	£4.50	
TO PARADISE AND BACK	D. H. Master	£4.50	
WANTON	Andrea Arven	£4.99	Apr

ANCIENT & FANTASY SETTINGS

CHAMPIONS OF LOVE	Anonymous	£3.99	
CHAMPIONS OF DESIRE	Anonymous	£3.99	
CHAMPIONS OF PLEASURE	Anonymous	£3.50	
THE SLAVE OF LIDIR	Aran Ashe	£4.50	
DUNGEONS OF LIDIR	Aran Ashe	£4.99	
THE FOREST OF BONDAGE	Aran Ashe	£4.50	
KNIGHTS OF PLEASURE	Erin Caine	£4.50	
PLEASURE ISLAND	Aran Ashe	£4.99	
WITCH QUEEN OF VIXANIA	Morgana Baron	£4.99	Mar

EDWARDIAN, VICTORIAN & OLDER EROTICA

ADVENTURES OF A SCHOOLBOY	Anonymous	£3.99	
ANNIE	Evelyn Culber	£4.99	
THE AUTOBIOGRAPHY OF A FLEA	Anonymous	£2.99	
CASTLE AMOR	Erin Caine	£4.99	
CHOOSING LOVERS FOR JUSTINE	Aran Ashe	£4.99	
EVELINE	Anonymous	£2.99	
MORE EVELINE	Anonymous	£3.99	
FESTIVAL OF VENUS	Anonymous	£4.50	
GARDENS OF DESIRE	Roger Rougiere	£4.50	
OH, WICKED COUNTRY	Anonymous	£2.99	
THE LASCIVIOUS MONK	Anonymous	£4.50	
LURE OF THE MANOR	Barbra Baron	£4.99	Jun
A MAN WITH A MAID 1	Anonymous	£4.99	
A MAN WITH A MAID 2	Anonymous	£4.99	
A MAN WITH A MAID 3	Anonymous	£4.99	

MAUDIE	Anonymous	£2.99
A NIGHT IN A MOORISH HAREM	Anonymous	£3.99
PARISIAN FROLICS	Anonymous	£2.99
PLEASURE BOUND	Anonymous	£3.99
THE PLEASURES OF LOLOTTE	Andrea de Nercist	£3.99
THE PRIMA DONNA	Anonymous	£3.99
RANDIANA	Anonymous	£4.50
REGINE	E.K.	£4.99
THE ROMANCE OF LUST 1	Anonymous	£3.99
THE ROMANCE OF LUST 2	Anonymous	£2.99
ROSA FIELDING	Anonymous	£2.99
SUBURBAN SOULS 1	Anonymous	£2.99
SUBURBAN SOULS 2	Anonymous	£3.99
TIME OF HER LIFE	Josephine Scott	£4.99
THE TWO SISTERS	Anonymous	£3.99
VIOLETTE	Anonymous	£4.99

'THE JAZZ AGE'

ALTAR OF VENUS	Anonymous	£3.99
THE SECRET GARDEN ROOM	Georgette de la Tour	£3.50
BEHIND THE BEADED CURTAIN	Georgette de la Tour	£3.50
BLUE ANGEL NIGHTS	Margaret von Falkensee	£4.99
BLUE ANGEL SECRETS	Margaret von Falkensee	£4.99
CAROUSEL	Anonymous	£4.50
CONFESSIONS OF AN ENGLISH MAID	Anonymous	£3.99
FLOSSIE	Anonymous	£2.50
SABINE	Anonymous	£3.99
PLAISIR D'AMOUR	Anne-Marie Villefranche	£4.50
FOLIES D'AMOUR	Anne-Marie Villefranche	£2.99
JOIE D'AMOUR	Anne-Marie Villefranche	£3.99
MYSTERE D'AMOUR	Anne-Marie Villefranche	£3.99
SECRETS D'AMOUR	Anne-Marie Villefranche	£3.50
SOUVENIR D'AMOUR	Anne-Marie Villefranche	£3.99

WORLD WAR 2

SPIES IN SILK	Piers Falconer	£4.50
WAR IN HIGH HEELS	Piers Falconer	£4.99

CONTEMPORARY FRENCH EROTICA (translated into English)

EXPLOITS OF A YOUNG DON JUAN	Anonymous	£2.99	
INDISCREET MEMOIRS	Alain Dorval	£2.99	
JOY	Joy Laurey	£2.99	
JOY IN LOVE	Joy Laurey	£2.75	
LILIANE	Paul Verguin	£3.50	
LUST IN PARIS	Antoine S.	£4.99	
NYMPHS IN PARIS	Galia S.	£2.99	
SENSUAL LIAISONS	Anonymous	£3.50	
SENSUAL SECRETS	Anonymous	£3.99	
THE NEW STORY OF Q	Anonymous	£4.50	
THE IMAGE	Jean de Berg	£3.99	
VIRGINIE	Nathalie Perreau	£4.50	
THE PAPER WOMAN	Francois Rey	£4.50	

SAMPLERS & COLLECTIONS

EROTICON 1	ed. J-P Spencer	£4.50	
EROTICON 2	ed. J-P Spencer	£4.50	
EROTICON 3	ed. J-P Spencer	£4.50	
EROTICON 4	ed. J-P Spencer	£4.99	
NEW EROTICA 1	ed. Esme Ombreux	£4.99	
NEW EROTICA 2	ed. Esme Ombreux	£4.99	Feb
THE FIESTA LETTERS	ed. Chris Lloyd	£4.50	
THE PLEASURES OF LOVING	ed. Maren Sell	£3.99	

NON-FICTION

HOW TO DRIVE YOUR MAN WILD IN BED	Graham Masterson	£4.50	
HOW TO DRIVE YOUR WOMAN WILD IN BED	Graham Masterson	£3.99	
HOW TO BE THE PERFECT LOVER	Graham Masterson	£2.99	
FEMALE SEXUAL AWARENESS	Barry & Emily McCarthy	£5.99	
LINZI DREW'S PLEASURE GUIDE	Linzi Drew	£4.99	
LETTERS TO LINZI	Linzi Drew	£4.99	

Please send me the books I have ticked above.

Name   ....

Address   ....

....

.... Post code   ....

Send to: **Cash Sales, Nexus Books, 332 Ladbroke Grove, London W10 5AH**

Please enclose a cheque or postal order, made payable to **Nexus Books**, to the value of the books you have ordered plus postage and packing costs as follows:

  UK and BFPO – £1.00 for the first book, 50p for the second book, and 30p for each subsequent book to a maximum of £3.00;

  Overseas (including Republic of Ireland) – £2.00 for the first book, £1.00 for the second book, and 50p for each subsequent book.

If you would prefer to pay by VISA or ACCESS/MASTERCARD, please write your card number here:

Please allow up to 28 days for delivery

— — — —   — — — —   — — — —   — — — —

Signature: _____